Lifting the Lid

A comedy thriller

Rob Johnson

XERIKA PUBLISHING

LIFTING THE LID

Published by Xerika Publishing

Copyright © Rob Johnson 2013

Cover design by Brian Ground from an original painting by Kostas Tsoukatos.

First published 2013 by Xerika Publishing
10 The Croft, Bamford, Hope Valley,
Derbyshire S33 0AP

ISBN: 978 0 9926384 2 9

http://www.rob-johnson.org.uk

For Penny,
who never stopped believing.

ACKNOWLEDGEMENTS

I am indebted to the following people for helping to make this book better than it would have been without their advice, technical knowhow and support:

Tom Doyle, Nuala Forde, Lisa Garvey-Williams, Richard Garvey-Williams, Bill Huntington, Judy Jagmohan, Trine Ejlskov Jensen, Rob Johnson (a different one), Jim Jones, Tina Keeley, Yiannis Kininis, Diane McDowell, Roddy McDowell, Huw Morris, Alexander Phillips, Derek Poulson, Jane Romans-Wilkins, Petros Stathakos, Nadia Tottman, Bob Uden, Dan Varndell, Naomi Varndell, Chris Wallbridge, Elizabeth Wallbridge, Nick Whitton, Rachel Whyte, Richard Wilkins

COVER DESIGN

Many thanks also to Kostas Tsoukatos for the original artwork and to Brian Ground for the overall design. (Sorry I kept changing my mind!)

1

Trevor stood with his back to the fireplace like some Victorian patriarch but without a scrap of the authority. Although the gas fire wasn't on, he rubbed his hands behind him as if to warm them. His mother sat in her usual chair by the window, staring blankly at the absence of activity in the street outside.

He knew exactly what her response would be. It was always the same when he told her anything about his life. Not that there was often much to tell, but this was different. This was a biggie. Almost as big as when he'd told her about Imelda's—

'It's of no concern to me.'

There we go. And now for the follow-on. Wait for it. Wait for it.

'I'm seventy-eight years old. Why should I care? I could be dead tomorrow.'

Trevor screwed up his face and mouthed the words of his mother's familiar mantra, but it became rapidly unscrewed again when she added, '...Like Imelda.'

'Don't,' he said. 'Just don't, okay?'

'No concern to me,' said the old woman with a barely perceptible shrug.

In the silence that followed, Trevor became aware of the ticking of the pendulum clock on the mantelpiece behind him. It had never been right since his father had died, so he checked his watch instead. 'You won't be... ' and he hesitated to say the word, ' ... lonely?'

If his mother had had the energy or inclination to have

laughed – derisively or otherwise – she would have done, but she settled for the next best option and grunted, 'Hmph.'

Trevor knew from experience that the intention was to pick away at his already tender guilt spot, and he looked around the room as if he were searching for the nearest escape route. His mother still referred to it as "the parlour", perhaps in a vain attempt to attach some kind of outmoded elegance to a room which, to Trevor's eye at least, was mildly shabby and darkly depressing even on the brightest of days. It was festooned with fading photographs of people who were long since dead, interspersed here and there with pictures of his more recently deceased brother and his very-much-alive sister. Of Trevor, there was only the one – an unframed snapshot of him and Imelda on their wedding day.

He became aware of the clock once again and cleared his throat. 'So... er... I'll be away then.'

This time, the shrug was accompanied by the slightest tilt of the head. 'No concern to me,' she said.

Again, he glanced at his watch. 'It's just that I have to—'

'Oh get on if you're going.'

Trevor stepped forward and, picking up his crash helmet from the table next to his mother, kissed her perfunctorily on the back of the head. For the first time, she turned – not quite to face him, but turned nevertheless.

'Still got that silly little moped then,' she said, repeating the comment she'd made when he had first arrived less than an hour before.

'Scooter, mother. It's a scooter. – Anyway, how could I afford anything else?' He was thankful she couldn't see the sudden redness in his cheeks or she would have instantly realised that he was lying.

He kissed her again in the same spot, and this time she

seemed to squirm uncomfortably. For a moment, he followed her line of vision to the outside world. – Nothing. He tapped his helmet a couple of times, then turned and walked towards the door. As he closed it behind him, he could just make out the words: 'Your brother wouldn't have gone.'

Out in the street, he strapped on his helmet and straddled the ageing Vespa, eventually coaxing the engine into something that resembled life. He took a last look at the window where his mother sat and thought he saw the twitch of a lace curtain falling back into place.

'Oh sod it,' he said aloud and let out the clutch.

At the end of the road, he turned right and stopped almost immediately behind a parked camper van. Dismounting the Vespa and still holding the handlebars, he kicked out the side stand and was about to lean it to rest when he decided that some kind of symbolic gesture was called for. Instead of inclining the scooter to a semi-upright position, he looked down at the rust-ridden old machine, tilted it marginally in the opposite direction and let go. With the gratingly inharmonious sound of metal on tarmac, the Vespa crashed to the ground and twitched a few times before rattling itself into submission. Trevor took in the paltry death throes and allowed himself a smirk of satisfaction.

Pulling a set of keys from his pocket, he kissed it lightly and walked round to the driver's door of the van. The moment he turned the key in the lock, a lean-looking black and tan mongrel leapt from its sleeping position on the back seat and hurled itself towards the sound. By the time Trevor had opened the door, the dog was standing on the driver's seat, frantically wagging its tail and barking hysterically.

'Hey, Milly. Wasn't long, was I?' said Trevor, taking the dog's head between both hands and rocking it gently from side to side. 'Over you get then.'

9

Milly simply stared back at him, no longer barking but still wagging her tail excitedly.

'Go on. Get over.' Trevor repeated the command and, with a gentle push, encouraged her to jump across to the passenger seat. Then he climbed in and settled himself behind the steering wheel. 'Right then,' he said, rubbing his palms around its full circumference. 'Let's get this show on the road.'

2

The lift was dead. The grey-haired guy in the expensive suit wasn't, but he looked like he was. Lenny had him pinned against the wall by leaning his back into him as hard as he could to keep him upright – no mean achievement since, although built like a whippet on steroids, Lenny was little more than five feet in height and well into his fifties.

'Come on, Carrot,' he said. 'What you messin' about at?'

Carrot – so called because of his ill-fitting and very obvious ginger toupee – jabbed at the lift button for the umpteenth time. 'Lift's not working. We'll have to use the stairs.'

'You kidding me? With this lard-arse?'

'So we just leave him here, do we?'

Lenny's heavily lined features contorted into a grimace. 'How many flights?'

'Dunno. Couple maybe?'

'Jesus,' said Lenny, taking a step forward.

The laws of gravity instantly came into play, and the Suit slid inexorably down the wall and ended up in a sitting position, his head lolled to one side and his jacket bunched up around his ears. Not for the first time, Carrot wondered why he'd been paired up with a dipshit like Lenny and even why the whining little git had been put on this job at all.

'Well you'll have to take the top half then,' Lenny said. 'Back's playing me up.'

Carrot snorted. Here we go again, he thought. The old racing injury ploy.

Lenny pulled himself up to his full inconsiderable height and shot him a glare. 'And what's that supposed to mean? You know bloody well about my old racing injury.'

'Doesn't everyone?' said Carrot.

Although Lenny's stature – or lack of it – gave a certain amount of credibility to his countless stories about when he used to be a top-flight steeplechase jockey, nobody in the racing business ever seemed to have heard of him. It was certainly true that he knew pretty much everything there was to know about the Sport of Kings, and most of his tales of the turf had a ring of authenticity about them, so he must have been involved in some way or other but more likely as a stable lad than a jockey. Hardly anyone bothered to doubt him to his face though, probably because his vicious temper was legendary and so was his ability with both his fists and his feet. For a little guy, he could be more than handy when it came to a scrap.

He looked like he was spoiling for one right now, so Carrot diverted his attention back to the Suit.

'Grab his ankles then,' he said and manoeuvred the man's upper body forward so he could get a firm grip under his armpits from behind.

Halfway up the first flight of concrete stairs, Lenny announced that he'd have to have a rest. Even though Carrot was doing most of the work, he decided not to antagonise him and eased his end of the body down onto the steps. Truth be told, he could do with a short break himself. He was already sweating like a pig and, besides, he needed at least one hand free to push his toupee back from in front of his eyes.

Lenny leaned back against the iron handrail and started to roll a cigarette.

Carrot's jaw dropped. 'Lenny?'

'Yeah?'

'What you doing?'

'Er…' Lenny looked down at his half completed cigarette and then back at Carrot. 'Rollin' a fag?'

His expression and tone of voice rendered the addition of a "duh" utterly redundant.

'We're not in the removal business, you know.' Carrot nodded towards the Suit. 'This isn't some bloody wardrobe we're delivering.'

Lenny ignored him and lit up. He took a long drag and blew a couple of smoke rings. Putting the cigarette to his lips for a second time, he was about to take another draw when he hesitated and began to sniff the air. 'What's that smell?'

'Er… smoke?' Two can play the "duh" game, thought Carrot.

'It's like…' Lenny's nose twitched a few more times and then puckered with distaste. 'Ugh, it's piss.'

'Dumps like this always stink of piss.'

'No, it's more…' Lenny carried on sniffing, his eyes ranging around to try to identify the source of the smell. 'Oh Jesus, it's him.'

Carrot looked in the direction he was pointing and, sure enough, the dark stain which covered the Suit's groin area was clearly visible despite the charcoal grey of the trousers. 'Oh for f—'

'Bugger's wet 'imself.'

'I can see that.'

Lenny took a pull on his cigarette. 'Fear probably.'

'Don't be a prat. The man's out cold. He doesn't know if it's Christmas Day or Tuesday.'

'Maybe it's like when somebody has their leg cut off – or their arm. They reckon you can still feel it even though it's not there any more.'

Carrot stared at him, unable to discern any logical

connection between amputation and pissing your pants.

'You know,' Lenny continued, apparently aware that further explanation was necessary. 'It's like your subconscious, or whatever, doing stuff behind your back without you realising.'

'I think it's far more likely it's a side effect of the stuff we injected him with.'

'Could be,' said Lenny, and he took a last drag on his cigarette before lobbing it over his shoulder into the stairwell.

'Ready now?' Carrot made no attempt to disguise the sarcasm in his tone.

'I'm not taking the feet this time though. My face'll be right in his piss.'

Carrot squeezed his eyes shut and counted to three. 'You want to swap?'

'Not necessarily. We could try taking an arm each.'

Because of the substantial difference in their heights, Carrot knew that this meant he would be taking most of the weight again, but he also realised there was no point in arguing. The priority was to get the guy up the stairs and into the flat before somebody spotted them.

3

The time wandered by, and the miles slid comfortably under the tyres at a steady fifty-five. Battered though it was, the converted Volkswagen Transporter was only twelve years old and could have gone faster, but Trevor was in no particular hurry. He was enjoying the ride, happy to be away and with the road stretching before him to an unknown destination. Milly seemed equally contented and alternated between sitting upright on the passenger seat, staring fixedly ahead, and curling up to sleep in the back.

It was Trevor's first real trip in the camper, and he liked the idea of having no fixed itinerary. After all, he reasoned, wasn't that the whole point of having one of these things?

To say that he had bought it on a whim would have been a gross distortion of the truth. Trevor didn't really do whims. His idea of an impulsive action was to buy an item that wasn't on his list when he did his weekly shop at the local supermarket. Even then, there would have to be a pretty convincing argument in favour of dropping the quarter-pound packet of frozen peas, or whatever it might be, into his trolley. Half price or two-for-one were minimum requirements.

The camper van hadn't fulfilled either of these criteria, and to begin with, he'd toyed with the idea of a motorbike. Something a bit flash, like a Harley. He'd have needed a halfway decent tent of course. A simple bedroll and sleeping out under the stars were all very well in Arizona or wherever but totally inadequate over here – unless you were one of those rufty-tufty outdoor survival types with an unnatural fixation about the SAS. He'd never understood the attraction of deliberately putting yourself in a situation where it was more than likely you would either starve or freeze to death or be attacked by a large carnivore or stung by something so venomous you'd have seconds to live unless you applied the appropriate antidote in time or got your best friend to suck out the poison. No, Scottish midges were about as much as he was prepared to tolerate, but even then he'd make damn sure he had a plentiful supply of insect repellent with him.

A hermetically sealable tent and a good thick sleeping bag would be indispensable as far as Trevor was concerned and, if space permitted on the Harley, an airbed – preferably with a pump which operated off the bike's battery. It had all started to make perfect sense until a small problem finally occurred to him. What about Milly? She was too big to ride in a rucksack on his back, and as for the only other possible option, the very idea of a Harley with a sidecar made him squirm with embarrassment.

A car was far too ordinary for his purposes, so a camper van had seemed to be the next best thing if he couldn't have a Harley. It still had a kind of "just hit the open road and go where it takes you" feel to it, and he'd once read a book by John Steinbeck where he set off to rediscover America in a camper with an enormous poodle called Charley.

The whole decision-making process had taken months of what Imelda would have called "anally retentive faffing", but which Trevor preferred to consider as an essential prerequisite to "getting it right". In his defence, he would have argued that it wasn't just about buying a van. There had been much greater life choices involved, such as whether to pack in his job at Dreamhome Megastores.

As it turned out, that particular decision had almost made itself for him. The company was in a bit of financial bother and was having to make cutbacks, so he and several of his colleagues had been offered voluntary redundancy. Although not exactly generous, the severance package was certainly tempting enough to cause Trevor a run of sleepless nights. But it wasn't until his annual staff appraisal that he'd finally made up his mind.

He had sat across the desk from the store manager and studied the thin wisps of hair on top of the man's head while he read out a litany of shortcomings and misdemeanours from the form in front of him.

'This simply won't do, Trevor. Really it won't,' Mr Webber had said, finally looking up and removing his glasses. 'I mean, there have been more customer complaints about you than any other member of staff.'

'I don't know why. I'm always polite. Always try and give advice whenever I—'

'But that's exactly the problem, Trevor. More often than not, the complaints are *about* your advice. We've had more goods returned because of you than... than...' The manager had slumped back in his chair. 'Good God, man, have you learned nothing about home maintenance and improvement in all the... What is it? Fourteen years since you've been here?'

'Fifteen.' And in all those long years, he'd never once heard Webber use the phrase "do-it-yourself", let alone its dreaded acronym.

'Quite honestly, I'm at a loss as to know what to—'

This time, it was Trevor who had interrupted. He couldn't be sure that he was about to be sacked, but he'd already had his quota of verbal and written warnings and thought he'd get in first with: 'About this voluntary redundancy thing...'

And that was that. Decision made and not a bad little payout. Added to what he'd squirreled away over the last couple of years or so, he could buy the van and still have enough left to live on for a few months as long as he was careful. He'd have to look for another job when the money did run out of course, but he was determined not to worry about that until the time came. At least, he was determined to *try* not to worry about it.

'What the hell, eh, Milly? This is *it*,' he said and shoved a tape into the cassette player.

He caught sight of the dog in the rear-view mirror. She briefly raised an eyebrow when the opening bars of Steppenwolf's *Born to be Wild* bellowed from the speakers above her head. Then she went back to sleep.

Trevor tapped the steering wheel almost in time with the music and hummed along when the lyrics kicked in. A song about hitting the open road and just seeing where it took you seemed particularly appropriate for the occasion, and when it got to the chorus, he'd begun to lose all sense of inhibition and joined in at the top of his voice.

Moments later, the van's engine spluttered and then abruptly died.

4

Carrot and Lenny hauled the Suit to his feet and, with an arm slung around each of their shoulders, half carried and half dragged him up to the first floor landing. As Carrot had predicted, Lenny's contribution amounted to little more than providing a largely ineffectual counterbalance, and by the time they'd lurched and staggered to the top of the second flight of steps, every muscle in his neck and back was screaming at him to stop whatever he was doing.

'I'm gonna have to... have a break for a minute,' he said, fighting for breath as he altered his grip and lowered the Suit to the ground.

'Come on, mate. We're nearly there now,' said Lenny, but his words of encouragement were meaningless, given that he did nothing to prevent the Suit's descent.

Carrot groaned as he sat him down against the frame of the fire door and so did the Suit.

''Ang on a sec. He's not coming round, is he?' Lenny squatted like a jockey at the start gate and brought his face to within a few inches of the Suit's. 'He is, you know.'

The muscles in Carrot's back grumbled as he crouched down to take a closer look and spotted the faintest flicker of the eyelids.

'You can't have given him enough,' said Lenny.

'What?'

'The injection.'

'Yeah, stupid me,' said Carrot, slapping his palm

against his forehead. 'I should've allowed extra time for all your fag breaks.'

Even though he resented Lenny's accusation, he'd worked with him on several other jobs and was used to getting the blame when things went wrong. Not that this was surprising since Lenny always avoided making any of the decisions, so any cockups were never his fault.

'We'll have to give him another shot,' said Lenny.

"We" meaning "you", Carrot thought and shook his head. 'Stuff's still in the van.'

'Jesus, man. What you leave it there for?'

Carrot bit his lip, aware from his peripheral vision that Lenny was staring at him, but he had no intention of shifting his focus to make eye contact. The Suit's eyelids were twitching more rapidly now and occasionally parted to reveal two narrow slits of yellowish white. Maybe the guy was just dreaming, but it was two hours or more since they'd given him the shot, so—

'Better bop him one, I reckon,' said Lenny.

It was Carrot's turn to stare at Lenny. 'Bop him one?'

'Yeah, you know…' He mimed hitting the Suit over the head with some blunt instrument or other and made a "click" sound with his tongue. 'Right on the noggin.'

Carrot continued to hold him in his gaze while he pondered which nineteen-fifties comedian Lenny reminded him of, but he was shaken from his musing by a strange moaning sound. The Suit's eyes were almost half open now.

5

The tiny room in the hotel near to York Minster was ridiculously expensive but all he could get. He and Milly had trailed round all the cheaper places in the city for a couple of hours, but they were all full. In the end, he'd been fit to drop and couldn't care less about the money as long as he had somewhere to sleep for the night.

The van was in a local garage, waiting for parts.

'Tomorrow lunchtime at the earliest,' the mechanic had told him.

'But I have to be at my brother's funeral in Newcastle by then,' Trevor had lied.

The mechanic had tutted and rolled his eyes, which could have been interpreted as an expression of sympathy or an indication that he didn't believe a word of it. 'As soon as we get the thing, we'll get straight onto it.'

He hadn't actually said "the thing", but Trevor had no idea what part it was that had to be replaced.

'So what do I do till then?'

'There's plenty of good hotels in the city.'

'Can't I sleep in the van?'

The mechanic had repeated the tutting, eye-rolling routine and said something about not being covered by the garage's insurance policy.

'Can't we push it out onto the road then?' Trevor had asked.

Just the tut this time and something about the local coppers taking a dim view of New Age Travellers.

'Well, thanks a bunch for your help, you greasy-arsed toerag,' Trevor hadn't said, but the idea of having his windows smashed in with police batons in the middle of the night hadn't appealed, so he'd pulled a few essentials from the van and wandered off into the city with his dog.

* * *

He lay sprawled on the single bed, listening to the sounds of dinner being prepared for a hundred-or-so residents directly beneath him and wondered why it was that people on their own were always given the crappiest rooms in hotels but still had to pay well over half the cost of a double.

The heat was becoming unbearable. Trevor guessed this was probably due to the restaurant ovens working overtime, and he went over to the sash window and raised it as far as it would go. He took a deep breath of the cooler air and caught a strong whiff of cabbage and onions before releasing his hold on the window. No sooner had he done so than it slithered slowly downwards and closed again with a dull thud. Rummaging around, he found a large Gideon Bible in a bedside cabinet and propped it open with that.

He fell backwards onto the scrawny little bed again with his feet hanging over the edge until he remembered where he was and how much he was paying. – His Doc Martens joined the rest of him on the bedspread and shuffled about to make themselves at home.

Milly looked up from her abortive sniffing of the empty wastepaper bin and then launched herself onto the bed. More precisely, she launched herself onto Trevor and wriggled between him and the wall until he gave way and she could lie down properly.

It had been a bit of a problem getting Milly into the hotel in the first place. Before he'd even overcome the initial shock of how much the room was going to cost him, he'd asked the receptionist if they allowed dogs. Milly was, at that moment, tied to a lamppost outside the hotel entrance and was shrieking wildly.

The receptionist had paused in the middle of entering Trevor's details onto her computer and given him a sickly and unconvincing smile. 'I'm sorry, sir, it's company policy not to allow pets within the hotel premises.'

'No, no, of course not,' Trevor had flustered. 'Glad to hear it.'

'Unless of course it's a guide dog,' the receptionist had added in a tone of voice that made it sound like an accusation.

'No, no, of course not,' Trevor had repeated and immediately wondered why he seemed to be apologising for not being blind. 'Just wanted to check. I'm er... I'm allergic, you see.'

The receptionist had smiled her unconvincing smile again and then returned her attention to the computer screen.

In the end, he'd gone up to his room and waited a few minutes before going out into the street to rescue the howling Milly. He could see the receptionist from where he stood, and as soon as she'd left the desk, he'd whisked Milly into the foyer and up the stairs to his room.

He put out his hand to where she lay next to him on the bed and stroked her head. 'Doesn't seem quite so bloody expensive now there's the two of us, I suppose.'

Trevor dozed for a while, and when he woke, realised that he was starving hungry. He was then faced with a dilemma. The restaurant would be closed by now, and if he went out to get something to eat, he would either have to smuggle Milly out of the hotel and back in again or leave her in the room. The first option was almost too tiresome to contemplate and, as for the second, he knew she would howl the place down the moment he'd gone. He tried to convince himself he really wasn't that hungry after all, but the sounds which came from his stomach reminded him otherwise.

'Bollocks,' he said as he manoeuvred himself upright on the bed. He looked down at Milly, who was snoring contentedly beside him. 'Listen, I'll do you a deal. If you stay here quietly, I'll bring you back a whole McDonald's McDoggyburger all to yourself.'

Milly shifted slightly in her sleep.

'And chips?' Trevor threw in as an extra incentive.

Milly shifted again and groaned.

'Okay, okay, *large* chips.'

Trevor eased himself from the bed and edged towards the door. All the while, he watched to see if Milly would wake. Just as his hand touched the door handle, Milly opened one eye and pointed it in his direction.

'But I'm bloody *starving,*' Trevor said. 'It's not as if there wouldn't be anything in it for you.'

Milly opened her other eye and then rolled onto her back, all four of her legs crooked playfully into the air.

'Oh for God's sake, Milly. Why can't you be a proper, well-behaved dog for once like other people have?'

Milly wriggled herself comfortable.

'Right, that's it,' said Trevor as he strode back towards the bed. He fixed her with a stare and raised a finger. 'I'm going to be out for ten minutes – twenty at most – and if you make a sound while I'm gone, I'll... I'll... Well, just don't even think about it.'

He backed up to the door, willing her to silence with his eyes. Out in the corridor, he'd gone no more than ten paces when he heard the sound of a wailing banshee. He burst back into the room to find Milly sitting squarely on the bed, her nose pointed vertically towards the ceiling, baying at an imaginary moon.

'Milly!'

She stopped abruptly mid howl and turned to face him, lowering her head as she did so, as if to convey her awareness that she had done a bad thing and that she was truly sorry, but to be perfectly frank, the situation he had placed her in had left her with very little alternative.

'And don't give me that butter wouldn't melt crap. You're a pain in the arse and you know it. – And get off the bloody bed, you... you... bitch.'

Milly slithered down onto the floor and under the bed. Trevor flung himself onto the mattress, and there was a yelp from beneath him.

'Serves you right,' he said. 'Because of you, I'm probably going to pass out through lack of food. I may even die. What about that then, eh? Who'd look after you then, eh? I mean, who'd be stupid enough to take on a... '

While he continued to rant, Milly emerged from under the bed and went in search of a safer, if not quieter, resting place. Making her way towards a small but comfortable-looking armchair beside the window, she suddenly stopped and began sniffing the air. After a few moments, she seemed to have located the source of olfactory interest and placed her front paws on the top of a low, oak-effect table in the corner of the room. Her sniffing intensified as she examined the contents of a round plastic tray – an electric jug kettle; a cup, saucer and teaspoon; a small wicker basket containing teabags, sachets of coffee and sugar, and individual pots of UHT milk; and— Just then, in her enthusiasm to investigate her discovery more closely, Milly's nose brushed against the cup and saucer.

Trevor snapped his head round to see where the sound of rattling china had come from.

'*Now* what are you doing?' he said. 'Get down off there before you break something.'

Milly stayed where she was, glanced briefly in his direction and then resumed her examination of the tea- and coffee-making facilities.

Trevor swung his feet over the side of the bed. 'I thought I told you to—' But he had completed only two of the three or four strides that lay between him and Milly when he spotted the object of the dog's attentions.

* * *

An hour or so later, Trevor sat on the toilet of the tiny en suite bathroom contemplating one of life's many little mysteries, as he was often wont to do at such times. On this occasion, he was attempting to resolve his newly formed hypothesis that hunger could be at least partially alleviated by the retention of bodily solids. The two small packets of biscuits (three custard creams in one and three shortbreads in the other, less half a custard cream and half a shortbread grudgingly given to Milly as a reward for her discovery) had, if anything, made him feel even hungrier.

His particular concern was that he might lose what meagre benefit he had derived from the biscuits if he had a dump, and his philosophical musings had almost convinced him to pull up his jeans and abandon the operation altogether when he remembered an article he'd once read. As far as he could recall, it had said that food takes several hours to pass through the digestive system, and that being so, the custard creams and shortbreads would not yet be anywhere near the disembarkation area. If he walked away now and then suddenly became desperate in the middle of the night, he might lose everything. On the other hand, if he did it now, the biscuits would still be safe until he was within sight of breakfast the following morning.

Smiling to himself at having satisfactorily resolved yet

another of life's conundrums, he coiled one down.

Mission accomplished and respectably dressed once again, his hand reached towards the chrome-plated flush handle. Trevor had believed his adventure had begun as soon as he had released the clutch and set off in his camper van, but in fact the adventure only began in earnest the moment he started to exert a downward pressure on the flush handle. It was like pulling a lever to let down the drawbridge to a whole new way of life.

Trevor, however, was totally oblivious to the momentousness of the occasion, particularly as, when he pushed the handle, nothing happened. There was no familiar sound of water cascading into the toilet bowl, just a dull mechanical clunk from somewhere inside the cistern.

6

Detective Sergeant Logan peered into the large, ornate mirror above the fireplace and plucked a single grey hair from his temple.

'And you've no idea where he is now,' he said.

'Who?' The old woman addressed herself to the window and the empty street outside as she had done for most of the time since they'd arrived nearly an hour ago.

Detective Constable Swann shifted her position on the battered, bottle-green settee, her pen poised above the small notebook on her knee in case something might be said that was worth recording.

'Your son?' Logan said, and Swann caught the sag of the head and the closing of the eyes in his reflection.

'What about him?'

The detective spun round. 'Oh for—'

'I think what DS Logan is wanting to confirm,' said Swann, pre-empting his outburst, 'is that you don't know where your son went after he left here at lunchtime.'

'Trevor, you mean?'

'That's right. Trevor.'

'No thought for me. No thought for his invalid old mother, oh no. His brother wouldn't have gone. God rest his soul.'

'The thing is, Mrs er...' Logan appeared to have recovered his composure but gestured to Swann for a prompt. She mouthed the name as clearly as she could, and he ran with it.

'Er... yes. The thing is, Mrs Dawkins—'

'Hawkins,' snapped the old woman. 'Mrs *Haw*-kins.'

'Sorry, yes. – Mrs Hawkins, if there's anything at all you can remember about the conversation with your son that might help us to find him, it would save a lot of valuable time.'

'All I know is he went off on that silly little moped of his and that was that.'

'So as far as you're aware, he could be absolutely anywhere.'

The old woman raised her shoulders by no more than half an inch and let them fall again.

Logan rested his arm on the mantelpiece and drummed his fingers. 'Mrs Hawkins, you do realise you've given us very little to go on here. You've made a very serious accusation about your son, and it's essential that we find him as quickly as possible. As it stands though, we don't even know where to start looking.'

'That's why you've got computers and all that stuff, isn't it?'

'Computers aren't crystal balls. You have to put something in to get something out. All we've got at the moment is a name and a photograph.'

'He's got a dog.'

'Sorry?'

'He's got a dog,' she repeated. 'Mangy little thing. He brought it here once, but that was the first and last time. I told him I didn't want it near this house ever again. He's probably taken it with him.'

'On a moped?'

'How should I know?'

'Well I suppose it might help to identify him if he *has* got the dog with him. What does it look like?'

'Mangy, as I said.'

'Colour?'

'I don't know. Black and brown probably.'

'Probably?'

'I just told you, I only saw it the once.'

'Size?'

'Medium?' It was more of a question than a statement.

Logan switched his attention to his colleague. 'You've got all this down, have you?'

'Yes, sarge,' she said, vaguely waving her notebook as if in confirmation.

'Right. Well in that case, we'd best be on our way... unless of course there's anything else you can tell us.'

Still with her back to them, Mrs Hawkins responded with an almost imperceptible shake of the head.

'Fine. Thank you for your er... assistance. We'll see ourselves out.'

* * *

DS Logan and DC Swann sat opposite each other at a corner table of The Hen and Chickens. For a Friday evening, the pub was surprisingly empty, although from the look of the place Swann wondered if it ever attracted more than a handful of the most committed of drinkers. It was one of those single storey, block-shaped buildings thrown up on the edge of housing estates back in the sixties, and the inside was overwhelmingly bright and smelt of stale beer and chip fat. She only hoped she wouldn't need to find out what the toilet was like while they were there.

'So what do we do now?' she said.

Logan took a long slug from his pint of bitter and wiped his mouth with the back of his hand. 'We do what all good detectives are supposed to do. We investigate.'

'You don't think she was making it all up then?'

'Possibly. But it's still a murder accusation and not just some complaint about the neighbour's dog fouling the footpath.'

Swann picked up the photograph which lay next to her

glass of orange juice. 'Doesn't look much like a murderer to me.'

Logan almost choked on his beer, 'Maggie, I really can't believe you said that.'

'All the same...' She continued to stare at the picture of Trevor and Imelda Hawkins on their wedding day, posing for the camera in all their finery – she with a forced grin on her face and he looking rather more genuinely happy. 'We've hardly got anything to go on. Even this photograph is years old.'

'Six, to be precise.'

'That's a bit odd in itself, isn't it? I mean, there were plenty of pictures of his brother and a fair few of his sister but only this one of Trevor. – Can't be very fond of him.'

'Well no. Turning in your own son for murder isn't what you'd normally expect from a doting mother.'

'Maybe inventing a story about Trevor murdering his wife is a way of getting back at him for the other son's death,' said Swann, flipping through her notebook for the name. 'Derek was definitely the apple of mummy's eye. – It's classic. Favourite kid dies. Mum resents the other kid for still being alive.'

'And shops him for a murder that never even happened?' Logan drained his pint and set the empty glass down in front of him, gazing at it as he twisted it back and forth between his palms. 'Look, I've no idea whether she's made it all up or not, but like I say, we have to do *something*. Otherwise the old bat'll put in some kind of official complaint. She's just the type who would.'

'Okay, Sherlock, so where do you suggest we start?'

'First, you go and get me another pint.' Logan gave her an exaggerated wink and slid his glass towards her.

'So how come it's my round again?'

'Forgot to bring my wallet.'

'Yeah, sure.' Swann got to her feet with a scowl and made her way to the bar.

When she got back, Logan was leafing through her notebook. 'God, your writing's atrocious,' he said without looking up.

'So? As long as I can read it, that's all that matters.'

'I mean, what's this supposed to say?' He pushed the notebook towards her, keeping the tip of his finger on a point halfway down the page.

'Married April 2007.' She read the words aloud as if it was perfectly obvious what they said.

'Oh I see. I thought it was "Maimed anvil soon".'

'Ha ha, very amusing.'

'Seriously. And what's this?' He pointed to another phrase on the same page.

'Er... ' She frowned as she stared at the words Logan had indicated. 'Actually, I'm not sure about that bit.'

'I rest my case,' he said, picking up his pint and sitting back in his chair.

'What the hell. We got so little out of her, I can remember it all anyway.'

'Yeah? Okay then, off you go.'

'What, now?'

'Good a time as any.'

Despite claiming total recall, DC Swann still used her notes for reference as she began to summarise the story the old woman had told them: 'Trevor Hawkins. Age forty-three. Married Imelda in April 2007. No children. Wife disappeared October 2011—'

'And Mrs H reckons our Trevor did her in and then—'

'Got rid of the body. Yes, I know. I was just getting to that.'

'And how does Mrs H know this?'

'Because he told her.'

'Figures.' Logan spoke the word with more than a hint of sarcasm.

'Maybe he couldn't live with his guilty secret any longer. Had to tell someone... someone he could trust not to turn him in.'

'What? His mother? He must have known she was just as likely to rat on him as anyone else.'

'Perhaps he didn't want to admit to himself that she couldn't stand the sight of him. Anyway, who else was he going to tell? Doesn't sound like he had any friends to speak of.'

'There's a sister though.'

Swann shrugged. 'Estranged? Not speaking? Who knows?'

'Too many questions and not enough answers,' said Logan, then gulped his beer and only half-heartedly attempted to stifle a belch. 'Come on. You've got work to do.'

7

Trevor could hear voices. He was almost certain of it.

He pressed his ear to the door once again. From somewhere along the corridor, he could just make out the sound. Two women, chatting and laughing. Every so often, the voices disappeared completely and then reappeared again a few minutes later, becoming gradually more audible each time. This was exactly the sound he had been hoping to hear for the past hour, and he prayed he was right about the people the voices belonged to.

He sucked on the knuckle he'd gashed whilst trying to fix the broken toilet flush. Although he was fully aware of his severely limited plumbing skills, he'd felt morally unable to simply leave the unflushed loo for someone else to find. Nor had it been an option to call reception and get somebody to come and repair it as this would have revealed that he was illegally harbouring a dog in his room. To his relief, however, when he'd removed the porcelain cistern lid and balanced it on the edge of the bath, the problem had seemed fairly straightforward. The bolt which had become dislodged from the lever hinge lay at the bottom of the cistern. It was merely a question of retrieving it and replacing it in its rightful position.

In hindsight, Trevor couldn't understand why he had been quite so cavalier about the difficulty of the task in hand. He would normally approach any such job in the sure and certain knowledge that if it appeared simple at first sight, it would be bloody difficult, and if it appeared difficult, it would be totally impossible. In this particular case, it had taken him an inordinate amount of time just to retrieve the fallen bolt due to the narrowness of the gap between the flush mechanism and the side of the cistern. He'd been able to slide his hand through, but his forearm had become trapped when the bolt was only half a centimetre from his fingertips, so he'd searched the room for anything which might resemble a pair of pliers. In the end, he'd had to make do with the nail scissors from his washbag, and after several attempts, he'd managed to get the blades to grip the bolt firmly enough for him to ease it upwards through the water. On three occasions, however, the bolt had slipped from the grasp of the scissors and fallen back to the bottom just as it was almost within reach of his free hand

When he had finally retrieved the elusive bolt, it had taken him a matter of seconds to insert it through the holes in the two parts of the lever hinge. He had realised that there was a small nut which would have secured the bolt in place, but since this also lay at the bottom of the cistern, he'd decided that he could still get the flush to work as long as he was careful. The first time he'd tested it, he was obviously not careful enough, and he had watched in horror as the bolt slipped from the hinge and sank rapidly down through the water.

'Dammit!'

Straightening up from his stooping position, he'd brushed against the cistern lid, and it had tottered for a moment and then fallen from the edge of the bath and broken into half a dozen pieces on the tiled floor below.

'Dammit!!!'

The noise must have woken Milly as she had instantly started barking to warn off the suspected but unseen intruder. Trevor had raced into the bedroom to find her standing on the bed, directing her attentions fixedly at the main door and in exactly the opposite direction to the bathroom.

He had hissed at her to be quiet, and for once, she had obeyed, turning towards him with a quizzical expression, which might have been interpreted as: So no intruder then?

After another half an hour of struggling, cursing and fiddling, the job was done. Gingerly pressing down the lever with one hand whilst simultaneously holding the bolt in place with the other, a gush of water had finally dispatched the contents of the toilet bowl on their long delayed journey.

So, what to do about the broken lid? One solution would be to leave the hotel early in the morning before anyone noticed the damage, but Trevor was one of those people to whom guilt came easily, and he was always keen to avoid it whenever possible. The logical answer would be simply to own up and pay for the damage when he checked out, but the room was already costing him a small fortune, and he was reluctant to shell out any more of his redundancy cash.

He had lain awake for most of the night, wrestling with the problem until a plan of sorts eventually began to evolve. But even when he was as satisfied as he could be that it might actually work, he had slept only fitfully. This was partly due to Milly's snoring, but mostly to the Richter Scale grumblings from his empty stomach.

Now, as he stood with his ear to the door, the women's voices in the corridor reappeared, and this time he could begin to recognise occasional words and phrases:

> VOICE 1: ... said to 'im... think you're... in 'ere with... bloody joking...
> VOICE 2: ... always... daft booger...
> VOICE 1: ... shove it where...

Trevor estimated that the sound of laughter which

followed couldn't have been more than a dozen yards away before it dissolved into silence. It was time to make his move.

He checked that Milly was still curled nose-to-bum on the bed. The nose was twitching a fraction out of time with her lip, more rhythmically accompanied by a *sotto voce* whimpering, and judging by the spasmodic jittering of her feet, she was chasing rabbits or – more likely – a rapidly escaping *cordon bleu* cowpat. But whatever the object of her subconscious quest, the important thing was that she was deeply asleep and therefore less likely to wake up and howl like a maniac when she realised he'd gone. So far, so good.

With his eyes fixed on Milly, he picked up his navy blue holdall and crept out into the corridor. He eased the door shut behind him and listened. He could no longer hear whimpering, but he breathed again when the expected shrieks of abandonment didn't materialise.

He looked to his left. Nothing. To his right, he could see one of those tall wire cages on wheels like they use in supermarkets, stacked with clean white towels and bed sheets. It was parked outside a room three along from his own. All was still quiet on the Milly front, so he advanced towards the cage, occasionally glancing over his shoulder to check whether anyone was watching. It occurred to him that this was faintly ridiculous since he hadn't done anything wrong yet, but he carried on doing it anyway.

As he came closer, the women's voices became more distinct:

> VOICE 1: You think so?
> VOICE 2: No doubt about it.
> VOICE 1: *Sharon*?
> VOICE 2: Sharon.
> VOICE 1: Well, who'd have thought it?

VOICE 2: Eee, there's nowt so queer as folk.
VOICE 1: 'Cept thee and me.
VOICE 2: And I'm not so sure about thee.

The two women exploded into laughter, and Trevor hesitated for a moment outside the open door. He practised a smile, assumed what he hoped might resemble an air of confidence, and then strode into the room.

'Oh,' he said in feigned surprise as he set down his holdall and took in the view of the two women bent low over either side of the single bed.

Neither of them missed a beat. They went on with their tucking and smoothing, and the older one with the badly peroxided hair said, 'Sorry, duck. Thought you'd still be at breakfast. Won't be a tick.'

'No problemo,' said Trevor and immediately thought: No problemo? *No problemo*? I've never said that to anyone in my life.

At the same time, he caught the glance that the slimmer, dark haired one gave to Peroxide and it read "prat".

'No problemo, ladies.' He couldn't believe he'd said it again, and for want of something better to do, he wandered over to the window and looked out on the street below. In a shop doorway opposite, a dog was casually relieving himself over the prone body of some poor sod who clearly couldn't afford these hotel prices.

'I'll just pop this over 'ere, shall I, duck?'

Trevor turned to see that Peroxide was dangling a black lacy bra from her fingertips, and without waiting for an answer, she draped it over the arm of a chair next to the window. The other woman had her back to him, but he could tell from the rapid rise and fall of her shoulders that she was struggling to control her sniggering. His face burned as a dozen unlikely

38

explanations flooded his brain.

'Er… yes, that's fine,' he said. 'It's um… it's my wife's.' Yeah, good one, Trevor, what with this being a *single* room in case you hadn't noticed.

'Course it is, lovie,' Peroxide said with a smirk. 'Anyway, we're all done 'ere now.'

As the two chambermaids gathered up their various sprays and polishes and slotted them into a plastic carrier, Trevor wondered if they had him down as one of those blokes who gets off on wearing women's underwear or whether they just suspected he'd had a woman in his room. He didn't even care if they thought it was a hooker. Far better that than being taken for a transvestite.

Still, no point worrying about that now. He had a job to do. The moment they closed the door behind them, he ignored the burst of laughter and snatched up his holdall. He knew he might not have much time. The real occupant could already be on his – or more probably, *her* – way back from breakfast. Not only that, but Milly might wake up any second and start howling the place down.

Oh shit. The thought suddenly struck him that he'd forgotten to hang the "Do Not Disturb" sign outside his room. This had been an integral part of his plan to make sure no-one went in and discovered Milly, and now the chambermaids were only minutes away from doing that very thing. Even more reason to work quickly.

He dived into the bathroom and was relieved to see the toilet was exactly the same as his own. Carefully – very carefully – he lifted the lid from the cistern. As he turned and placed it gently on the floor, his mind did a doubletake. What was that?

8

Sandra sat eyeing the last piece of toast in the silver rack in front of her.

Hell, it's only half a slice. It's not as if I'd be shoving down half a loaf. I mean, *half a bloody slice*. Get a grip, woman. You don't even need to put much butter on it.

Maybe you could just do the marmalade and forget the butter altogether. Yeah, that's it. Marmalade. No butter. Well you'll have to have marmalade at least 'cos it's been sitting there for a while now, and it's going to be as dry as the driest thing in Dryville on Saint Dry's Day without something or other spread on it.

'Would madam care for more coffee?'

'Jesus,' she said, snatching back the hand that was already reaching for the toast.

'I'm sorry, madam. Did I startle you?'

She turned to see a waistcoated and bow-tied waiter with a dome of a forehead and an absurdly pointed chin hovering above her with a china coffee pot.

'Er... No. Er, no, not at all. I was only...'

'Would madam like some fresh toast?' said the waiter with a slight inclination of his head towards the lonely piece in the rack.

He reminded her of someone, but she couldn't quite place him. In any case, he was obviously on to her with the toast thing. She could read it in his wide-set eyes, and what he really meant by all the madam this and madam that was: Okay, fatty, I can see you're gonna scoff down every last scrap of food on this table, so why don't I get you some more and you can have yourself a frigging party?

'Excuse me?' Her tone was indignant.

'Would madam like more *toast*?'

'Oh, I'm sorry. I was miles away. Er, no. No thanks.'

'Coffee?' He tilted the pot towards her empty cup.

Was it the chin or the heavy, dark eyebrows that made him seem so familiar? Or perhaps it was the mouth, which looked like it couldn't decide whether it wanted to pout or sneer. But where had she seen him bef—

'Of course,' she said with a click of her fingers. 'Quentin Tarantino.'

'What?' said the waiter, losing the ever-so-slightly-French accent in that one solitary word.

'You know. *Reservoir Dogs* and all that. *Kill Bill*? *Inglourious Basterds*?' Sandra beamed at him, delighted she had cracked the mystery.

"Quentin" now stood erect and bristling. 'No coffee or toast then,' he said in a seriously Birmingham accent as he began to turn away.

'No, no. Both. Bring it on.' She sat back, flamboyantly folding her arms and staring at the lonely piece of toast, a beatific grin still spread across her face.

Quentin leaned forward and poured coffee into her cup. 'As madam wishes.' The words came through teeth that appeared to be intent on grinding each other to dust.

Sandra watched the flow of dark liquid and inhaled the bittersweet aroma. When the waiter had gone, she added a dash of cream and a teaspoon of sugar, hesitating for the briefest of moments before adding a second. She raised the cup level with her eyes. 'Here's to me,' she said. 'Sandra Gray. Private detective.'

Taking a sip, she thought how good life could be sometimes, and her tongue tingled with the anticipation of the crisp, fresh toast that would belong to her, and her alone, in a few short minutes. A touch on the underdone side of overdone and cut triangularly. It always tasted so much better like that, so why was it she always cut it straight across on a right-angle when she made it at home? It wasn't as if it involved any more effort.

Hang on though. Yes it did. She vaguely remembered her geometry from school and something about Pythagoras's hypotenuse – or was it isosceles? Or even Isosceles's pythagoras. Whatever. Anyway, it was definitely true that the slopey bit was much longer than the straight bit, and to confirm it she traced a right-angled triangle with a fork on the tablecloth.

To hell with it. I'm having extra butter *and* marmalade when it comes, and bugger the consequences. I should be celebrating, not fiddle-fannying around about a few calories here and there.

She took a generous slug of coffee and leaned back in her chair. Two grand and all expenses paid. Not bad for a couple of days' work, and she'd only been in business less than six months. Easy-peasy lemon-squeezy. All she had to do now was—

'Your toast, madam.'

Sandra looked up into the face of a scrawny, raven-haired girl with multiple piercings and skin the colour of anaemic alabaster. She had never fully understood the allure of the Goth look.

'What happened to Quentin?'

'Quentin, madam?' said the Goth in a monotone and without any attempt at eye contact as she placed the silver rack of toast within easy reach.

'The guy with the pointy chin and the eyebrows who was here before.'

The girl finally met Sandra's gaze. 'Don't know, madam. I expect he's doing other guests.'

'What makes you think he isn't on a plane halfway to Costa Rica?'

The Goth clearly didn't recognise Mr Pink's line from

Reservoir Dogs, and she gawped for a moment before reciting, 'Would madam like more coffee?'

'Yes please. Oh, and could you bring a little more butter while you're at it?'

9

Taped to the underside of the cistern lid was a transparent plastic wallet, and inside this Trevor could see a brown paper envelope. Perhaps all it contained were the instructions for... For what? How to flush the toilet? Okay, so maybe it was the guarantee or—

Curiosity got the better of him, and he peeled the wallet from the porcelain. He took out the envelope and, turning it over in his hand, saw that it was unmarked and seemed to have been opened and then resealed again. He prised open the flap and removed the contents. A ticket and two white index cards, one of which had a small yellow Post-it note attached and a bronze coloured key stuck to the back.

Both cards had been printed with some kind of stick-on letters. The one with the Post-it note said:

> FLAT 12
> CABOT TOWER
> MILTON STREET
> BRISTOL

On the Post-it, someone had written in block capitals:

> LEAVE THIS CARD IN LOCKER.
> DESTROY POST-IT NOTE.

Trevor read the second card:

> LOCKER NUMBER C9
> COMBINATION 357716

MOTHER'S MAIDEN NAME = HURST

MEMORABLE DATE = 30/07/66

Then he examined the ticket:

LEEDS FESTIVAL

BRAMHAM PARK

24th – 26th AUGUST

DAY TICKET ONLY

SATURDAY 25th AUGUST

He frowned and scratched his head as he scanned each of the items again. The address of a flat in Bristol – and presumably a key for it. Something about a locker and a festival ticket for 25th August... Today in fact.

But what's it all doing inside a toilet cistern? And what's with destroying the Post-it note? Weird or what? Still, it's nothing to do with me. Need to get on.

Trevor replaced the cards and the ticket in the envelope and slipped it back into the plastic wallet, but no sooner had he sealed it than he heard the cacophony of Milly launching into one of her famous barking frenzies, unmistakable even at this distance.

'Shit,' he said aloud and dropped to his haunches. He re-taped the wallet back inside the cistern lid while a voice in his head told him this was not a very sensible idea, but he had no time to listen. Milly's barking had reached a crescendo, and Trevor thought he could hear the sound of a woman screaming – or was that two women?

He wrenched open the canvas holdall and emptied the broken pieces of porcelain onto the floor, making a vague attempt to arrange them so it looked as if this was where the cistern lid had fallen. Then he laid the intact lid in the holdall and zipped it shut.

Grabbing the bag by the handle, he fled from the bathroom, through the bedroom, and out into the corridor. As he had feared, the wire cage with the towels and linens was parked immediately outside his room, but how had the chambermaids got there so quickly? He scuttled along the hallway and soon had his answer. The two intervening rooms on his side of the corridor had "Do Not Disturb" notices hanging from their door handles, and on the floor outside the second on the right was a large silver tray laid with breakfast.

He was almost level with this particular door when it opened, and an overweight man in a white towelling dressing gown appeared and stooped down to pick up the tray.

'What an idiot,' said Trevor.

The man in the dressing gown paused mid-stoop and stared up at him, a baffled expression on his bloated face. 'Excuse me?'

'Oh sorry. Not you. Me. I'm the idiot,' Trevor said without breaking his stride and continued to chide himself for having forgotten to put a "Do Not Disturb" sign on his own door.

So intent was he on getting there, he scarcely registered the words, 'You know, I think you're probably right'.

The barking had reached a ridiculous level of decibels by the time he burst into the room, and he was not in the least surprised by the awful scene which greeted him. Milly stood in the middle of the bed, baying wildly in the direction of the two chambermaids, who were pinned against the far wall with a look of abject terror on their tear-stained faces. One of them – the younger of the two – was just completing an excruciatingly ear-piercing scream when Trevor came through the doorway.

'Milly!' he yelled.

Milly, who was quite clearly having a whale of a time,

stopped barking long enough to look round at her master and then, after giving him what could only be described as a conspiratorial wink, turned back towards her cornered prey and resumed her deafening assault.

Trevor rapidly approached the bed. 'Milly, I'm warning you...'

Apparently realising he was serious this time, she gradually reduced her barking to a barely audible level and contented herself with an occasional growl, supplemented here and there with a teeth-baring snarl. If it hadn't been for the seriousness of the situation, Trevor would have found Milly's display of aggression highly amusing. He knew as well as she did that it was all show, and if the chambermaids had stood up to her, she would have run a mile.

'That your dog?' said Peroxide.

'Er...' Trevor glanced round at Milly as if noticing her for the first time.

'It's a bloody menace, that's what it is.'

'Ought to be... put down... if you... ask me.' The younger woman could barely get the words out through her tears.

'You may well have a point there,' Trevor muttered, and he gave Milly a withering glare, which she completely ignored and directed a particularly threatening growl towards the two women.

'I'll 'ave you reported, I will,' Peroxide said, seeming to regain her composure a little. 'And what was yer doing in t'other room?'

'Long story I'm afraid, and I'm a bit pushed for time at the moment.'

With that, Trevor disappeared into the bathroom and closed the door. But as he removed the cistern lid from his holdall, he spotted the plastic wallet taped to the underside, and straight away he understood the reason for his sense of unease a few minutes earlier.

Oh bloody Nora. How could you have been so stupid?

He stared at the wallet and tried to think what to do with the damn thing. There was no point leaving it here... Perhaps he could sneak back into the other room and— No, that wouldn't work. The door had locked as soon as he'd closed it behind him... Maybe he could hand it in at reception when—

He suddenly became aware that Milly had cranked up her vicious-killing-machine act with some blood-curdling growling and snarling, and the two women had started screaming again. The reception plan would have to do. Ripping the wallet from the lid, he tossed it into his holdall and then carefully positioned the lid on top of the cistern.

Back in the bedroom, he saw that the chambermaids had pressed themselves against the wall once again, and the younger one was about to let out another scream. He stuffed his few belongings into the holdall and turned to the two cowering women. 'Er... Sorry.'

'Aye, right,' said Peroxide with a snarl that even Milly would have been proud of.

'She wouldn't have hurt you, you know.'

'Tuh.'

Trevor headed for the doorway. 'Come on, Milly. Hurry up.'

Milly jumped down off the bed and took a step towards the two women. This time, both of them screamed as if they really were being savaged by a demented hound from hell.

Trevor was almost at the stairs when Milly came bounding up behind him, her tail held almost perpendicular and wagging like a hyperactive windscreen wiper.

10

With a full stomach and the prospect of being two grand richer in the next couple of days, Sandra Gray felt nothing but utter contentment as she strode out of the hotel dining room. When she reached the foyer, she saw there was a queue for the lift.

What the hell, she thought. It's only two flights, and the exercise will help salve my conscience about the extra toast.

She made her way to the staircase and started to climb. Rounding the corner onto the first floor landing, she had little time to register the man who was hurtling down the stairs towards her. The collision was inevitable, and she almost went down under the force of the impact but managed to stay on her feet by grabbing hold of the handrail.

She pulled herself upright and realised that the guy seemed to have come off worse than she had. He'd dropped his canvas holdall and was supporting himself with one hand against the wall and the other clutched to his chest as he fought to catch his breath.

'You all right?' she said.

'S... sorry... 'bout that.' He wheezed out the words between gulps of air.

If she hadn't been feeling quite so pleased with herself, Sandra would probably have given him a good tongue-lashing, but instead she settled for: 'That's okay. No harm done.'

She waited for him to recover, not knowing what else

to say until she spotted the black and tan mongrel gazing up at her and frenetically wagging its tail.

'That your dog?'

'Er, yes.'

'I didn't think you were supposed to—'

'No, you're not. But we're leaving now anyway.'

'Ah.'

His breathing seemed to have returned to normal, and he stooped to pick up his bag. 'Look, I don't want to be rude, but I'm in quite a hurry and I—'

'Sure.' Sandra smiled and stepped to one side to let him pass.

'Sorry about…'

'Don't worry. No broken bones.'

'Come on, Milly,' he said and nodded a goodbye.

Sandra reciprocated and watched him scurry down the staircase with his dog and disappear from view into the foyer.

Nice enough, she thought as she began to climb the second flight of stairs, and not bad looking in a rabbit-in-the-headlights kind of way. The eyes were a bit on the boggly side, and the thick, mousey hair could have done with a trim, not to mention a comb, but other than that, not bad at all. Sexy? Five out of ten maybe, although, to be fair, the grey fleece jacket didn't do him any favours, and the jeans were much too saggy to tell whether he had a decent arse on him. There was something odd about him though. Something… furtive. Perhaps it was just that he was in a hurry, or possibly it was her private detective mind being a little overactive.

By the time she reached her room, Sandra had all but forgotten him and was planning what she would need to do in the next few hours. She closed the door behind her and headed straight for the bathroom. Too much coffee always had this effect on her.

What the f—

The open-topped cistern and the pieces of broken porcelain on the floor stopped her in her tracks. A moment later, her heart almost stopped as well.

Oh Christ, no.

She dropped to her knees and rummaged frantically amongst the shattered remains of the cistern lid.

No, no, no. This can't be happening.

Sandra's bladder reminded her of her pressing need, and as she sat, she leaned forward and continued to sift through the broken porcelain. But it was no good. The bloody thing just wasn't there.

Okay, girl, calm down. It can't have vanished into thin air. It was here last night when you arrived, exactly where you'd been told it would be, and it was still here an hour ago when you went down to breakfast. So somebody must have taken it. Why though? And more importantly, who?

All right, think about who had access to the room, who had been in here last... Then she remembered passing a metal laundry cage in the corridor a few minutes earlier. Of course. The cleaners must have accidentally dropped the cistern lid and then spotted the envelope and put it somewhere else.

She scanned every surface in the bathroom as she got to her feet and rearranged her clothing. Not here.

She rushed into the bedroom and searched desperately but fruitlessly, all the while trying to suppress the rising panic in her chest.

The buggers must have nicked it. But why would they? What possible use could it be to them?

Sandra immediately realised the futility of asking herself these questions when the culprits themselves were probably still just along the corridor.

She swept out of the room and almost ran along the hallway to where the linen cage was parked outside an open door. Without even thinking of knocking, she marched into the bedroom and saw two women in white housecoats, one of them talking on the telephone and the other sitting on the edge of the bed, her head in her hands.

'Excuse me.' Sandra's voice was firm to the point of authoritarian.

The woman on the phone barely acknowledged her presence and continued her conversation, anxiously fiddling with a loose strand of heavily bleached hair. '... That's right. A bloody dog... '

The girl on the bed slowly lifted her head and stared myopically in Sandra's direction, her eyes red from crying.

'Have you just been in to clean my room?'

'Dunno,' sniffed the chambermaid.

'What do you mean, you don't know?' Sandra's patience was already strained to the limit.

'We clean loads. What number?'

'Twenty-five.'

''Appen we musta done.'

'Well, in that case...' Sandra peered at the card pinned to the girl's housecoat. '...Denise. Perhaps you could explain to me how you came to break the lid of the toilet cistern and what you've done with the...' She tailed off, not wanting to give out too much information in case the chambermaids might actually be innocent. 'There's also something missing from my room.'

'Eh?'

'Do I have to call the manager?'

'Sorry, I just dunno what you're on about.' She turned towards her colleague. 'Maureen?'

Maureen was still in mid conversation and gestured to her to be quiet. '... Well, it were one of you lot let him in in the first place...' She was clearly involved in a heated argument with whoever was on the other end of the line.

'I think you'd better come with me.' The fact that

Sandra's tone and choice of words made her sound like a police officer at the end of her tether was not entirely unintentional.

'Eh?' said Denise, blowing her nose on a tissue she'd taken from the box beside her on the bed.

'If you're going to play dumb, I'm obviously going to have to show you what I'm talking about. Come on. Up.'

'Oh chuffin' 'eck. As if I 'adn't 'ad enough to cope with already for one day.'

'Tell me about it. Now shift your arse.'

As the chambermaid forced herself to her feet, Maureen slammed the phone down. She looked from Denise to Sandra and back again. 'What's going on?'

'Dunno,' said Denise. 'Broken toilet or summat.'

Maureen eyed Sandra with undisguised contempt. 'Sorry, madam, but you'll 'ave to contact reception and 'ave 'em send up a plumber. Not our job, see.'

'Now listen to me, *Maureen*.' Sandra spoke the name with heavy disdain. 'I don't give a shit about the bloody toilet. What I do give a shit about – a very big shit in fact – is what you've done with the envelope that was inside it.' Instantly, she regretted that her anger had got the better of her resolve for discretion.

The two chambermaids exchanged sideways glances.

'Which room?' said Maureen.

'Twen-tee-five,' said Sandra, clearly enunciating each syllable.

Maureen turned back to Denise. ''Ang on a bit. That's the room where the bloke came in.'

'Oh yeah. It were.'

'Bloke? What *bloke*?' Sandra could feel her blood pressure mounting.

'Summat bloody odd goin' on 'ere if you ask me,' said Maureen. 'Broken toilet, you say?'

'Yes, but—'

Maureen brushed past her and was out of the door

before Sandra could get any further. A moment later, the younger chambermaid trotted after her.

'Oh Jesus,' said Sandra, rolling her eyes heavenwards and setting off in pursuit.

* * *

Immediately after his brief encounter with the woman on the stairs, Trevor found himself in the hotel foyer and advanced towards the reception desk.

The woman on duty was the same one that had checked him in the evening before. She was staring intently at the computer screen in front of her and occasionally tapping on the keyboard.

Trevor dropped his holdall to the floor and reached for the wallet in his back pocket. 'Can I have my bill, please?'

'I won't keep you a moment, sir,' said the receptionist without diverting her attention from the monitor.

'Ninety-five quid, wasn't it?'

'I'll be right with you, sir.' Her tone bristled with irritation.

'Actually, I'm in a bit of a hurry,' said Trevor and slapped five twenty-pound notes onto the desk.

The receptionist ponderously removed her heavy, black-rimmed glasses. 'I'm sorry, sir, but—' She broke off abruptly and leaned forward as if to confirm that her eyes had not deceived her. 'Is that your dog?'

Milly sat staring up at her and panting slightly.

Trevor was getting tired of having to answer the "Is that your dog?" question and chose to ignore it. He patted the banknotes on the counter. 'That's a hundred quid there. Okay?'

'Sir, I did tell you last night about the hotel's policy with regard to—'

'You did indeed, and now you've caught me red-handed.' He raised his hands in a gesture of mock surrender, surprised at how cocky he must have seemed. 'You owe me a fiver by the way.'

'I'm afraid I'll have to call the manager,' said the receptionist and reached for the telephone.

'Look, I haven't got time for all that.' He bent down and picked up his holdall. 'I tell you what. Why don't you keep the five quid as compensation for the dog and we'll say no more about it?'

He crossed the foyer to the main exit and held open the glass door, waiting for Milly. The receptionist had been joined by a tall, pasty-faced man in a dark blue suit and a pink and white striped tie. Both were looking in his direction, and the receptionist was pointing at him.

Trevor called to Milly to get a move on, and she was almost at the door when she suddenly squatted down and deposited a small puddle on the richly carpeted floor.

'Hey!' The man in the tie began to make his way out from behind the reception desk.

Out on the street, the holdall bashed repeatedly against Trevor's knee as he and Milly ran, but by the time Trevor heard the manager shout again from the hotel steps, they were just about to turn a corner and disappear.

11

His reaction wasn't unexpected, but there was no way of breaking it to him gently, so DC Swann had come straight out with it and then braced herself for the response. Logan was sitting at his desk reading a newspaper. He folded it roughly and slapped it down in front of him.

'Gone?' he said. 'What do you mean, it's gone?'

'As in… not there any more?'

He snatched up the newspaper and pointed it at her as if it were a loaded weapon. 'Don't get smart with me, constable.'

'Hey, I'm only the messenger,' said Swann. 'There's nothing on the system, and I even got Records to check the file hadn't been put back in the wrong place.'

'But that's ridiculous. A missing persons file can't just vanish.'

Swann decided this wasn't the time to remark on the irony of his statement. Instead, she told him how she'd asked around and found out who'd led the investigation into Imelda Hawkins's disappearance.

'Tom Doyle?' said Logan. 'But he retired months ago.'

'Still lives locally though.'

He drummed his fingers on the edge of the desk. 'I suppose we ought to pay him a visit then.'

'Two o'clock suit you?'

Logan raised an eyebrow. 'You've spoken to him?'

Swann could detect a gradual easing of the volcanic

tension as she summarised her phone call with Doyle. He'd denied all memory of the case at first, but she'd chipped away at him with the few details they had until he eventually admitted to having "some vague recollection". Even then, he'd become defensive, almost to the point of abusive, and had been doggedly resistant when she'd suggested a meeting. In the end, it had taken all her reserves of womanly wiles and the oral equivalent of some serious eyelash fluttering to bring him round.

'Always was a bit of a one for the ladies as I recall,' said Logan. 'Didn't get the name Donger Doyle for nothing.'

'Ee-yuck,' said Swann, guessing that the guy must be into his sixties by now and trying to blot out the inevitable mental image. 'Did you know him then?'

'Not really. I never worked with him directly, and he kept himself to himself most of the time. As far as us blokes were concerned anyway. – You ask him if he thought it was murder?'

'I decided I'd leave that to you.'

'Good plan.' He leaned back in his chair, swung his feet onto the desk and opened his newspaper.

Not for the first time, Swann wondered how he'd ever made it to detective sergeant and was about to leave when the phone rang.

'Get that, will you?' said Logan, without looking up from his paper. 'I'm a bit busy at the moment.'

Swann reached across the desk for the receiver. 'Yes?'

It was a result at last. Not a major one but a result nevertheless. She grabbed a pen and wrote down the details.

'Oh yes,' she said, putting down the phone and pumping the air with her fist. 'Detective Constable Maggie Swann strikes again.'

Logan cocked an eye at her over the top of his newspaper. 'Don't tell me you've done something useful for once.'

But her self-satisfaction was more than a match for his sarcasm, and she rode the punch without flinching. 'The whole bloke and dog on a moped thing seemed a bit unlikely to me, so I thought I'd—'

'—Find out whether there are any other vehicles registered in his name?'

This time, her smugness took the full force of the blow and threw in the towel. 'Camper van,' she said in a bland monotone. 'VW Transporter.'

'We'll make a detective of you yet,' said Logan with a wink and a click of the tongue.

Swann held up the middle three fingers of her right hand, the knuckles towards him.

'Read between the lines,' she said.

12

Sandra's contentment of earlier that morning had evaporated completely, and she was in no mood to be messed about. She had interrogated the two chambermaids until she was satisfied they really didn't know anything about the missing envelope. They'd told her about the strange man who had come into what they now knew to be her room and about how he had retrieved the mad dog from the room that was actually his.

Their story was far too bizarre to have been invented, Sandra had eventually concluded, and she doubted they would have had the wit to have concocted such a tale even if they'd wanted to. However, partly to reassure herself and partly out of spite, she had insisted that they turn out their pockets. Not surprisingly, they had objected strongly, but they had given in when she'd threatened to call the police.

There could only be one explanation for the missing envelope. The chambermaids' strange man with the mad dog must have taken it, but how he knew it was there and why he had stolen it was a total mystery. She was almost certain it must have been the same man she had bumped into on the stairs since it was unlikely there had been more than one guy with a dog in the hotel. She also recalled how furtive he'd seemed. At least she'd be able to recognise him again, so this chance encounter had been fortunate indeed. Even so, a few more details wouldn't go amiss.

'Don't muck me about,' said Sandra, glaring at the hotel manager from the opposite side of his desk. 'Just give me the name and address, and I'll be on my way.'

'The thing is, madam, we can't go giving out the details of other guests willy-nilly,' the manager said with his best attempt at an ingratiating manner.

'Willy-nilly? Willy-nilly? Now you listen to me, matey. I've had a very valuable item stolen from my room – a room in *your* hotel, I might add – and I'm still not entirely convinced that one of your staff wasn't responsible.'

'That's a very serious accusation, and I really must insist that—'

'Insist all you like, pal, but unless you give me what I want I'll have you so deep in scandal this place will be about as popular as a Chernobyl Travelodge.'

She knew she was bluffing and the manager probably did too, so after some further exchanges of Sandra's threats and the manager's flustered protestations, she decided to try a different approach. Softening her voice, she pointed out that this particular guest had broken the rules by bringing a dog into the hotel, so why should he show him any loyalty?

She could tell from the pause which followed and the expression on his face that this idea held some appeal for him. Perhaps he saw it as a way of exacting revenge on the wilful transgressor of his precious rules, or maybe he was beginning to believe that this she-devil in front of him really could cause serious trouble. Whatever the reason, his fingers hovered briefly over his computer keyboard and then started rattling away at the keys. Peering into the monitor, he read out a name and address while Sandra wrote them into her notepad.

'Thank you *so* much for your cooperation,' she said. 'You've been most helpful.'

Just as she opened the office door, he called out after

her. 'There will of course be a charge for the broken cistern lid I'm afraid.'

'Quite right,' said Sandra. 'I'll tell him when I see him, shall I?'

* * *

Trevor was happy to be back behind the wheel of his camper van once again and by the look of her, so too was Milly, who lay curled up asleep on the passenger seat beside him.

He had arrived at the garage to find his van raised high up on a hoist, and the mechanic he had spoken to the previous afternoon was tinkering away at the underside with a large spanner.

'You're in luck,' the mechanic had said. 'The part arrived earlier than I'd expected. Few more minutes and you should be on your way. What time did you say your brother's funeral was?'

'What?' Trevor had completely forgotten the lie he had told in an attempt to get the van repaired as quickly as possible.

'Newcastle, wasn't it?'

'Oh, er... yes, that's right, Newcastle. Brother's funeral, yes. Er... three-thirty, I think.'

'Don't you know?'

'Er, well... we weren't that close really.'

The mechanic had stopped what he was doing and given him a look before resuming his work.

A little less than an hour later, the van was rolling along at a steady forty-five miles per hour. Trevor's wallet was almost £200 lighter as a result, and with the hotel on top, he had already spent nearly £300 on unforeseen expenses.

'We might have to cut down on your dog food at this rate, Mill,' he said.

Milly lazily opened one eye and then immediately went back to sleep.

The traffic began to increase as Trevor looked out for signs to Bramham Park and the Leeds Festival. He still wasn't convinced this was a good idea, but he'd realised when he'd got to the garage that he'd forgotten to hand in the ticket and the index cards at the hotel reception. Returning to the hotel had not been an option, and at first, dropping them all into the nearest litter bin had seemed to be the most sensible alternative. But wasn't that part of the reason for this whole trip? To stop being sensible for once in his life and just go wherever his fancy took him? Be open to whatever might come his way, like Steppenwolf said in *Born to be Wild*?

Well, the ticket had come his way, so why not make use of it? What had he got to lose? It wasn't as if he had any other plans for the day, and besides, he'd guessed from the index cards that there must be something in a locker at the festival site, and his curiosity nagged at him to find out what.

He eventually located the car park that was designated on his ticket, and after queuing for about twenty minutes, a young woman in a fluorescent yellow tabard approached his open window.

'Can I see your ticket please?'

Trevor handed it to her, and she examined it before tearing off the perforated stub. Passing the larger portion back to him, she suddenly noticed Milly, who was now sitting bolt upright on the passenger seat and intently observing all the activity around her.

'You do realise you can't take dogs into the main arena, sir?'

Trevor glanced at Milly as if he had forgotten she was there. 'Oh right. Of course.'

'Unless it's a guide dog or a hearing dog, that is.'

'A what?'

'Hearing dog. You know, for deaf people. Mind you, I don't know why any deaf people would want to come to a thing like this.'

'Quite,' said Trevor and then followed the directions she gave him until he found a parking space.

'I hadn't thought about you not being allowed in,' he said to Milly. 'You'll be all right here for a bit though, won't you? I'll probably only be gone for an hour. Two at most.'

The dog looked directly into his eyes and wistfully cocked her head to one side.

'Oh Jesus, Milly. – Okay, half an hour tops.'

She cocked her head to the other side and gave a flick of her tail.

* * *

A thickset man with a shaven head and wearing one of the ubiquitous yellow stewards' vests started to hold out his hand for Trevor's ticket and then stopped. 'Sorry, mate, but there's no dogs allowed into the main arena.'

'Pardon?'

'I said there's no dogs allowed into the main arena,' the steward repeated but at a slightly increased volume.

Trevor responded with a faint shrug and tapped his right earlobe with his forefinger.

The steward gestured towards Milly and shook his head with exaggerated emphasis. 'Dog. No. Not here,' he shouted, and with a sweep of his arm he indicated the area beyond the ticket barrier behind him.

'I'm sorry, I don't understand. I'm very deaf, you see.'

'Might be one of them hearing dogs,' another steward chipped in.

'Oh yeah,' said Shaved Head. 'Don't we need some sort of proof though?'

'Dunno, mate. Never 'ad one before.'

Shaved Head turned back to Trevor and clearly enunciated the words, 'Do – you – have – a – certificate – or – summat?'

Trevor tilted his head forward as if straining to hear the steward's words more clearly. 'Sir... ?'

'Cer – tif – i – cate.'

'Get on with it for God's sake,' came a male voice from further back in the queue.

Shaved Head craned his neck to identify the voice's owner, and to judge from the narrowing of his eyes, whoever it was would be getting a hard time of it when his turn came to have his ticket checked.

'Oh just let him in, Phil,' said the second steward as he fixed a blue plastic tag around the wrist of a middle-aged woman with long, greying hair. 'We'll be here all day otherwise.'

'Quite right,' said the woman. 'This man clearly has a severe disability, and you're treating him like some kind of criminal.'

'And who asked you, Mrs Gandalf?' Phil's apparently tenuous grasp of the concept of customer relations seemed to be being tested to the limits.

'Well really,' said the woman. 'I've a good mind to report you to your employers.'

'Yeah? And how you gonna do that when I've banned you from the site? Now piss off on yer broomstick and let me get on with my job.'

The woman stood open-mouthed for a moment and then stormed off, shouting 'Fascist pig' over her shoulder.

'Come on, baldy. Get yer finger out.' It was a different male voice from the queue, and once again Phil appeared to make a mental note of his soon-to-be victim.

'Oh for—' he muttered and held out his hand. 'Give us yer ticket then.'

Trevor stared blankly back at him.

'Here.' The steward snatched the ticket from him and attached one of the blue plastic bands to his wrist. 'Next.'

Trevor turned to walk away but immediately turned back again. 'Oh, excuse me.'

'Now what?'

'Can you tell me where the lockers are?'

The steward flung out an arm and pointed at a large marquee about a hundred yards away. 'See the big yellow tent? T'other side of that is the food area. Through there, and the lockers are on the left.'

'Thank you,' said Trevor and instantly realised he'd forgotten the deaf act. Still, the steward didn't seem to have clocked it, and he set off towards the marquee with Milly trotting contentedly at his heels.

'Oi! You with the dog! Get back 'ere!'

Trevor didn't need to look round to know who was yelling at him, and he quickened his pace until he had merged into the thick of the crowd.

13

She was well aware that a hundred and twenty quid for a one day ticket was extortionate, but Sandra didn't have time to shop around. Her only priority was to get into the festival and catch up with the bastard who'd nicked the envelope before he screwed up her job completely. What was the name the hotel manager had given her? Terry...? No, Trevor. Trevor Hawkins. That was it.

'So how do I know it's genuine?' she asked the first tout she had come across outside the main entrance.

'Trust me, lady,' he said in a heavy Cockney accent.

'And why should I do that exactly?'

'Listen, love, everybody'll tell yer I'm honest as the day is long.'

'In Finland in December maybe.'

The tout bristled, his jaws visibly clenching and unclenching beneath the taut, suntanned skin. 'Look, d'you want it or not?'

'Hundred quid.'

'Leave it out. I've already come down from one-thirty.'

Sandra grunted and took her purse from the pocket of her cream cotton jacket. 'It better had be genuine for your sake. Because if it isn't, I shall come and find you and cut off both your nuts with a pair of very rusty and very blunt garden shears.'

'Oh yeah?'

She paused in the middle of counting out the banknotes and looked up to see the tout grinning at her.

He was missing two of his front teeth, and those that remained were clearly in need of some serious dental attention. She fixed him with a penetrating and emotionless stare, and the tout's grin subsided as he shuffled from one foot to the other.

'Okay, lady, keep yer 'air on. I'm only tryin' to make a livin'.'

After a few more seconds of watching him squirm, she released him from her gaze and finished counting the money. 'Here.'

The tout reached for the cash but stopped when Sandra quickly withdrew it from his grasp.

'Ticket first, I think,' she said, raising a menacing eyebrow.

He mumbled something under his breath and pulled a ticket from a bundle of about a dozen. Sandra snatched it from him and examined it closely before giving him the money.

Placing the ticket in her pocket alongside her purse, she began to walk in the direction of the main entrance and then suddenly turned.

'Don't forget,' she called out and mimed the action of opening and closing a pair of garden shears.

* * *

Trevor's senses were being battered from every direction as he walked towards the bright yellow marquee. There was the pounding rock music from the main outdoor stage, which morphed into the thundering rhythms of a group of Japanese drummers he glimpsed through the open sides of the marquee as he passed.

There were the vivid and clashing colours, not just of the clothes the people were wearing as they scurried this way and that, but of the numerous stalls selling all kinds of goods ranging from garishly painted wooden toys to outrageously flamboyant hats and plastic angel wings.

Beyond the marquee, his nose was bombarded with a bizarre blend of cooking smells emanating from the impressive range of mobile kitchens arranged on three sides of a large square. Each scent vied with the other to attract his attention but merely succeeded in creating a distinctly unappetising stink involving curry, hot dogs, garlic, roasting chicken, candyfloss, chip fat, onions, barbecued sweetcorn, frying bacon and other odours which were impossible to identify from the mix.

Ravenous though he still was from having eaten nothing but a handful of biscuits since yesterday lunchtime, Trevor found it surprisingly easy to resist temptation. Milly, on the other hand, was evidently much more impressed with the aroma, particularly when she discovered the drool-inducing assortment of half-eaten food which had been dropped on the ground.

'Come on, Milly,' Trevor shouted when he turned to see his dog enthusiastically devouring what appeared to be a polystyrene tray of tapeworms but which, in reality, were probably some kind of noodles.

Now it was Milly's turn to pretend to be deaf. Only when she had finished her meal did she canter jauntily over to him, scooping up half a sausage as she went without even breaking stride.

Glad to leave the nauseating stench of the food stalls behind him, Trevor spotted the locker area, which was surrounded by a temporary but sturdy-looking steel fence. Fixed to this was a large metal sign bearing the words "Safe and Sound" in black letters on a pale green background. Approaching the open gate in the centre of the front section of fencing, he noticed that a CCTV camera was mounted high up on each of the compound's four corner posts and pointing inwards. He hesitated for a second and pulled up the hood of his fleece jacket to cover his head. He wasn't entirely sure why except that he knew he was probably doing something he ought not to be doing and thought it would be wise not to have his identity recorded on film while he was doing it.

He walked over to where an attractive young woman and a slightly older man with Too Many Pies Syndrome sat behind a small trestle table immediately to the right of the gate. Each wore a tight-fitting T-shirt printed with the same words and in the same colours as the sign.

'Hello,' said the woman, beaming up at Trevor and displaying an impossibly white and immaculately proportioned set of front teeth.

'Um, I need to get to my locker,' he said and reached into his jacket pocket.

'Certainly, sir. Which number?'

Trevor pulled out the brown paper envelope and extracted one of the two index cards. It was the one with the Bristol address printed on it.

'Sorry. Wrong one.' He smiled weakly at her and took out the second card.

The male attendant, who had been staring at Trevor without any trace of expression from the moment he had arrived, seemed suddenly distracted.

'That your dog?'

Oh not again, thought Trevor. 'Pardon?'

'The dog. Is it yours?'

He followed the nod of the attendant's head and saw Milly sauntering through the open gate and into the compound.

'Ah. Yes, she's a hearing dog.'

'Good for her,' said the man and proceeded to clean the dirt from under his fingernails with the plastic fork from an empty takeaway container.

Realising the attendant neither knew nor cared what a hearing dog was, Trevor turned his attention back to his female colleague, relieved that he didn't have to reprise the deaf act. 'C nine,' he read out from the index card.

'C nine,' she repeated and began riffling through the pages of a large plastic-covered folder. 'Here we are. C nine. I'll just have to ask you a couple of security questions if that's okay, sir.'

'Fine.'

'Could you tell me your memorable date?'

Trevor glanced at the index card in his hand. 'Thirtieth of July, sixty-six.'

'Football fan, eh?' She treated him to the same dentally perfect smile as before.

'Sorry?'

'World Cup Final? England four, West Germany two? They think it's all over?'

'Oh yes, of course.'

She looked back at the file. 'And your mother's maiden name?'

'Hurst.'

'Quite a coincidence that,' she said, closing the file.

'It is, isn't it?' said Trevor, not having the slightest clue what she was talking about.

'Right, that's all, sir. You can carry on now.'

'Thank you.'

'You're welcome.' She beamed at him once again while the male attendant studiously continued to clean his fingernails with the fork.

Trevor headed towards the banks of lockers in the middle of the compound. By now, Milly had investigated the area thoroughly and, having apparently discovered little of interest, lay down for a nap.

Each of the blue-fronted lockers was about a foot wide and six inches high, and they were stacked in columns of ten. He located C nine with little difficulty and began entering the numbers from the index card into the chunky combination lock. Hearing a faint click when he punched in the final number, he removed the lock and

70

cautiously opened the small metal door as if afraid that he was about to be attacked by whatever lay inside.

14

The ground was hard, and MacFarland's arse was killing him. Not only that, but he was getting desperate for a pee. He shifted his position on the sloping grass bank and winced. Two bloody hours he'd been sat there, pretending to read the festival programme whilst keeping a careful eye on the locker area twenty yards in front of him. And where the hell was Humpty Numpty? He should have taken over from him ages ago. For the third time in as many minutes, he tried to reach him on his mobile phone but, as before, the unavailable message cut in straight away.

Idle bastard must have switched it off. Probably getting himself bladdered in the beer tent.

He scanned the small groups of people scattered here and there along the embankment, most of whom were in their early twenties or younger. They sat or lay chatting, eating and drinking, and every one of them seemed to be having the time of their lives except for the two older men who had been sitting in the same spot ever since he'd arrived. One was short and slightly overweight and wore a smart tan-coloured leather jacket. The other was of medium height and pipe-cleaner thin with a blue denim jacket and a matching baseball cap. Both wore sunglasses even though the sun had yet to make an appearance that day.

MacFarland had decided they didn't look much like your average festival goers when he had first noticed them, and he'd become convinced that they too were taking an unusual interest in anyone entering the locker area. Right now, he was certain they were watching a man in a hooded fleece who was heading towards the block of lockers.

He followed their gaze, thinking this would be yet another false alarm until he realised the man seemed to be making for C nine. He sat upright. Jesus, he's going for it. I'm bloody sure he is. – Hang on a sec though...

He snatched up his phone again and punched rapidly at the keys. It rang only twice before Delia answered. 'What's up, Mac?'

'I thought ye said it was a woman supposed to be making the pickup.'

'That's right.'

'Well, seems to be a wee blokie opening the locker.'

'Maybe she's got a partner. I wouldn't worry about it for now. Just make sure you don't let him out of your sight.'

'Fair enough.' MacFarland twisted round to see that one of the two men he'd been watching had produced a fancy looking camera with a long lens and was aiming it at the locker area. 'Oh aye, an' I reckon there's a coupla other guys watchin' him as well.'

'Probably Special Branch – or whatever they call themselves these days. Hardly surprising in the circumstances, I'd say.'

'Fair enough,' he repeated and hung up.

He got to his feet and grimaced as he felt the stiffness in his legs and backside. At the same time, a man in a white singlet with a severe stoop and extraordinarily hairy shoulders sidled up to him.

'Anything happening?' he said.

'Where the fuck have you been?' MacFarland said without taking his eyes off the locker compound.

'Sorry, Mac. There was this really good band on the main stage, and I lost track of the time.'

'Yir no here tae enjoy yirself, Humpty. We've got a bloody job tae do.'

'Sorry,' Humpty said again, his already flushed cheeks reddening with contrition.

'Anyways, looks like we have liftoff at last.'

Humpty peered in the same direction as MacFarland. 'The guy in the grey fleece with the hood?'

'That's the one.'

'But I thought it was supposed to be a woman.'

'I know. That's why I phoned Delia.'

'And?'

'Said she might have sent an errand boy. He's oor man though, whoever he is.' MacFarland pulled the band from his ponytail, scraped back his hair and replaced the band.

Humpty's eyes strayed from the locker compound. 'Bloke over there seems to be taking photographs.'

'Special Branch probably. Hardly surprising in the circumstances,' said MacFarland, almost exactly repeating Delia's words. 'My guess is that one o' 'em will go straight tae the locker as soon as our friend has gone, and the other'll follow him. Ye stick wi' the locker one and I'll go after the fleece guy. – And keep yir bloody mobile switched on this time.'

'Er, right. Battery must be on the blink.'

With his gaze still fixed on the locker area, MacFarland heard a faint bleep, which could only have been Humpty turning his phone back on.

'Here we go. He's on his way oot.'

Both of them watched as the man in the hooded fleece chatted with the security woman on the gate while her male colleague seemed to be fiddling intently with his fingernails. Moments later, he walked briskly away, a black and tan mongrel dog trotting at his heels.

'That his dog, d'you think?' said Humpty.

'How should I know? Just dae what I tellt ye, okay?'

He glanced at the men with the sunglasses. As he'd expected, the taller of the two was already making his way towards the lockers while the other brushed some loose grass from his pale beige trousers and set off after the fleece guy.

MacFarland waited for a few seconds to let him get ahead. More out of habit than any real need to check it was still there, he slid his hand inside his jacket and ran his fingertips over the textured rubber grip of his gun.

15

It was official. Sandra was definitely not having a good day.

'What the hell are you talking about?' she said to the shaven-headed steward. 'I paid a hundred and twenty quid for that.'

'Sorry, love. Not my problem.' The steward grinned smugly and waved the ticket in front of her face. 'It's a dud.'

'Okay, okay, so what's it worth?'

'Not even the paper it's printed on, darlin'.'

In normal circumstances, Sandra would have vehemently objected to being called "darling" and "love", but on this occasion it was essential she kept the guy sweet.

'No, I mean how much do you want?'

'Eh?' His grin vanished.

'How much do you want to let me in? Twenty cover it?' She began to reach in her pocket for her already much-depleted purse.

'You trying to bribe me, lady?'

'Listen, it's really important that I get in, and I'm willing to pay whatever you—'

'Bugger off, will you?' He looked over her shoulder at the next person in the queue. 'Ticket, please.'

'Oh for God's sake.' Sandra was at a loss what to say or do next and peered past the intransigent steward at the throng of people milling around beyond the barrier. She was pondering the idea of making a run for it and losing herself amongst them when she noticed a black and tan mongrel trotting in her direction from about thirty yards away.

It was the dog from the hotel, she was certain of it, and the guy it seemed to be with looked a lot like the one she had bumped into on the stairs. It was hard to tell though because much of his head was obscured by the hood of his fleece, but he was clearly in a hurry and making for the exit.

She pushed and jostled her way back through the incoming queue and reached the end just after he passed the small group of stewards who were making sure nobody sneaked in the back way. She increased her pace to catch up with him, and when she was within range she opened her mouth to call out but immediately closed it again as a shortish man in a tan-coloured leather jacket came up behind her quarry and placed a hand on his shoulder.

The guy in the fleece turned to face his assailant, and she caught a glimpse of his rabbit-in-the-headlights eyes. Trevor Hawkins. No doubt about it. She edged her way closer so she could hear what was being said.

'...few questions,' she heard the man in the tan jacket say when she came within earshot.

'Er, what about?' Trevor looked like he was about to crap his pants, and she almost felt sorry for him. Almost, but not quite. She noticed he was holding his right arm rather awkwardly across his stomach as if he had something concealed inside his jacket and was preventing it from falling out.

'It might be better if we went somewhere a little more private. We need to wait for my... friend though. He'll be along any minute.' So saying, he raised his wrist to his face and spoke into his sleeve. 'Subject apprehended. Outside arena entrance.' He cocked his head to one side as if straining to hear something, and Sandra spotted the thin curly wire which ran from his right ear and disappeared inside his jacket collar.

'I'm in a bit of a hurry actually,' said Trevor.

'Won't keep you long, sir.' The man in the tan jacket smiled without a hint of sincerity and transferred his attention to the dog, which was staring up at him and whining. 'This your dog?'

'Yes.' The voice sounded weary.

'Cute. Does he bite?' He tentatively held out the back of his hand towards the dog, who eyed it suspiciously.

'He's a she, and no she doesn't,' Trevor said and then added, '...usually.'

'I see.' He withdrew his outstretched hand and pretended to check his watch.

'Who are you anyway?'

Sandra could see that Trevor was becoming increasingly agitated and possibly even a little braver at the same time.

'Oh I'm sorry. Didn't I introduce myself?' His words were heavy with mock politeness. 'Patterson's the name.'

'What are you? Police?'

'Something like that, sir.'

'So do you have any identification?'

'Indeed I do,' said Patterson but made not the slightest move to produce anything. 'And while we're at the introductions stage, you are...?'

'Er... Wolf. – Stephen Wolf.'

Patterson smirked. 'In sheep's clothing, eh?'

There was no response.

Just then, three men wearing nothing more than the minutest white skirts-cum-loincloths, sandals, and plastic laurel wreaths on their heads appeared from nowhere and advanced towards Patterson. Each carried an elaborately shaped plywood bow and arrow, and all of them were in their early to mid forties and of varying degrees of unattractiveness. Even so, they moved elegantly as if in slow motion with every step exaggerated and precise. Pouting theatrically all the while, they surrounded their prey and stared at him with the intensity of a hunter.

Sandra watched as the oldest and chubbiest of the three crouched down in front of Patterson and ever so slowly drew himself upright, lingering momentarily over the crotch area, until their faces were only two or three inches apart. The other two Cupids slid to either side of their target and brought their own faces to within the same distance.

For a few seconds, they stood motionless as they gazed at their victim, their bows and arrows now pointing at the ground. Then, and at exactly the same instant and without any visible cue passing between them, they each began to caress his hair and face with tender sensuality.

A small crowd started to gather, and Sandra moved closer to maintain her uninterrupted view.

By now, Patterson's body was completely rigid, his head tipped backwards and his teeth bared in a fixed grin which managed to convey both embarrassment and annoyance. If he was trying for "Hey, I'm just an ordinary festival guy like the rest of you and isn't this fun", he'd failed badly.

The three Cupids rotated around him, and their caresses ventured steadily downwards from his head to his shoulders and beyond, a face always directly in front of his own, eyeball to eyeball and pout to grimace. There was a movement at the edge of Patterson's mouth, and Sandra could just make out the words, 'Piss off, you arse bandits, or I'll nick the lot of you.'

Apparently she wasn't the only one to have heard him, and someone in the crowd shouted out, 'Jeez, mate. Relax, will ya? They're only having a bloody laugh.'

Patterson's remark seemed to be a not unexpected

response for the Cupids, and they immediately intensified their efforts. Still stroking him with their hands, they proceeded to rub their entire bodies against his in an up and down motion, sometimes with their backs and sometimes with their fronts. Without resorting to unseemly violence, Patterson was locked to the spot.

The crowd, which had tripled in size by now, was roaring with laughter and encouragement, and Sandra also found herself clapping her hands and laughing like a loon until she suddenly remembered why she was there. She felt the panic rise from somewhere deep inside her as she turned towards where Trevor had been standing, knowing full well that she'd see an empty space.

'Shit.'

As she set off, she was aware from her peripheral vision that Patterson tried to do precisely the same thing but instantly fell headlong in the dirt with an almost naked Cupid hugging his ankles.

16

'Come on, Milly. Shift.'

Trevor was almost sprinting towards the camper van when it finally came into view, and he glanced back to see that Milly was lagging behind and clearly intent on seeking out additional sources of food.

His hand trembled, and he struggled to get the key in the lock. He took a few deep breaths and concentrated... Click. Milly was beside him now and leapt onto the driver's seat the moment he opened the door. Trevor unceremoniously bundled her over to the passenger side as he climbed in and fired up the engine. He reached down to release the handbrake and then jumped at the sound of a sharp tapping noise on the glass to his right. So swiftly did he turn that he felt a sudden but fleeting spasm of pain in the back of his neck.

The woman's face seemed familiar. She was smiling, but her eyes gave him the distinct impression the smile was far from genuine. She rotated her index finger to indicate that she wanted him to wind down the window, and he reluctantly obliged.

'Well, well. Fancy bumping into you again,' she said. Milly stared at her and wagged her tail. 'Hello, doggie.'

He remembered now. It was the woman he'd collided with on the hotel stairs.

'I'm sure you'll forgive me if I'm wrong, but I believe you have something that doesn't belong to you.' The smile remained, but her eyes widened as she arched an eyebrow.

Trevor clutched at his chest, and he felt the bulge of the package through the soft material of his fleece.

'Oh dear. Touch of heartburn perhaps?' The smile evaporated, and she held out her hand, palm upwards.

Heart *attack* was more likely, thought Trevor, and wiped the sweat from his brow. He took the tag of his jacket zip between his forefinger and thumb and, millimetre by millimetre, pulled it down with such slow deliberation that he might have been performing a striptease.

'Today would be good.'

She was obviously getting impatient, and he was about to rip open the rest of the zip when a man's face loomed over her shoulder. Trevor's hand froze, and his jaw dropped. He could see the gun reflected in the window of a nearby car.

'Oh yeah,' said the woman with a scowl. 'Someone behind me, is there? Well if you think I'm going to—'

'I wouldnae turn round if I were ye, hen.'

Trevor's focus was drawn to the heavy scar on the man's cheek, the chunky gold earring and the long black hair which was scraped back so tightly into a ponytail it must have been impossible for him to blink. Definitely not the sort of person he'd want to meet on a dark night in some deserted alley. Come to that, not the sort of bloke he'd want to meet in broad daylight in the middle of a busy festival car park either.

'I see ye have something for me.'

Trevor stared down at the corner of the padded, green Jiffy bag protruding from inside his jacket. Oh God, how he wished he'd never set eyes on the bloody thing, that he'd never checked into the hotel, that he hadn't broken the toilet lid, that he'd—

'Don't piss me about, pal. I'm nae in the mood for playing games. Giz it here.'

He edged the woman to the side, and his left hand

82

reached in through the open window. The right hand followed, and this one was holding a rather heavy looking gun, which was aimed directly at his head. It was at this point that Milly apparently decided she wasn't at all keen on this intrusion, and she started barking at him like a deranged Rottweiler.

'Shut yir racket.' The muzzle of the gun shifted a few degrees, away from Trevor's head and towards the dog's.

What happened next was almost too quick for Trevor to take in. The woman's arm snapped upwards and caught the guy on the elbow so sharply that the gun was now directed at the roof of the van. At exactly the same moment, her hand whipped up from the small bag slung at her hip and shot a fine spray straight into his face. He roared in pain and staggered backwards, clutching at his eyes, then tripped and fell heavily to the ground, dropping the gun in the process.

Trevor grabbed at the handbrake, but before he could even engage first gear, the woman appeared in front of him through the windscreen. He watched the movement of her lips as they made some kind of "tut tut" sound, but he took even more notice of the gun which had been pointing at his head only a few seconds earlier. She waved it back and forth as if wagging an admonishing finger and then aimed it at his chest.

He eased his foot from the accelerator pedal, and she edged around to the passenger door and climbed in. Milly, who had stopped barking and was looking faintly bemused by this whole chain of events, obligingly and uncharacteristically jumped down from her seat and scuttled off into the back.

'Drive.' The woman's voice was calm and assured.

Trevor's palm hadn't left the gear shift, and he yanked it backwards as he continued to stare wide-eyed at the pistol. He was beginning to turn away when a powerful hand slammed onto the steering wheel. Crimson eyes blazed in at him through the still open window, tears streaming down the contorted features.

There was a dull thud and a faint crunching sound as the woman brought the butt of the gun crashing down onto the back of the intruding hand. It vanished instantly to the accompaniment of an anguished shriek of extreme pain.

'Drive!'

Trevor let out the clutch far too quickly, and the van lurched forward, almost flattening a shortish guy in a tan-coloured leather jacket, who just managed to fling himself out of the way.

'Shit,' said Trevor, glancing into his wing mirror to see the man he had almost killed lose the battle to stay upright and go sprawling onto the ground. 'Wasn't that—'

'Your policeman buddy?'

'Patterson.'

'Whatever.'

Out of the corner of his eye, Trevor could see she was still aiming the gun at him. He felt an unpleasant disturbance deep in his guts, and it wasn't because all he'd had to eat in the last twenty-four hours was a handful of biscuits.

17

A light breeze rippled the material of the patio umbrella, and a sudden gust threatened to blow the notebook off the slatted wooden table beneath. Maggie Swann made a grab for it and caught it just in time. So far, there had been very little that was worth writing down. Doyle had been reticent on the phone to put it mildly, but now, face to face, he was honing his blood-out-of-a-stone act to perfection. For some minutes, Logan had been drumming his fingers on the edge of the table – a sure sign that his patience tank was running on empty.

'I must say I'd hoped for rather more cooperation,' he said after another lengthy pause.

Doyle spread his palms wide but said nothing.

'I mean, all you've told us is that you led the investigation into Imelda Hawkins's disappearance, that you never found her and that you didn't suspect foul play or even that she was dead at all.' Logan leaned forward across the table. 'Why not?'

'As I said before, it was a long time ago.'

'Long time? Eighteen months?'

'Memory's not what it used to be, I'm afraid.' Doyle tapped the side of his head as if to emphasise the point.

'Oh come off it, Doyle. That's bullshit, and you know it.'

Again the spread palms and the sealed lips.

Logan stopped drumming and ran his fingers through his hair. 'What happened? Someone get to you, did they? Told you to drop the case?'

'Don't be ridiculous.'

'Freemason, are you?'

Doyle gripped the arms of his chair. 'What the hell has that got to—'

Both Doyle and Swann were facing towards the house, and they could see his wife step out through the sliding patio door with a tray of tea things. Unseen by Logan, he opened his mouth to speak, but Swann shook her head at him to keep quiet.

There was something incongruous about a woman serving tea in a figure-hugging black dress that would have been far better suited to some swish cocktail party at the Savoy. Swann was no fashion expert, but she guessed it was expensive designer gear, and the double string of pearls round her neck looked like the genuine article too.

'Sorry it's taken so long,' said Doyle's wife. 'Phone rang just as I'd filled the pot. The tea had gone cold by the time I'd finished, so I had to start all over again. It never ceases to amaze me how some folks can jabber on. Hah, I'd like to see their phone bills. Still, I suppose it is Saturday, and most people have that free-calls-at-the-weekend thing nowadays, don't they? Now, who's going to be mother?'

Swann pretended to study her notebook, partly to conceal a giggle and partly because she was aware that three pairs of eyes were probably trained on her.

'Pop it down here, love. I'll do it,' she heard Doyle say.

'It was Jessica by the way, darling. Wants to know if we're going to the Ladies' Night at the Lodge again this year.'

Swann looked up to clock the pained expression on Doyle's face and the broad wink that Logan threw at her.

'Can we talk about it later?' said Doyle. 'We're right in the middle of something at the moment.'

'Catching up on old times, eh? Okay, I can take a hint. I'll leave you to your reminiscing then.'

She gave her husband an affectionate pat on the shoulder and headed back towards the patio door.

'Speaking of old times,' said Logan loudly enough for her to hear. 'You still see anything of Veronica from Admin these days, Tom?'

There was a choking sound and the clatter of cups and saucers as Doyle came close to dropping the teapot. Swann thought she detected a slight hesitation in his wife's step, but she might have been mistaken.

'What the bloody hell did you have to say that for?' said Doyle as soon as his wife had disappeared back into the house.

It was Logan's turn to spread his palms wide, and he added a self-satisfied smirk for good measure.

'Attractive woman, your wife,' he said. 'Must be, what? Twelve, fifteen years younger than you?'

'You threatening to blackmail me, Logan?'

'But I'm a police officer. How could you think such a thing?' He sat back in his chair and folded his arms. 'Mind you, I seem to remember that Tony Ambrose took a fair few photos at your retirement bash. I wonder if—'

'All right. All right. What is it you want?'

'Three sugars, please.'

Swann wondered if it was physically possible for someone to actually explode from smugness. Doyle was showing no sign of picking up the teapot again, and Logan was obviously far too busy congratulating himself. She was gasping for a cuppa, and if she was ever going to get one, it seemed she'd have to be mother after all. She stood up and pulled the tea tray towards her.

'Either of you wearing a wire?' said Doyle.

Logan and Swann exchanged glances.

'A what?' said Logan.

'I'm not saying another word till I know this isn't being recorded.'

'And why would we want to do that exactly?'

'You want me to frisk you?'

Doyle's "Donger" nickname flashed into Swann's brain, and she felt a wave of nausea at the idea of a full body search. He wasn't nearly as repulsive as she'd imagined he would be, and despite the wavy white hair, baggy eyes and sagging jowls, she could tell he'd probably been not bad looking in his day. Even so, a letch was a letch, and she had no desire to have his hands all over her.

'Trust me,' said Logan. 'We're not wearing wires.'

'Trust *you*?'

He ignored the jibe and ploughed straight on. 'So what made you think Imelda wasn't dead?'

'Call it… a copper's intuition.'

Logan waited for him to continue. He didn't. 'Care to elaborate?'

'For a start, we never found a body.' Doyle raised a hand to silence Logan, who seemed to be on the point of interrupting. 'You want to let me finish? – Nor was there any kind of motive for murder. No enemies to speak of. No-one stood to gain financially. Not even the husband.'

'You interviewed him presumably.'

'Of course we interviewed him,' said Doyle, his tone clearly conveying his resentment at being taught how to suck eggs. 'Several times in fact. You know as well as I do that the husband is always the most likely suspect in cases like this.'

'And?'

'Well he was either bloody clever and an exceptionally gifted actor, or he was totally innocent.' He took a sip of his tea and winced. 'Put it this way,' he added, spooning sugar into his cup. 'He was certainly no Einstein in the brains department.'

'He have an alibi?'

'For what?'

Logan sighed. 'For the time she disappeared.'

'But that's the thing of it. No-one knew precisely *when* she went AWOL. She was a sales rep for a pharmaceutical company, so she was often away for days at a time. On this particular occasion, she'd checked into a hotel in Birmingham for four nights, but nobody'd seen her from the moment she signed the register till she was due to vacate the room.'

'So it could have been any time during those four days.'

Doyle nodded.

'What about her employers?' said Logan. 'You check with them?'

'Course I checked.' Again the sucking eggs tone of voice. 'At least, I tried to.'

Logan raised an eyebrow.

'No such company ever existed apparently. We found some letterheads at her house, but the address turned out to be an abandoned warehouse in Cheam.'

'And you didn't think that was suspicious?'

Doyle rolled his head back and gazed up at the sky. 'God give me strength.'

'Okay, okay,' said Logan. 'So what did Trevor have to say about it?'

'Seemed genuinely gobsmacked. Went all pale and vacant, like he'd gone into some kind of trance.'

Logan started drumming his fingers on the edge of the table once again. 'Then what?'

'Then nothing. No body. Trail had gone cold. We couldn't pin anything on the husband, so that, as they say, was that.'

'You're kidding me, right?'

Doyle fixed him with a Mona Lisa smile.

'And what happened to the file?' said Logan.

'End of interview, I think.' Doyle pushed back his chair and got to his feet.

'So who was it that got you to drop the case and make out it never happened?'

Doyle was already making his way across the patio towards the house. 'Use the side gate on your way out, will you?' he called back over his shoulder.

Logan jumped up and almost sent his chair flying. 'Who was it, Doyle? How much they pay you, eh?'

Swann thought she heard a faint chuckle as Doyle stepped inside and slid the patio door shut behind him.

* * *

As Logan began to back the car up the gravel driveway, Swann could see Doyle in the front room window. He was on the phone and gesticulating wildly at whoever he was talking to.

'I think we might have rattled him,' she said.

'Stroke of genius, wouldn't you say? The stuff about Veronica and the photos.'

She decided not to feed his already bloated ego. 'D'you think he really did take a bribe then?'

'Expensive house. Fancy car. Wife dripping with designer fashion. Must be on a bloody good pension if he didn't.'

18

This was the second time in the space of a few minutes that Patterson had been subjected to the ridicule of a small group of total strangers, and he was less than happy about it. He had never liked being the centre of attention even in social situations – not that he ever encountered many of those – but it was part of his job to be as inconspicuous as possible. Being publicly groped by three almost naked, middle-aged Cupids would hardly conform to anyone's notion of blending in with the crowd, and now here he was, sat on his arse in a puddle of muddy water, being watched by a bunch of guffawing buffoons. He scrambled to his feet and scowled as he felt the cold wetness of his pale beige trousers clinging to his lower regions.

'You all right, chief?'

Patterson rounded on his denim-clad colleague, his mouth loaded with a variety of abusive remarks, but his brain seemed unable to select any one in particular. Instead, he pointed at the guy with the ponytail who was staggering away and bouncing off the occasional parked car. 'Get after him, Colin. I want a word.'

'Who is he?'

'I don't know yet, but I reckon there's a good chance that if we lose him, we're stuffed.'

Colin Statham set off at a trot, and Patterson dabbed his handkerchief at the damp patch on his trousers, which had begun to spread slowly downwards. If it hadn't been for those damn Cupid poofters, this would never have happened. Not only that, but he'd have got to the van a couple of minutes earlier and would probably have a better idea of what the hell was going on. All he'd seen was the guy with the ponytail reeling backwards from the side of the camper and then the van lurching off and almost running him over. He was pretty sure the man behind the wheel was the same one he'd collared at the arena exit, but who the woman was, he hadn't got a clue.

He raised his wrist to his mouth and spoke into the sleeve of his jacket, 'Come in, Sneezy. Do you read me?' Not for the first time, he wondered which idiot had had the bright idea of codenaming this job Operation Snow White.

His earpiece hissed momentarily, and he winced as he heard the words, 'Sneezy here. Go ahead, Grumpy.'

Patterson thought he could hear a stifled snigger in the background. 'There should be a white VW camper van passing your position any second now,' he said. 'Registration whiskey six three five papa juliet tango. Keep on its tail but do not intercept. I repeat, do *not* intercept. – And don't bloody lose it. I want to know exactly where it goes.'

'Will do, Grumpy. Van just passing us now.'

He was certain he heard a giggle this time. 'Who've you got with you?'

There was a brief pause and then: 'Sorry, sir. Can't tell you that.'

'What are you talking about, you can't tell me?'

'It's just that... ' Sneezy was obviously trying to compose himself. 'He's *Bashful*, guv.'

The suppressed giggling suddenly erupted into an explosion of laughter so loud that Patterson snatched the earpiece from his ear to avoid being deafened.

'Oh ha bloody ha. And now you've had your little joke, just remember this, Mr Sneezy. You two clowns lose that van and you'll be sneezing out of your sodding arseholes. Got it?'

Through his earpiece, which he was now holding a couple of inches from the side of his head, he heard a car engine starting up and possibly the word "tosser".

* * *

Despite his lean and athletic appearance, Colin Statham had a long history of avoiding anything which remotely resembled physical exercise, and so he was not the best equipped for a high speed chase on foot. Fortunately for him, however, his target on this occasion was going nowhere fast.

Must be completely trollied, he thought, as the man weaved this way and that, his arms flailing around in front of him as if he were negotiating his way in total darkness. His lack of forward progress meant that even Statham had little trouble gaining on him, and when he was within ten feet or so, he contemplated a headlong dive to bring the guy down in a spectacular looking rugby tackle. But he immediately decided against it when he noticed the bogginess of the ground. Instead, he drew the Glock 17 pistol from the holster inside his jacket and held it flat against his hip, pointing downwards so as not to arouse unnecessary attention. He grabbed hold of a flailing arm and spun the man round to face him. A pair of severely bloodshot eyes blinked back at him several times as they attempted to focus.

'Get off o' me, ya wee shite.'

Statham easily dodged the wayward punch and thrust the barrel of his gun into the man's groin. 'Shut up and keep still if you value your nuts.'

'What d'ye want? Money or wha'?'

Statham raised the cuff of his jacket to his mouth. 'You there, Grumpy? This is Sleepy. I have our man.

Repeat. I have our man. Where are you?'

'Grumpy? Sleepy? Yir havin' me on, right?'

Statham did not respond.

'Ye Special Branch or somethin'?'

'Nasty cut you've got there,' said Statham, nodding at the blood dripping from the gash on the back of the man's hand. 'I'd get that seen to if I were you.'

''Cos if ye are, yir making a very big mistake here, pal.'

'Oh really?'

'Anything happens ta me an' the whole deal's off. Ye know what I'm sayin'?'

Statham was beginning to feel uneasy about this whole situation and stole a glance over his shoulder to see if Patterson was about to come to his rescue in deciding what to do next. What he saw instead, and for the briefest of moments, was a large fist and something dark and heavy looking. He barely even had time to register the savage pain in the side of his head, but it returned quickly enough when he opened his eyes to see Patterson crouching over him.

'Jesus Christ,' said Statham as his hand made tentative contact with the fiery swelling just above his right ear.

'Well?' Patterson's bedside manner left a lot to be desired.

Statham propped himself up on one elbow. 'Somebody jumped me.'

'The guy with the ponytail?'

Statham shook his head and instantly regretted it. 'Someone else. I'd caught up with the ponytail and was waiting for you. Next minute, bang. Goodnight Vienna.' Still nursing his wound, a thought suddenly occurred to him, and he scanned the ground around him. 'Damn.'

'What's the matter?'

'Bastard nicked my gun.' He pushed himself into a sitting position, and a memory forced its way into his throbbing brain. 'He said something about the deal being off if anything happened to him.'

'What the hell are they playing at?' said Patterson. 'The whole point of "the deal" was to leave the address in the locker, and they haven't. The only reason I stopped the joker who made the pickup was because you'd told me the locker was empty. And now he's buggered off in a bloody camper van.'

'Anyone after him?'

Patterson nodded. 'But I told them not to intercept. For all we know there may not even *be* an address so if they're mucking us about, I want to know where he ends up.'

'Who's tailing him?'

'Sneezy and Bashful?'

Statham's laugh was cut short by the flash of pain that shot through his head. 'Thank God it's not Dopey, I suppose.'

'Quite.'

19

Trevor drove the van as fast as he dared but slow enough to avoid knocking anyone else down. All the while, he continued to give himself a good mental kicking and asked himself the same question over and over again. Why oh why had he ever got involved in all this? Okay, so not all of it was his fault. The van breaking down, ending up in that hotel in that particular room with a dodgy toilet flush. That was just chance. And it wasn't as if he'd broken the cistern lid deliberately.

Even then, it was guilt that had driven him to try and replace it, so he could hardly be blamed for that. Looking in the wallet which was taped inside the lid? Natural curiosity. He was only human after all. As for taking it away with him... All right, so he'd panicked. Perfectly normal in the circumstances and so was the fact that he'd been in a hurry and forgotten to hand it in at reception like he'd intended. Actually using the ticket to get into the festival and taking the package from the locker was...

Well that was a little trickier to work out, but the upshot was that he had someone who may or may not be a copper after him as well as a gun-wielding psychopathic Scotsman. Then there was this crazy woman sat next to him – also with a gun.

'Which way?' he said when they reached the main road.

'Whichever. For now, I just want to get away from this place.'

Trevor turned left, purely on the basis that he had entered the site from the right, and it somehow seemed like a good idea to head in the opposite direction.

'So who are you, and why exactly did you nick the envelope from my toilet?' the woman said after a couple of miles of silence.

'Believe me, I keep asking myself the same question.'

'Which one? The who are you one or the nicking one?'

'The nicking one. I'm Trevor Hawkins.' He decided there was little point in giving a false name this time. He didn't have a clue who this woman was, but she did have a gun.

'I know what your name is. What I want to know is who you're working for.'

'Me?'

'No, I was talking to the bloody dog,' she sneered. 'Yes, *you.*'

'Well I suppose you could say I'm unemployed at the moment. I've just packed in my job at Dreamhome Megastores, you see, and—'

She rounded on him and aimed the gun at his face. 'Are you taking the piss?'

'Pardon?' Trevor frowned back at her.

'You tell me you don't know why you stole the envelope from my room, so I can only assume somebody told you to but didn't give you a reason.'

'Look, it was a mistake. That's all. I know it was a stupid thing to do, but there was nobody else involved. I promise you.'

'A *mistake?*'

The pistol persuaded him that his best course of action was to tell her the whole story from when he'd first set off in the van the day before to the moment he took the package from the locker.

'Speaking of which...' she said when he'd finished

97

and held out her free hand towards him, nodding at his chest.

Trevor unzipped his jacket and pulled out the padded, green Jiffy bag. He passed it to her and, on the edge of his vision, noticed her lay the gun down on top of the dashboard. Not that this was particularly significant. Making a grab for it and forcing her to get out of the van at gunpoint simply wasn't an option. Hell, he barely knew one end of a gun from the other, and she wasn't going to sit there and wait while he figured it out.

'So you haven't opened it then,' she said. 'That's something, I suppose.'

Trevor wondered how critical this might be to saving his life. Perhaps if he knew what was inside the Jiffy bag, she'd have to kill him, but because the seal was still intact she might just take the damn thing and let him go. – Perhaps.

'What about the index cards?' she said. 'You leave the one with the address and the key in the locker?'

Uh-oh. She was going to kill him after all. He considered telling a little white lie, but his hesitation and flushed cheeks must have given him away.

'Oh great,' said the woman. 'Well that's me totally screwed then. Two grand for what should have been a perfectly simple job and, thanks to you, I doubt I'll see a single penny of it now. And then of course there's the small issue of a dissatisfied client who's probably got a contract out on me already.'

Trevor kept half an eye on the top of the dashboard. Please don't pick up the gun. Please don't pick up the gun. Please don't p—

She picked up the gun.

Oh bloody Nora. – But surely she wouldn't shoot him while he was driving. She might end up getting killed herself. That was it. Keep driving. As long as he kept going, she wouldn't be able to do anything. If she told him to pull over, he'd refuse. Simple as that.

He glanced across at her and saw the last thing he expected to see. Instead of staring into the barrel of the pistol, he was looking at the side of it, and it was pointing straight up under the woman's chin.

'May as well end it all now,' she said. 'No sense prolonging the inevitable.'

She was joking of course. Or was she? Maybe the woman was a total headache, and he'd tipped her over the edge by messing up her—

There was the sudden blare of a horn, and Trevor had to swerve sharply to avoid the oncoming car.

'Jesus. Keep your eyes on the road, will you? You want to get us both killed?'

Nothing further was said for the next several minutes. The only sounds were the hum of the engine and Milly snoring loudly on the back seat. Trevor caught a glimpse of her in the rear-view mirror and realised at the same time that the dark blue Ford Mondeo was still there, about sixty or seventy yards behind them.

'I wish he'd overtake if he's going to,' he said.

'Who?' Her voice seemed wearily unconcerned.

'The car that's been behind us ever since we left the festival site. He's had plenty of chances to get by.'

The woman skewed her head to look in her wing mirror. 'Slow down a bit.'

Trevor eased off the accelerator pedal and watched the Mondeo drop back.

'Now speed up again.'

He accelerated and so did the Mondeo, maintaining the same distance between them as before.

'Shit,' she said. 'That's all I need.'

'Are we being followed?'

'Looks that way.'

'Who is it?' Trevor knew that this was probably a silly question the moment the words left his lips and wasn't surprised when he didn't get an answer. Presumably, they must be something to do with the Scottish bloke or Patterson.

'We'll have to try and shake them off whoever they are.'

Despite the seriousness of his situation, Trevor couldn't help but laugh. 'In this?'

'Why? What speed will it do?'

'Sixty? Sixty-five maybe if it's going downhill with a following wind.'

'Oh terrific.' She continued to monitor the progress of the Mondeo in the wing mirror, a heavy frown indicating that she was deep in thought. 'You got much fuel?'

'Plenty. I filled up before I got to the festival.'

'How big's the tank?'

'Dunno exactly. About eighty litres, I think.'

'Right,' she said, staring into the wing mirror. 'I think I've got an idea.'

20

For a dead man, Harry Vincent didn't look too bad at all. In fact, apart from the roll of belly spilling over the waistband of his brightly striped swimming shorts, he appeared to be in remarkably good condition. His skin was tanned to a pale teak colour, and his thick sandy hair, combed backwards from his forehead, was only just starting to show signs of thinning.

Lying on the sun lounger beside the pool, he had been watching his wife swim back and forth for the past ten minutes or so, sipping his rum and Coke and occasionally pulling on his cigar. They had been childhood sweethearts, and even now, forty-odd years later, he loved her as much as he had done during those heady days of teenage romance. Harry knew she felt the same way about him.

He exhaled a large cloud of cigar smoke and smiled. He had worked hard all his life to be where he was now, lazing in the late afternoon sun at his Greek villa while Donna sent ripples of silver across the surface of the pool. By his own admission, his labours had rarely been within the boundaries of what might be considered legal, but there again, as he often told himself, how many bankers, stockbrokers, lawyers or politicians were there who could honestly say they had never once broken the law in pursuit of their goals? Okay, so maybe very few of them had actually had people killed during the process, but what about the arms dealers whose apparently legitimate trade resulted in the slaughter of countless thousands of innocent men, women and children? At least he'd never been responsible for the deaths of any women or children, and most of the men had pretty much deserved what they'd got.

As far as he was concerned, he was little different from any of the so-called captains of industry who are driven to succeed at all costs and no more ruthless than the chief executive of some blue chip multinational. Where his own ambition and work ethic had originated from, he couldn't be sure. He certainly hadn't inherited them from his father, who had been a builder by trade but a drinker by inclination. Like so many of his contemporaries growing up in the East End of London, he had simply wanted to escape – to carve out a better life for himself – and this of course meant making money. Lots of it.

Some of his own mates had looked to the boxing ring as their way out, but Harry had seen at first hand the physical cost to too many of the older kids who had explored this route and failed. Apart from joining the army, the only other alternative was crime. Not the petty pilfering, burglary and car theft sort of crime, but the big league, where the risks were inevitably greater but the rewards immeasurable. Harry had witnessed the consequences of failure in this area too, but he had believed himself to be far smarter than those who had got caught, and to a great extent, he had been proved right over the following years.

He took another sip from his rum and Coke and set the glass down on the low table beside him. Donna was beginning to climb the ladder out of the pool, and he went to meet her with a gaudily patterned beach towel. She squeezed some of the water from her long and unnaturally auburn hair when she got to the top step, and Harry reached behind her to drape the towel over her shoulders. She hugged it around her and kissed him lightly on the lips.

'Thanks, love,' she said, looking into his eyes as if in the aftermath of the first passionate kiss on their first date.

Harry took a couple of paces backwards and gave a sweepingly flamboyant bow. 'We aim to please, madam.'

Donna laughed and gave him a playful tap in the ribs with the side of her foot as she walked past him. He feigned falling sideways onto the tiled floor, theatrically rolling in fake agony until he fell off the edge and into the pool with a dull splash.

By the time he'd clambered out, Donna had already put on her sunglasses and had settled onto her own lounger, reading a *Hello* magazine.

Harry stood gazing down at her with the water dripping from his body and forming a small puddle by his feet. She still looked good even now, he thought, especially in that one-piece black swimsuit with the gold plastic clasp just under the cleavage. He hawked and then turned sideways to propel the resulting phlegm into the pool.

Donna dropped the magazine onto her lap and stared up at him. 'Harry,' she said with obvious disgust. 'Why do you *do* that?'

'Chlorine, love. Plays 'avoc with me sinuses.'

She picked up her magazine and snapped it open with a long-suffering sigh.

'Besides,' said Harry, 'it gives the pool cleaner something to do.'

'Did I ever tell you you have the manners of a warthog?' she said without looking up.

'No, but you did tell me once that I was 'ung like a donkey.'

'Dung beetle, I think I said.'

'Oh really?' Harry manoeuvred himself into a position

103

astride Donna's lounger.

She snatched the magazine away from the dripping water. 'Bugger off. You're getting my *Hello* all wet.'

He squatted lower over her chest.

'Zair was a time when zair was more of you I could get wet than your *'Ello* magazine,' he said in an accent which sounded like Arnold Schwarzenegger playing Inspector Clouseau.

As he spoke the words, he tucked his thumbs into the waistband of his swimming shorts and eased it down slightly to reveal a glimpse of pubic hair. 'Hee-haw, hee-haw?' he said, still pretending to be a Frenchman rather than a mule.

Donna looked up at him and slowly removed her sunglasses. She lowered her eyes to his minimally exposed manhood, and a smile began to spread across her face.

Harry followed her gaze. 'Aha, I see we eff lift-urf.'

She reached up her left hand and lightly caressed his cheek. At the same time, she rolled the magazine into a tight club with her other hand and whacked him in the area which was not quite so soft as before.

This time, Harry wasn't faking when he rolled sideways onto the floor, clutching at the front of his shorts, his mouth opening and closing wordlessly like a beached guppy.

Donna replaced her sunglasses and unrolled the magazine. 'Now stop being annoying and get me another drink... darling.'

'I suppose... you think... that was... funny,' said Harry, still gasping to catch his breath.

'Hmm?' She flicked over a page of her magazine. 'What was that, love?'

'Bloody 'urt that did.'

'Oh come here, you big wuss, and I'll kiss it better.'

In the hope that this might be a genuine offer, Harry

forced himself onto his knees and then onto his feet, his hand still firmly between his legs.

'You all right, Harry?'

It was a male voice, and Harry turned towards it. A well-built man in his late thirties was standing on the veranda of the house, the short sleeves of his Hawaiian shirt rippling gently in the breeze.

'Yeah yeah, I'm fine, Eddie. Just 'avin' a bit of a... laugh. Know what I mean?'

'Right you are, boss.'

Harry picked up a towel and moved somewhat awkwardly towards the elevated veranda. 'Something 'appened?'

'Just had a call from MacFarland.'

'Oh yeah? And?'

'You're not going to like this, I'm afraid.' Eddie shifted his weight from one foot to the other and back again.

Harry stopped drying his hair with the towel and lowered it to his side in slow motion. He stared up at Eddie, waiting for him to continue.

'Seems like there was a bit of a cockup.'

'What?' Harry felt his blood pressure beginning to rise.

'Delia hired some woman to make the pickup apparently, but it was a bloke turned up instead. Then he gave MacFarland the slip.'

'Oh for f...'

'He also reckons that the pickup guy didn't leave anything in the locker.'

'Reckons? What do you mean "he reckons"?'

'MacFarland said that Humpty didn't actually check it, but from the reaction of the—'

'Christ almighty,' said Harry, looking up at the clear blue sky. 'What do I pay these people for?'

The veins in his temples were throbbing like pistons.

'Where are they now?' he called over his shoulder as he walked back to his sun lounger and collected his half-smoked cigar from the ashtray.

'Still at the festival. They're waiting for your instructions.'

'Coursh they are,' said Harry, his teeth clamped around the cigar as he struck a match. 'Can't bloody think for themshelves, can they? Useless fucking twats.'

Donna lowered her magazine. 'What's up, love?'

He took a deep draw on the cigar and combined a dismissive wave of the hand with extinguishing the match. 'Nothin' I can't deal with, darlin'. Don't worry about it.'

'Just watch your blood pressure, that's all,' she said and returned to her reading.

'Yeah yeah, don't fuss.'

'You know what happened last time you got yourself into a tizz.'

'Tizz? Huh,' Harry muttered and retraced his steps to the veranda. 'Anything from Carrot?'

'Not since last night, no,' said Eddie with a slow shake of the head.

'Well let's just 'ope *that* part of it's still going to plan anyway.' Harry studied the glowing tip of his cigar for several seconds and then jabbed it in Eddie's direction. 'Get MacFarland back on the phone and tell the stupid Scotch git to get his lazy arse to the drop-off point. I don't suppose anybody'll turn up now, but I wanna be certain. And while you're at it, tell Delia to get hold of this woman he hired and find out what the fuck she thinks she's playin' at.'

'Right you are, boss.' Eddie started back towards the house.

'Oh yeah,' Harry shouted after him. 'And you can tell MacFarland that if there's any more cockups, he'll be singing falsetto in the heavenly fucking choir by the time

106

I've done with 'im.'

'Language,' said Donna and flipped over a page.

21

The dull ache in Sandra's lower back had become progressively worse, and she rolled her head to try and ease the stiffness in her neck. The passenger seat of the camper van was not the most comfortable in the world, and they'd been going for almost three hours now without a break.

During the earlier part of the journey, she had continued to quiz Trevor about what his involvement was and why he had taken the index cards from the toilet cistern.

She had asked him who the guy was that had tried to stop him at the festival exit. Trevor had told her he had no idea except that he'd said his name was Patterson, and he seemed to have something to do with the police.

She had asked him who the Scottish guy with the ponytail was that had pulled the gun on them in the car park, and Trevor had said he was about to ask her the same question.

He had asked *her* what was in the package, and she'd told him she didn't know, which was true. He'd been surprised she wasn't curious to take a look inside, which wasn't true, but she'd had strict instructions not to open it.

He had asked her where she'd got her instructions from, and she'd told him to mind his own business and that if he hadn't poked his nose in in the first place she wouldn't be in the mess she was now.

Since then, they'd driven on in almost complete

silence apart from the occasional sound of Milly snoring peacefully from the back seat. Sandra's mobile phone had gone off at one point, but she'd recognised the number and hadn't picked up. She had no desire to speak to her client until they had at least shaken off the Ford Mondeo that was tailing them.

'What's up?' she said, finally breaking the silence when she noticed Trevor shifting awkwardly in his seat for the umpteenth time in the last twenty minutes.

'I'm knackered. I need a rest.'

'Not possible, I'm afraid.' She craned her neck to look into the wing mirror. 'Our friends are still with us unfortunately.'

'If they really are following us like you say—'

'Of course they're following us. Why else would they still be there after a hundred and twenty-odd miles?'

'All I'm saying is that they don't seem to be making any effort to hide the fact.'

'I don't know. Perhaps they're not very good at their job.'

'But who are *they* and what exactly is their *job*?'

Sandra counted to five before she replied. 'What do you want to do? Stop and ask them? – Excuse me, gents, but we've noticed you've been behind us for quite some time now and we were wondering if you were following us and, if so, whether your intentions are honourable or otherwise.' She ended the sentence with a contemptuous sneer.

Trevor said nothing.

She glanced across at him and saw he was chewing on his bottom lip. Even though she was seriously hacked off with the guy, Sandra realised she had offended him and felt an unaccountable twinge of guilt.

'Look,' she said in a stern tone of voice to disguise any trace of sympathy she might have had for him. 'As far as I'm concerned, this was going to be a nice straightforward little earner until you came along and made a total bollocks of the whole thing. I don't know if you're telling me the truth or not, and I sure as hell don't know who the good guys are and who the bad guys are. Shit, I don't even know if there *are* any good guys in all this. What I do know is that I don't intend to hang around to find out which is which. Okay?'

Trevor merely grunted in response.

God, what was it with men and sulking? She closed her eyes but opened them again immediately as she felt a wave of tiredness rolling her towards a sleep she could ill afford. She yawned and rubbed her face with both hands to try to bring some life back to her flagging consciousness. Peering at her reflection in the wing mirror, she recoiled at the dark rings under her eyes, the furrowed brow, the blotchy skin, the – Shit, what was that? Surely she wasn't getting a double chin? She raised her head up and down a few times, closely observing the area in question and prodding the flesh with the tips of her fingers.

Right, that settles it, she thought. It's diet time for you, my girl. But what about the baggy eyes, the lines, the strawberries and cream complexion but with all the strawberries in the wrong place? A diet wasn't going to cure those. Maybe it was the job. She was certain she hadn't looked this rough when she'd first set up in business. All those long nights sat in her car outside some house or other waiting to get a photograph of an errant husband or wayward wife were bound to take their toll, not to mention the endless succession of hastily grabbed burgers and doner kebabs. Stress had a big part to play in it too, and this current job was turning out to be a severe test of what little composure she had left. Hell, it should have been one of the simplest *and* most lucrative cases she'd had yet.

This last thought prompted her to adjust her focus in

the mirror.

'Aha,' she said aloud and leaned forward to get a better view.

'What?' said Trevor.

'I do believe they've finally...' Her voice tailed off as she watched even more intently. The Mondeo seemed to be falling behind and lurching as if it was being driven by a novice who'd barely begun to master clutch control.

'At bloody last,' she said, seeing the reflected image of the car grow ever smaller. She sat back in her seat. 'I was beginning to think they'd never run out.'

'So now what?'

'You drive me back to the festival so I can pick up my car. You drop me off. I never see you again as long as I live.'

'The festival? But we've been driving for hours.'

'Yes, but we've been going pretty much in a circle. I'd say it's no more than thirty miles away.'

Trevor shifted his position and flexed his fingers.

'Okay,' he said, 'but I'll have to have a break first. Everything aches, and I've hardly eaten a thing since yesterday lunchtime.'

'Fair enough. We'll stop at the next services or whatever. I'm feeling a bit peckish myself.'

There was a faint whimper from the back seat of the van. Milly was sound asleep and dreaming that she was chasing an enormous chicken nugget on legs.

* * *

Patterson was sitting bolt upright in the passenger seat of a green Skoda Octavia, rigid with fury.

'How the hell did you manage to lose a beat-up old camper van?' he yelled into the onboard radio.

'Ran out of petrol, guv,' came the crackled reply.

'Oh terrific.'

111

'Yeah, they must have seen the film about that Irish bloke – IRA I think he was. Anyway, he knew he was going to be followed by the police so he'd got a spare can of petrol in the boot of his car, and when they—'

'For Christ's sake, just shut up and tell us where you are.'

Radio static was the only response.

'You still there?' Patterson said after a few moments.

More static.

'Sleepy? Bashful?'

This time, he heard what sounded very much like stifled laughter amongst the static, and Statham coughed and spluttered in the seat beside him.

Patterson shot him a withering look and then spoke into the radio again. 'Right. That's it. I've had enough of all this Snow White nonsense. You're back to Jarvis and Coleman from now on. Understood?'

'Okay, Grump— um, guv.'

'We'll get your location from the GPS, so just stay where you are and we'll come and pick you up.'

The radio interference intensified, but Patterson thought he heard the words "going anywhere", "petrol" and "duh". He replaced the microphone in its holder on the dashboard and sat back with a sigh, rubbing the palms of his hands down his face.

'Then what?' said Statham, dropping down a gear and accelerating hard out of a bend.

'Put out a trace on the camper van first, I suppose, and then report in to see what the brass has to say.'

'Rather you than me.'

Patterson slammed his hand down onto the dashboard. 'What a God almighty balls-up.'

'Watch it, guv. I nearly did an emergency stop then.'

He looked across at Statham and saw that he was smiling. He was about to let fly with a stream of abuse but checked himself. What was the point? It wasn't his fault that the operation was on the brink of disaster. Mind you, if he ever laid eyes on those bloody Cupids again…

22

Trevor turned into the car park of the roadside diner and found a space at the rear of the building where the van wouldn't be spotted from the road. He switched off the engine, and Milly stood up on the back seat and stretched herself, seemingly refreshed from her long sleep.

He waited for Sandra to finish her phone call. She'd rung someone about a lunch date the next day and told them she might not be able to make it. – A friend or maybe a relative, but not a boyfriend or husband by the sound of it. She'd started off with 'Hi, it's Sandra', so at least he knew her name now even if pretty much everything else about her was a complete mystery.

She ended the call and put the mobile back in her bag. 'I hope you're not thinking of doing anything silly while we're here,' she said, picking up the gun from the dashboard and depositing it in the bag with her phone.

'Like what exactly?' Trevor was tired and aching from the long drive, and he made no attempt to conceal his irritability.

'I think I'd better have those.' She held out her hand as he took the keys from the ignition.

He dropped them into her outstretched palm and then made his way through the gap between the driver and passenger seats into the back of the van. He opened one of the small fitted cupboards above the sink and took out a box of dog biscuits. Milly leapt on the half dozen that he threw on the floor and devoured them as if she hadn't had a scrap to eat in days.

'Here,' said Sandra. 'You may as well stick this in there for now.'

She tossed the padded, green Jiffy bag at him, and he caught it one-handed. He placed it in the cupboard along with the box of dog biscuits and closed the door.

Five minutes later, Sandra and Trevor sat opposite each other at a red Formica-topped table, each of them studying a garishly designed, laminated menu, which gleamed under the brightness of the fluorescent lights. The restaurant was almost full, and the general hubbub of chatter mingled with the jangle and clatter of cutlery and crockery. Above all this, a baby was screaming as if determined not to be consoled.

'I'll have a cheeseburger and chips and a large coffee,' said Sandra, scraping back her chair and getting to her feet. 'I'm desperate for a pee.'

She picked up the van keys from the table and dangled them in front of Trevor's face. 'No tricks, eh?'

'And what d'you reckon I'm going to do without those?' he said, looking up from his menu.

'Let's just say I don't entirely trust you,' she said with a faint smile before turning and heading towards the toilets with apparent urgency.

Trevor watched her go, and as he did so, a girl of about sixteen in a red and black uniform arrived at his table, notepad and pen at the ready. Despite her rake-like physique, she was partially obscuring his view, and he had to lean to one side so he could continue to observe Sandra's progress.

'You ready to order?' said the girl and flicked her head backwards to dislodge a lock of dyed black hair from in front of her eyes.

'Er... yes,' said Trevor without diverting his gaze to either her or the menu. 'Cheeseburger and chips and a large coffee please.'

The waitress started scribbling on her notepad and then paused. 'Chips?' she said as if the word was completely foreign to her.

'Oh, er, fries I mean.'

'Regular, large, or super?'

'Small,' said Trevor and stood up when he saw the heavily sprung door to the ladies' toilet swing shut behind Sandra.

'We don't do small. We only do regular, large, or—'

'Super. Yes. – Make it super then,' Trevor called out over his shoulder as he strode towards the exit.

Outside in the car park, he broke into a run and pulled the spare set of van keys from his pocket.

* * *

Sandra got to the exit, via the empty table, just in time to see the van turn left onto the main road.

'Shit, shit, shit,' she said and stared at the keys in her hand for a few moments until the penny dropped. She chided herself for her stupidity – and her bladder for its limited capacity – until her eyes focused on the yellow cardboard tag that was attached to the keyring. It was printed with the name and logo of a car dealer, but what particularly caught her attention were the letters and numbers written on the back of the card in red ink – the vehicle's registration number.

She walked over to the table which Trevor had so recently vacated and sat down. She took out her mobile phone and was scrolling through her contacts list when a skinny waitress with dyed black hair came over and asked her if she was ready to order.

'Cheeseburger, chips and a large coffee,' said Sandra without taking her eyes from her phone.

The waitress tutted and started writing on her notepad. 'Cheeseburger, *fries* and a large coffee,' she said, but with heavy emphasis on "fries". 'So will that be regular, large or super *fries*?'

'Regular,' said Sandra but then suddenly looked up at her. 'No, hang on. Make that super. I think I'm in need of a serious carbohydrate fix.'

'Whatever,' muttered the girl and wrote on her pad once more before slouching off towards the counter.

Sandra found the number she was searching for on her mobile and pressed the Call button. A familiar voice answered almost immediately.

'Martin, it's Sandra. I need a favour.'

23

The glare from the early evening sun was starting to make him squint, so he reached up and pulled down the sun visor. He vaguely registered that he must therefore be heading west, but other than that, Trevor neither knew nor cared where he was making for. All he did know was that he wanted to put as much distance as possible between himself and Sandra and the various other people who seemed intent on either arresting him or doing him serious physical harm.

He'd estimated that an hour's driving would put him beyond the reach of any pursuers for the time being at least, and the straightness and smooth surface of the road had encouraged him to push the van almost to its limits. He'd covered about fifty miles now, and the appalling smells that were emanating from the back seat reminded him that Milly must be getting desperate for a squat-break, so he began to look out for campsite signs.

Eventually, he spotted one which claimed that there was a site two miles from the main road. He took the turning and, about five miles later, drove in through the main gate of the Riverside Farm Campsite.

He checked in at the small wooden office inside the entrance and found a spot near to a slow flowing river, from which he assumed the campsite derived its name. He jerked on the handbrake, switched off the engine and sat back in his seat, surveying his surroundings. The campsite was large but sparsely populated, with gravel tracks criss-crossing the neatly trimmed grass, which sloped gently down to the river.

This will do nicely, he thought, as Milly leapt onto the passenger seat beside him and began to lick his face with eager enthusiasm.

'Okay, girl,' he said, patting her on the head. 'I get the message.'

He opened the driver's door, and Milly bounced off his lap and out onto the grass.

'Don't go far. And don't go annoying anybody,' Trevor shouted after her, increasing his volume so she could hear him as she sped away, zig-zagging this way and that with her nose to the ground like some manically out-of-control mine detector.

He went to the back of the camper and lifted the tailgate. He pulled out a small folding picnic table and chair and set them up next to the side door of the van. Sliding the door open, he climbed inside and randomly grabbed a packet of Simmer 'n' Serve from the cupboard behind the driver's seat. There were half a dozen varieties of dried ready-meals to choose from, but he was in no mood to be picky. He'd already begun to feel light-headed with hunger, and his stomach was threatening to implode. He needed to get something solid inside him, and fast.

Half filling a saucepan with water, he placed it on the three-ring hob and turned on the gas, but when he clicked on the ignition button, the expected flame failed to materialise. Click-click-click-click-click. – Nothing.

'Oh bloody hell. Don't tell me…'

He jumped out of the van and hurried round to the far side. Wrenching open the other sliding door, he snatched up the small blue gas bottle and shook it. – It was empty.

He rammed it back into its compartment and slammed the door shut.

This was the first time he'd tried to use the cooker, and it had never occurred to him to check there was at least some gas on board when he'd bought the van. They probably sold refills in the campsite shop, but it was already closed. What an idiot.

Still, no need to panic. He could always make a sandwich and—

Then it struck him. He'd intended to pick up bread and milk and a few other bits and pieces once he'd left his mother's place and was on the road, but what with the breakdown and all the other comings and goings, it had completely slipped his mind.

Back inside the van, he rummaged through the cupboards in search of anything edible that didn't require some form of heating, but his quest was in vain. Not even a tin of baked beans, which he would have gladly eaten cold on this occasion. He dropped to his knees and examined the contents of the tiny fridge. A couple of boil-in-the-bag cod in parsley sauce and a six-pack of beer. Now there's an idea. Quite a lot of protein in beer.

He peeled off a can and went to the locker above the sink to fetch a glass. When he opened it, the box of dog biscuits caught his eye. – Oh, come on. He was ravenous, yes, but not quite that desperate... yet. Reaching in for the glass, the back of his hand brushed against the Jiffy bag. He'd been trying to put it out of his mind, curious to know what it contained but afraid that opening it might land him in even more trouble than he was already. – But maybe... just maybe, and talking purely hypothetically of course... he could probably... if he really wanted to... and he wasn't convinced he did... be really really careful unsealing it, have a quick peek inside and close it again so nobody'd be any the wiser.

Taking hold of a corner between forefinger and thumb, he eased it from the cupboard as if it were contaminated with some deadly virus.

He stepped out of the van and placed the can of beer, the glass and the Jiffy bag on the table and sat down.

Fastidiously positioning the padded envelope so that one of its long sides was exactly parallel to the edge of the table, he poured the beer, never taking his eyes off the package for a moment. He took a long drink and continued to stare at it. What the hell was he doing with the bloody thing? More importantly, what the hell was inside it that had so suddenly turned his quiet and ordinary life into a nightmare of guns and mayhem?

For several more minutes, he looked and pondered, taking frequent sips from his beer until the temptation became far too strong. He put down his glass and slowly reached out both hands towards the Jiffy bag. Again, he used only his forefingers and thumbs to take a tentative hold of the two nearest corners.

Just then, Milly came bounding over and almost knocked the table flying. Trevor let go of the package to save the table and swore at her. He glared at the dog and noticed she had something in her mouth – something that looked a lot like a string of half a dozen sausages. The words 'Oh shit' had barely left his mouth when he heard a man shouting, and the shouting was getting rapidly nearer.

'Oh shit,' he said again but with greater emphasis when he looked round to see a very large bearded man in a grubby grey T-shirt and faded denim cutoffs bearing down on him at speed.

'That your dog?' The man stabbed a nicotine-stained finger in Milly's direction as she disappeared inside the van with her prize.

By the colour of his face, Trevor thought the guy either had a serious blood pressure problem or he was very very angry. However, circumstantial evidence tended to suggest the latter might prove to be the better but far less welcome bet.

'Well is it?' The man was now standing directly in front of him on the opposite side of the table, his hands

121

on his hips and his considerable bulk almost entirely eclipsing the setting sun behind him.

Besides being so hungry he could almost have eaten a string of raw sausages himself, Trevor was physically and mentally shattered and not at all in the best of moods. He was also getting rather irritated by the number of times he could be asked the "Is that your dog?" question during the course of a single day. It wasn't bravery but some form of exhaustion-induced hysteria which prompted him to respond in a way he wouldn't normally have dared. He looked up at the man's crimson, bushy features.

'Er, no,' he said and drained his glass of beer.

The man's enormous tattooed hands left his hips and clenched at his sides. 'Don't mess with *me*, shithead, or I'll bloody clatter you. If that's not your dog, then what the fuck's it doing in your van?'

Trevor shrugged and poured the rest of the can of beer into his glass. 'Visiting?'

The man's face turned an even deeper shade of scarlet, and his knuckles grew white with the increased force of the clenching. 'Listen, you. That mangy mutt of yours has just nicked a buncha sausages from my barbecue, and I wanna know what you're gonna do about it.'

Trevor was aware of chomping sounds coming from inside the van as he said, 'What? You want them back?'

'Course I don't want 'em back. Not after your bloody mutt's been slobbering all over 'em.'

'Well I'm sorry, but I really don't know what you want me to do about it. In any case, I didn't see her with any sausages.'

'Okay, so how about we 'ave a little look then, eh?'

With that, he marched round the table and gawped in through the sliding door of the van. Trevor, who could no longer hear any chomping noises, got to his feet at the same time and also looked inside. Milly was lying on the back seat and licking her lips, but there wasn't a single sausage in sight.

'See? No sausages,' said Trevor with a wry grin.

'You calling me a liar?' The man squared up to him, clenching and unclenching his fists.

'No, but if there aren't any sausages, I can't give them back to you, and if there were any sausages, you wouldn't want them anyway. So what exactly *do* you want?'

'You can bloody well pay for 'em for starters.'

Trevor sighed and pulled out some change from his pocket. 'Okay, okay. How much?'

It was obviously a much trickier question than he'd realised because there was a pause while the man seemed to be wrestling with an especially complex calculation.

'Fiver.'

'What? Five quid for half a dozen sausages?'

The man's face brightened as if he'd scored some major victory. 'Ah, so you did see 'em then.'

Trevor sighed once again but decided it was worth every penny just to get rid of the knuckle scraping headcase. 'All right, Poirot, you've got me bang to rights,' he said, counting out five one-pound coins and dropping them into the man's dinner plate of a palm.

The knuckle scraper studied the coins for a moment as if to satisfy himself that they were genuine and then thrust them into his pocket. 'You wanna keep that mutt on a lead.'

'Good idea,' said Trevor with heavy sarcasm.

'You wanna watch out I don't bloody report you.' He wagged a finger in Trevor's face, then turned on his heel and stomped off across the grass.

'Dickhead,' muttered Trevor, making sure he spoke quietly enough so the man wouldn't hear. 'Sod off back to your hog roast and your fat ugly wife and your eighteen fat ugly kids.'

He climbed into the van and saw that Milly was in the same position on the back seat and still licking her lips. She seemed more than a little pleased with herself and was apparently oblivious to the fact that her master had come within an inch of having the living shit kicked out of him by a Neanderthal with fists the size of bowling balls.

Trevor gave her the most withering look he could muster. 'Right, young lady, you obviously can't be trusted, so you'll have to stay tied up from now on.'

He took a length of rope from one of the cupboards and tied one end to Milly's collar and the other to the handle of the sliding door. She now looked considerably less pleased with herself, and she watched Trevor with doleful eyes as he grabbed another beer from the fridge and stepped back outside.

Sitting down at the picnic table and filling his glass, he took a drink and gazed at the Jiffy bag. After a few moments, he picked it up as tentatively as before and turned it over in his hands. There were no markings of any kind on either side. He eased his finger under one end of the flap and took some time in sliding it along until the flap was completely free. He paused and took three large gulps of his drink, looking up and all around him to check that no-one was watching. Setting his glass down on the table, he opened the neck of the envelope by little more than half an inch. He peered inside, aware that his heartbeat was setting the rhythm for some unseen marching band.

'Eh?' he said aloud and immediately opened the Jiffy bag to its fullest extent. 'That's ridiculous.'

He tipped the contents out onto the table. Six packets of Silk Cut cigarettes. All this cloak and dagger stuff for half a dozen packets of fags? It didn't make sense. Picking one up, he examined every side for some indication that they might not be what they seemed. Although he'd never smoked in his life, he'd been around enough people who did to recognise a fag packet when he saw one, and that was exactly what this was. A perfectly ordinary packet of cigarettes.

He scanned the other packs on the table. All were exactly the same, and all of them were cellophane sealed, so they couldn't have been tampered with. Each bore the same health warning: "Smoking seriously harms you and others around you".

Yeah right, thought Trevor, and apparently it can get you chased by the police and mad people with guns too. What could be worse for your health than that?

He stuffed the cigarette packets back into the Jiffy bag and resealed it as best he could. Clutching it to his chest, he took a long drink and wondered why anyone would want to make so much fuss over a few fags. He'd no idea how much a packet cost these days, but it couldn't have been much more than six or seven quid, and thirty-odd quid's worth hardly amounted to tobacco smuggling.

Milly's whimpering from inside the van interrupted his ponderings. Despite her substantial sausage snack, she was making it clear to Trevor that it was way past time for her evening meal. He returned the Jiffy bag to the locker above the sink and opened a tin of dog food. Spooning the chunks of meat into her bowl, his rumbling belly tried to persuade him to save some for himself and only narrowly failed.

He spent the next hour sitting outside, drinking beer and trying to figure out a rational explanation for the contents of the Jiffy bag and what his next course of action should be. Eventually, however, he realised his brain was far too tired and addled to come up with anything even remotely coherent and decided that his best option now was some much-needed sleep.

Promising himself he'd get up early and head straight

for the nearest café and a slap-up breakfast, he left the picnic table and chair where they were and set up the bed in the van. He grabbed a pillow and a duvet from a shallow cupboard above the cab, and although his mind and grumbling stomach seemed intent on preventing it, he was asleep within seconds with Milly curled up beside him, snoring softly.

24

Trevor had no idea how long he had been asleep when he was awoken by a tapping noise. It took him a few moments to reconfigure his brain cells into consciousness, and then he heard the sound again. Someone seemed to be knocking on the side of the van. The events of the previous day came flooding back to him, and his immediate instinct was to panic. He glanced at his watch. It was just after eight o'clock.

'Mr Hawkins?'

He didn't recognise the man's voice, but that didn't mean a thing. He knew of at least three people who were after him, and quite likely there were others.

'Mr Hawkins?' The voice was louder this time.

'Er... yes?' Pulling the duvet around him, he sat upright and wriggled himself towards the foot of the bed.

'I wonder if we could have a word.'

Oh God, thought Trevor. That sounds like police talk. Surely the fat slob with the sausages hadn't really reported him. But even if he'd gone to the campsite manager, there's no way they'd call in the—

'Mr Hawkins.' It was more of a statement than a question now, and whoever was speaking was getting impatient.

He pulled back the curtain on the side door and slid back the window. The broad chinned face of a man with slicked back dark hair was smiling in at him and holding up some kind of identity card. 'Sorry to disturb you, sir. I'm Detective Sergeant Logan from the Metropolitan

Police and this is Detective Constable Swann.'

Trevor peered over Logan's shoulder at the face of the woman who was standing behind him. She too was smiling.

'I'd like to ask you a few questions,' said Logan.

'What about?'

'I'll explain at the station.'

'Station?'

'The local police station, sir. Now if you wouldn't mind getting dressed...'

Milly's face appeared next to Trevor's at the open window, and she surveyed their early morning visitors as if trying to decide whether they presented a sufficient threat to merit the effort of barking. She apparently concluded that they didn't and contented herself with panting and dribbling.

'This your dog, sir?' said Logan.

Trevor scowled. 'Yes.'

'Cute,' said the woman detective.

'It'll take me a few minutes to pack up the van if you want me to follow you.'

'That won't be necessary, sir. We'll give you a lift and drop you back here afterwards,' said Logan and almost inaudibly added, 'All being well.'

Trevor closed the curtain and threw on his clothes. The marching band had taken up residence in his chest again, and his brain was turning somersaults. This has got to be about that bloody Jiffy bag, he thought, and he looked up at the locker above the sink. Perhaps he should just hand it over right now and have done with it. No, said another voice in his head. Find out if that's what they're really after first. Anyway, they might think you're trying to bribe them. – What, with half a dozen packets of fags?

'You nearly ready, sir?' Logan's voice sounded weary.

Trevor was sitting on the end of the bed, tying his boot laces. 'Two seconds,' he said and noticed that Milly was standing on her hind legs with her front paws up against the door, her head under the curtain, staring out at the detectives. 'What about the dog?'

'Can't you leave it here?'

He took Milly by the collar and slid open the door. 'Depends how long for.'

'Hard to say,' Logan said with a shrug.

DC Swann stepped forward and stroked Milly's head. 'Maybe we should take her with us. Most nicks have some kind of facilities for animals.'

'Okay, okay,' said Logan. 'Bring the dog, but can we please get going?'

Trevor and Milly sat in the back of the Volvo with Logan driving and Swann beside him in the passenger seat. The detectives refused to answer any of his questions, and they spent the rest of the journey in total silence.

Once inside the police station, Swann spoke to a uniformed officer at the front desk, and he took Milly's lead from Trevor and began to walk away with her – or rather, he walked and she slid as the officer half dragged her across the tiled floor.

Logan and Swann led the way along a brightly lit corridor and into a small windowless room that was furnished only with a table, which was set at right-angles halfway along one wall, and two chairs on each side of it. On top of the table and against the wall was some kind of black box that Trevor assumed was a recording device. Logan motioned him to one of the two nearest chairs, and he and Swann sat down opposite him. The latter tossed a buff coloured folder onto the table but left it unopened.

Logan leaned forward and clasped his hands together. 'So, Mr Hawkins. You want to know what this is all about.'

'Hang on a sec, sarge,' said Swann.

'Ah yes,' said Logan with a grin. 'I'd forgotten.'

Swann pressed a couple of buttons on the recorder and a red light came on. 'Preliminary interview with Trevor Hawkins. Sunday 26th August, commencing at...' She checked her watch. '... Zero eight fifty-eight. Officers present, DS Logan and DC Swann.'

Trevor stared at the lights on the front of the recorder and felt the colour drain from his face.

Logan indicated the recording machine with a nod of his head. 'That's just a formality. All we want is to clear up one or two loose ends about your wife's... disappearance.'

Trevor almost choked. He'd been mentally preparing himself for a grilling about envelopes, toilet cisterns and lockers, but *this*? He also didn't like the way Logan had hesitated at the end of the sentence.

'I'm sorry to have to rake up the past as I know it must be painful for you, but...' The detective tapped the folder three times with his index finger. 'We've received certain new information which—'

'New information? What sort of new information? You don't mean you've found her?'

'No, I'm afraid not.'

'What then?

'Perhaps you could begin by telling me precisely where you were when your wife... disappeared.'

Again the hesitation. It was as if they didn't believe Imelda had gone missing at all. As if they suspected instead that she'd been– Wait a minute. Wait a minute. Trevor sat back in his chair and looked up at the cracked plaster on the ceiling with the faintest of smiles. 'This wouldn't have anything to do with my mother, would it?'

He diverted his gaze from the ceiling just in time to

catch the look that went between the two detectives.

'Well, er...' Logan faltered. 'We have in fact spoken to Mrs... er... your mother, and she expressed her concern that—'

Trevor's smile widened. He was starting to relax now he had begun to understand the real reason for the police's interest in him.

'You find something amusing about all this, do you?' said Logan.

'Of course not. It's just that my mother got it into her head after Imelda vanished that she'd been murdered and that it was me who killed her. She's not exactly been firing on all four cylinders for years.'

Logan coughed to clear his throat. 'Well that's as may be, but an accusation has been made, and we have a duty to investigate.'

'Even though the accusation comes from a batty old woman who thinks Princess Di was abducted by aliens and the London Eye is some kind of massive surveillance system?'

'It's not for me to judge the state of your mother's mind. It's my job to find out the truth.'

'But surely that amounts to the same thing.'

There was a lengthy pause while Trevor and Logan locked eyes, and Swann glanced back and forth between the two of them.

It was Logan who broke the silence. 'You do not have to say anything, but it may harm your defence if you do not mention when questioned anything which you later rely on in court. Anything you do say may be given in evidence.'

Long before the detective got to the end of the caution, the increasingly familiar marching band in Trevor's chest had been joined by the group of Japanese taiko drummers he'd seen at the festival. 'Am I... under arrest?'

'Not yet,' said Logan. 'But I think you should be aware of your rights before we go any further – before you start to incriminate yourself.'

'You *are* kidding, aren't you? I mean, how can I incriminate myself when there hasn't even been a crime?'

'So you say.' Logan picked up the folder. 'Unfortunately for you, though, there appear to be one or two grey areas about this case, so I'll ask you again. Where were you when your wife went missing?'

'Look, I went through all this at the time,' said Trevor and pointed at the folder. 'It's all in there, isn't it?'

He thought he spotted another exchange of looks between the two detectives but had no idea whether this had any significance.

'We'd like to hear it again if it's all the same to you,' said Logan.

Trevor's mind leapt back to the caution and particularly the bit about not having to say anything. But there was also the part about harming his defence. 'They don't even know *when* she disappeared, so how can I say—'

'They?'

'The police. The hotel. Anybody.'

'Okay, so where were you during the four days she was away in Birmingham?'

'At home and at work.'

'Any witnesses?'

'You mean do I have an alibi?'

'That's the one,' said Logan with a sardonic grin.

'At work, yes. At home, no,' said Trevor. 'And don't you think I'd have made damn sure I did have an alibi if I was planning to murder my wife?'

'Might not have been planned. Might have been a... crime of passion.'

Trevor threw his head back. 'Oh for—'

'Heat of the moment and all that. You know the sort of thing. You find out she's having an affair, the red mist comes up, and bang... So was she having an affair?'

'Imelda?' Trevor wondered if the guy was being deliberately offensive to try and trap him into saying something he'd regret.

'Well she was quite an attractive woman,' said Logan, pulling out the wedding photograph from the file and waving it in front of him.

'Yeah yeah, that's right. I found out she was screwing my best friend... and... and... and the entire string section of the Birmingham Philharmonic Orchestra – women included.'

'I really don't think sarcasm is going to help your case one little bit, Trevor... D'you mind if I call you Trevor, by the way?'

Trevor responded with a snort and folded his arms across his chest. He'd been married to Imelda for four and a half years, and never once in all that time had it occurred to him that there might be someone else. Not that she hadn't had plenty of opportunity. All those business trips away, and then of course there was the non-existent company she was supposed to have worked for. But that had only come out after she'd disappeared, and—

'So what was his name?' said Logan.

'Who?'

'This best friend of yours. The one she was having an affair with.'

Oh for goodness' sake. This was getting more absurd by the minute, and he was beginning to feel light-headed again from lack of food. He darted a glance from side to side and then behind him before looking back at Logan. 'Sorry, I was just checking for the hidden camera. I mean, this has got to be *Trigger Happy TV* or something, right?'

Logan was about to respond when there was a knock on the door. Whatever words he was about to utter before the interruption, they now came out as 'Damn it' and then, rather louder, 'Come.'

The door opened, and a uniformed female officer came into the room.

'I *am* trying to conduct an interview here, you know,' said Logan.

'Sorry, sir. There's an urgent message for you.'

'Oh? Who from?'

The officer hesitated, her eyes drifting towards Trevor, who had turned in his seat to face her. 'Er... I think it might be better if I told you in er... private, sir.'

'Christ,' said Logan, getting to his feet. 'This better had be urgent, constable.'

'Interview suspended at zero nine zero five,' said Swann and switched off the recorder as Logan followed the uniform out of the room. Then she opened the folder and began to read.

Trevor tried to make out what was written on the upside-down page but failed. 'So what does it say in there?'

Swann looked up at him and smiled. 'Sorry, sir. Confidential I'm afraid.'

'You do realise that this whole thing is totally ridiculous, don't you?'

'Sorry, sir, but I can't discuss your case until the interview restarts formally.'

She went back to reading the file – or pretending to. As far as Trevor could tell, there were no more than two or three pages. He still couldn't believe what was happening to him. Not only did he seem to be in serious trouble over the package-in-the-locker business, but now he was being accused of murdering Imelda. At least this lot didn't seem to know anything about the Jiffy bag. So who was the Patterson guy that had stopped him when he was leaving the festival? What was it he'd said when he'd asked if he was the police? – 'Something like that.' What the hell did that mean? Either you're police or you're not. Simple as that.

He suddenly became aware of the dryness in his mouth. 'I don't suppose there's any chance of getting a coffee is there? I haven't even had breakfast yet. Come to that, all I've had since Friday lunchtime is a handful of biscuits.'

Swann raised her eyes from the folder. 'I'll see what I can do when DS Logan gets back. I'm not sure I can promise bacon and eggs, but I expect we can—'

She broke off as the door to the interview room was flung back on its hinges and Logan stormed in with a face that looked like it could launch a thousand nuclear missiles. 'You can go,' he said.

Trevor's head swivelled to face him. 'What?' he and Swann said in almost perfect unison.

'You heard me. Go.' Logan was holding the door open, his gaze fixed on the lino covered floor at his feet.

Trevor stood up and walked towards the doorway. He had no intention of jeopardising this unexpected offer of freedom by asking any of the questions that had flashed into his mind.

'Go with him and get him a lift back to the campsite,' said Logan as Trevor went past him into the corridor.

Swann paused when she got to within a couple of feet of the sergeant and opened her mouth to speak.

'Just do as you're told for once, will you?' Logan yelled.

Not a happy bunny, thought Trevor, as Swann led the way along the corridor and he heard the door of the interview room slam shut behind them.

25

'In… one… hundred… yards… turn… right,' said the robotic staccato voice of the satellite navigation system.

Sandra did as she was instructed, but when she reached the entrance of the Riverside Farm Campsite, she was almost certain she recognised the dark blue Ford Mondeo that was parked a little further up the road. Instead of turning into the campsite as she'd intended, she drove past the Mondeo, noticing the two men in the front seats. One was reading a newspaper, and the other seemed to be asleep. She carried on until she came to a dirt track on the left, which ran alongside the six-foot chainlink fence of the campsite. She took the turning and drove slowly, partly because of the rough surface and partly because she was trying to spot Trevor's camper van through the fence.

She still hadn't seen it by the time the track opened up into a parking area and ended next to a river. She stopped the car and got out. There was a narrow footpath between the river and the bottom fence of the campsite, and she walked along it until she reached a small wooden jetty that jutted out at right-angles to the riverbank. Half a dozen rowing boats were tethered to it, pitching and bobbing in the water, and a faded metal sign indicated the hourly hire rate.

Opposite the near end of the jetty there was a steel framed gate set into the fence with another, less faded, sign fixed to it, announcing that the gate was FOR THE USE OF CAMPSITE RESIDENTS ONLY. Sandra slid back the bolt and stepped inside. Almost immediately, she saw the object of her quest. The white VW van was parked near to the fence and about fifty or sixty yards to her right.

Lazy bugger must still be asleep, she thought when she noticed the camper's curtains were all closed. So much the better. The element of surprise is always a bonus.

She strode across the grass and banged the palm of her hand several times against the side of the van. When there was no response, she repeated the action and called out, 'Come on. I know you're in there. Open up.'

Still there was silence, so she went around the van trying to find the slightest gap in the curtains but without success.

'He's not in, duck.'

Sandra spun round to see a middle-aged woman with plaited hair, who was carrying a red plastic washing-up bowl piled high with plates and pans.

'Police took him away first thing this morning.'

'Police?'

'Well, they was plain clothes of course, but I can always spot 'em.'

'Right,' said Sandra distractedly as her brain struggled to work out the most logical reason for the police's interest in Trevor, but there were too many possibilities. More importantly, had they taken the Jiffy bag?

'He didn't look much like a criminal though, I must say. And believe you me, I've known quite a few in my time, I can tell you.'

'Right,' Sandra said again and smiled at the woman, wishing she would clear off and let her get on with finding out if the Jiffy bag was still in the van.

'Friend of his, are you?'

'Kind of,' said Sandra and started to rummage through the contents of her shoulder bag.

'What's he supposed to have done then?'

'No idea.'

'Here, he's not a murderer, is he?'

'Ah, here we are.' Sandra exhibited the set of keys she had taken from Trevor the day before. 'Good thing he gave me the spare set.'

'Or one of those pervies even? I mean, I've got kids here and—'

Before the woman with the washing-up bowl had finished her sentence, Sandra had opened the sliding door and jumped inside. 'Thanks for your help,' she said and slammed the door behind her.

She went straight to the locker above the sink and was relieved to see that the green, padded envelope was still there. She was about to stuff it into her bag when she noticed that the seal seemed to have been tampered with. Her instructions had been very precise. On no account was she to look inside the package. Her job was simply to collect it and then deliver it. The contents were none of her business.

Sandra hesitated. Well maybe not, but it had already been opened so... She took hold of the envelope and peeled back the flap.

'Eh?'

She pulled out a packet of cigarettes and stared at it before upending the Jiffy bag onto the sink drainer. Five more packs fell out, and all were identical by the look of them. She'd suspected the envelope probably contained a substantial amount of cash, but whatever she'd expected, it certainly wasn't cigarettes.

No, this can't be right. Why pay her two grand to collect something you could get for a hell of a lot less at your local tobacconist, and why were people apparently prepared to kill for them? Maybe Trevor had pocketed the cash, or whatever else was in the Jiffy bag, and substituted the fag packets. But why bother? He couldn't have known she was about to catch up with him. – Damn and bollocks. Her original plan had been to grab the package and leave, but now she'd have to hang around till Trevor got back so she could ask him a few questions.

She sat down on the end of the bed, almost dizzy from the rapidness of her breathing. Her eyes darted around the interior of the van as if it were a cage and she was desperate to find some means of escape. She told herself she needed to keep calm and concentrated on controlling her breathing. Coffee might help. Most people would have considered this counter-intuitive, but Sandra often found a burst of caffeine strangely calming in situations like this.

She picked up the kettle from the hob and half filled it with water, but when she tried to light the gas, nothing happened.

'Sod it.'

There was a small fridge, which was partly obscured by the bed, but she managed to open it just enough to see that its only contents were a couple of boil-in-the-bag cod steaks and three cans of beer. A little early, she thought, and then remembered she'd grabbed a can of Coke when she'd stopped for petrol. She searched in her bag. The Coke was a bit on the warm side, but at least it had some caffeine in it, and she was desperate for a fix.

Sandra had just taken her third mouthful when the shrill ringtone of her mobile phone startled her into inhaling rather than swallowing. Most of the Coke shot out of her mouth in a fine spray, and she spluttered as she fought to control the coughing spasms. She fished around in her bag with one hand while she held the palm of the other tight against her heaving chest. Despite being half blinded by tears, she could focus sufficiently on the phone display to recognise the number. She had ignored it before, but now she was in possession of the

Jiffy bag again she had something positive to report even though she was doubtful that its contents were quite what her client was expecting. She let the phone ring a few more times to allow her lungs to recover as much as possible before answering.

'Hello?' Her voice was husky, and uttering even this single word almost provoked another coughing fit.

'Sandra Gray?'

'Speaking.'

'Where the hell have you been? Mr Vin— er, my boss is not at all happy about what he's been hearing.'

'Sorry. My mobile must have been out of range.'

'Do you have the package?'

'Of course. It's right here in front of me.'

Sandra had always known her innate ability to lie convincingly would be of great benefit to her as a private investigator, and she answered the ensuing barrage of questions with confidence.

– Had she looked inside it?

– Certainly not.

– Why hadn't she picked it up from the locker herself?

– She'd been running late and sent one of her employees.

– Why hadn't he left the card with the address details in the locker?

– He'd forgotten, he's an idiot, and she'd already sacked him.

– Why had she attacked one of "our people"?

– She hadn't known he was one of "their people", and she'd thought he was trying to steal the package. (At least that part was true.)

– Was she being followed?

– No.

– Was she sure about that?

– Positive.

– Was she now in a position to be able to deliver the

package?

– She said she was and did her best to disguise the hesitation in her voice.

'How long will it take you to get to Sheffield from where you are now?'

'Sheffield?' said Sandra, roughly calculating the distance in her head. 'Dunno. Couple of hours maybe?'

'Just get there as quick as you can, okay? Arundel Gate Hotel. Room two-seventeen.'

'Any name I should—?' Sandra began, but the phone had gone dead.

* * *

She had almost finished her can of Coke when she heard a key being inserted into the lock of the sliding door. She sat upright on the end of the bed and pulled her bag closer to her, feeling inside for the gun she'd taken from the Scottish guy at the festival. The door slid open a couple of feet and then stopped.

There was a moment's pause before Trevor's head appeared in the opening.

'Welcome home,' said Sandra and tightened her grip on the butt of the pistol but without removing it from the bag.

Trevor opened his mouth to speak but was interrupted by Milly, who had apparently recognised Sandra's voice and was inside the van and up on the bed next to her before he could utter so much as a syllable.

'Well the dog seems pleased to see me even if you don't,' said Sandra, using her free hand to ward off Milly's frenzied attempts to lick any undefended part of her face. 'Why don't you join us? After all, *mi* camper van *es su* camper van.'

He hesitated, so she ostentatiously moved the gun inside her bag, and he seemed to get the message.

'Sit yourself down,' she said and nodded towards a space on the floor that was furthest from her.

Trevor climbed into the van but instead of doing what he was told, went to the back of the passenger seat and bent forward from the waist.

Sandra thrust Milly away from her and whipped the gun from inside the bag, pointing it at the small of his back. 'I said *sit*.'

Trevor may have been amused – and even impressed – if he had been able to see Milly instantly drop down on her rear end and gaze eagerly up at Sandra as if awaiting further instructions. If he had also known there was a gun pointing at him, he would no doubt have stopped what he was doing and straightened up with both hands in the air. Without the benefit of having eyes in the back of his head, however, he muttered something about sorting the chair out, pulled a small lever and swivelled the passenger seat through a hundred and eighty degrees so that it faced inwards towards Sandra. He sat down, and his hands reached upwards to shoulder level when he finally noticed the gun.

Sandra lowered it and smiled. 'Wondered what you were up to for a moment there. Thought you might have some kind of hidden weapon.' Then she laughed as another thought struck her. 'Maybe even an ejector seat.'

Trevor grunted. 'Yeah, that's right. This van used to belong to James Bond, you know. Traded in his Aston Martin for it in fact. Oh the Aston had all the fancy gadgets like bulletproof shields and spikes coming out of the wheels and a thing for making smokescreens and spreading oil on the road, but there was nowhere to cook a decent meal or even do the washing up. As for somewhere to sleep, well...' He spread his raised palms outwards.

'You can put your hands down now if you want,' said Sandra in a quiet, almost soothing tone. Flippancy wasn't a reaction she would have anticipated from someone who had a gun pointing at them, and she interpreted it as a sign that Trevor had been pushed to the edge of rational thought. In that state, he was potentially dangerous and needed to be handled with care – for the time being at least.

She picked up one of the packets of cigarettes from the small pile on the sink drainer. 'So then, Trevor,' she said. 'I think there are one or two things you and I need to talk about.'

26

Logan was sitting with his face in his hands when DC Swann came back into the interview room.

'So what was all that about?' she said and flopped down onto the chair opposite him. Logan's response was muffled, so she asked him to repeat what he'd said.

He placed his palms on the table and slowly raised his head as if the effort required all of the strength he had left. 'Spooks.'

'What?' Swann's expression would have been much the same if he'd punched her on the nose.

'Yep, MI5,' said Logan with a sour grin and performed a brief drum roll on the edge of the table with his fingertips. 'The very same.'

'But what's it got to do with them?'

'Oh yeah, and they're going to tell *me* that, aren't they? A detective bloody sergeant.'

'Well what did they say exactly?'

'I haven't spoken to them. The message just now was to phone the guv'nor, so I did. He tells me that the spooks had got wind of our little investigation and were not at all happy about it. Apparently, they're after our friend Trevor for something a whole lot bigger, and we were getting in their way.'

'Oh right,' said Swann with a scowl. 'So now he's some kind of international terrorist?'

'No idea. All I know is we were to release him immediately and drop the whole thing altogether – or at least till MI5 have finished with him.'

'What do you mean, "finished with him"?'

'I think the precise words were "satisfactorily concluded their own enquiries".'

Swann slumped back in her seat. 'So that's that then, is it?'

'Hardly.'

'But if the guv'nor says—'

'Sod the guv'nor. I've got my own "enquiries to conclude",' said Logan, snatching up the buff coloured folder from the table and brandishing it at her. 'I don't care if this guy is Osama Bin Laden's wicked bloody uncle. I just want to know if he murdered his wife or not.'

'But if we get found out, we'll be lucky if we end up on traffic duty.'

Logan tossed the folder back onto the table. 'Well we'll just have to be discreet then, won't we? In fact, we won't be able to do anything at all until we know where he ends up.'

'So we still keep a tail on him?'

'Certainly. And as long as the plods don't mess up, nobody'll be any the wiser.' He glanced at his watch. 'Anyway, I make that about coffee time.'

'And you'll be wanting me to fetch it, I suppose.'

'No, no, no. Not a bit of it,' he said, getting to his feet. 'Let's go and see what the canteen in this fine establishment has to offer.'

'Blimey. You feeling flush or something?'

'I don't remember saying I was going to *pay*.'

Swann rolled her eyes as he opened the door and waited for her to join him. 'Okay, I'll do you a deal,' she said. 'I'll get the coffees, and you can buy me lunch at some quaint little country pub.'

Logan nodded at the table behind her. 'You forgot the file.'

27

Patterson peeled back the top slice of white bread and peered at the three thin rashers of fatty bacon, poking at each one in turn with his knife.

'And what's this supposed to be?'

Statham had just taken a mouthful of scrambled egg, and he washed it down with a gulp of tea from a chipped white mug before answering. 'I'm no expert of course, but I'd say it was a bacon sandwich.'

'You forgot, didn't you?'

'Forgot what?'

'When you put in the order. You forgot to ask for crispy.'

'No I didn't.'

Patterson jabbed at one of the rashers. 'So what do you call this then? It's certainly not crispy by most commonly accepted definitions of the word.'

Statham put down his own knife and fork and leaned forward to examine the bacon more closely. 'Oh yeah, I see what you mean. Not crispy at all. More like... fatty, I'd say.'

'Exactly.' Patterson slammed his knife down onto the once cream-coloured tabletop and sat back heavily in his chair. 'I mean, I know this is hardly the Savoy Grill, but surely even a crappy little caff like this knows what crispy bloody bacon looks like.'

'Probably more sho,' said Statham through a piece of blackened sausage, which seemed to be burning his mouth. 'Should almosht be a shpeshiality in a plaish like thish.'

'What?'

The irritation in his colleague's tone would have been unmistakable to most, but Statham apparently misinterpreted the question as encouragement to continue with his explanation.

'Transport caffs,' he said, swallowing the sausage and wafting a hand in front of his mouth. 'You'd think they'd know how to do a decent bacon sarnie a damn sight better than somewhere like the Savoy Grill, wouldn't you? Of course, if it was something like steak tartare or lobster au something-or-other, for instance, then you'd expect the boot to be on the other foot because they've—'

'Colin?'

'Mmm?' said Statham, taking a slug of tea.

'Why don't you just shut up and pass me the HP sauce?'

'Oh, okay.' He picked up the plastic bottle of brown sauce at his elbow and handed it to Patterson. 'Good idea. Smother it with enough of this stuff and you'll never know the difference.'

'Yes... I... will,' said Patterson as if he were addressing a three-year-old whose first language was Swahili. 'Because although it might disguise the *taste*, it's not going to persuade me for one moment that this bacon is anywhere approaching crispy like I asked for in the first place.'

Unlike the other half dozen customers in the café, Statham seemed oblivious to the dramatic rise in volume with which this last sentence was delivered and chomped noisily on a generous slice of black pudding.

'You know what?' he said, leaning forward again and gesticulating with his fork at the bacon, which by now was almost entirely invisible under a blanket of sauce. 'You could always cut out the fatty bits and just leave

147

them on the side of the plate.'

With careful deliberation, Patterson replaced the lid on the sauce bottle and set it back down on the table. He looked up and registered the childlike enthusiasm in Statham's eyes. 'In case you hadn't noticed,' he said, 'this is what is commonly referred to in the meat trade as *streaky* bacon.'

Statham sat back, deflated. 'Yeah, I see what you mean. I suppose you wouldn't be left with a great lot if you sort of... filleted it.'

'Not only that, Colin, but I'd need to be a bloody neurosurgeon with a very sharp scalpel and about a couple of hours to spare.' With that, Patterson slapped the top slice of bread back onto his sandwich and took a large bite. It took only a few moments of chewing before he realised he'd seriously overdone the HP sauce. He grabbed a paper napkin and spat most of the mouthful into it, and there was a loud clattering noise as the remainder of the sandwich connected with the plate in front of him.

'I guess the sauce didn't do the trick after all then,' said Statham with what appeared to be a sympathetic smile.

Patterson drained half a mug of tea and then reached for a fresh napkin to wipe away the traces of brown sauce from his chin.

'Bloody tea's cold too,' he said and looked at his watch. 'Christ almighty, what the hell are they doing? They should have reported in twenty minutes ago.'

'You want me to call them?'

'No,' said Patterson with a heavy sigh. 'I'll do it. You go and get me another tea – and make sure it's hot this time. And get some crisps or biscuits or something. At least they won't have messed those about.'

* * *

Jarvis roughly folded the sports section of *The Mail on Sunday* and slid it onto the top of the dashboard. He glanced across at Coleman, who had tilted the passenger seat as horizontally as it would go and was lying back with his eyes closed and his mouth open.

'You asleep?'

There was no response.

He turned his attention to the campsite entrance and began to tap out a rhythm on the steering wheel. After a few seconds, he added an improvised melody, humming it at first and then whistling as he became more confident in the way the tune was developing.

'Not bored, are you?' said Coleman.

Jarvis stopped whistling but continued his tapping as he looked to his left to see that Coleman's eyes were still shut.

'Didn't wake you, did I?' he said.

'Wasn't asleep.'

'Course you weren't. That's why you've been snoring your head off for the last half hour.'

Coleman's eyes snapped open and he turned his head to fix them on his accuser. 'I don't snore.'

'How do you know?'

'The missus would have told me.'

Jarvis laughed. 'You've been divorced for three years.'

'So?'

'So to my certain knowledge you haven't slept with anyone since. So how do you know it's not something you've developed since you were married?'

There was a brief pause as Coleman held his partner's gaze. Then he yawned and stretched. 'Anything happening?' he said with a cursory nod towards the campsite entrance.

Jarvis stopped his drumming. 'Not since the boys in blue dropped him off, no.'

149

The two men lapsed into silence for a few minutes until Jarvis rubbed his stomach with the palm of his hand and said, 'I could murder a bag of chips and a couple of saveloys right now.'

'You and me both, mate.' Coleman checked the dashboard clock. 'I haven't had anything to eat since— Oh shit. Look at the bloody time.'

Jarvis looked. 'Yeah? So?'

'We were supposed to report in twenty minutes ago.' He grabbed his mobile phone from the top pocket of his jacket just as it began to play the opening bars of *The William Tell Overture*. He didn't need to look at the display screen to know who was calling him. 'Hello?'...

... 'Yeah, sorry, guv. Bit of a bad signal here.'

... 'It's fine now, yes, but we had to move up the road to—'

... 'Not since they brought him back, no.'

... 'A what? Sorry, guv, the signal's going again.' He smirked at Jarvis and made a circle with the index finger and thumb of his free hand while flexing his wrist up and down.

... 'Oh right. Yeah, we put a tracker on the camper while he was away.'

... 'But there's only one entrance, guv.'

... 'Okay.'

... 'Okay, we'll get right onto it.'

... 'Yeah, fine. By the way, we haven't had anything to eat for hours. I don't suppose there's any chance we—? ... Hello? ... Hello?' He held the phone in front of him to look at the display. 'Bastard hung up on me.'

'Maybe his signal went,' said Jarvis with a broad grin. 'So what exactly are we getting right onto?'

'He wants us to check out the van and make sure the guy's still actually in there... without being spotted ourselves of course.'

'Well where else is he gonna be? There's only one

way out, and we've been watching it the whole time.'

'That's what I told him, but he still wants us to make sure.' Coleman reached into his pocket and pulled out a coin. 'Toss you for it.'

'What?'

'We can't both go, can we?' He flipped the coin into the air, caught it in the palm of his right hand and slapped it onto the back of his left.

'Heads,' said Jarvis and watched carefully as Coleman revealed the coin. 'Best of three?'

'On your bike, pal,' Coleman said as he returned the coin to his pocket. 'And while you're at it, see if the site shop's open yet.'

Jarvis grunted and opened the driver's door a few inches. He stopped abruptly and snatched it back towards him when his peripheral vision caught sight of a small white hatchback speeding past from behind.

'Jesus,' he said. 'Not a single car goes by in over an hour, and then Lewis bloody Hamilton comes along and nearly takes the sodding door off.'

'Mirror, signal, manoeuvre,' muttered Coleman and reached for the newspaper on top of the dashboard.

28

Sandra swerved slightly to avoid hitting the door of the dark blue Mondeo. She glanced in the rear-view mirror as she accelerated away and caught sight of Trevor, who was half lying and half crouching on the back seat with Milly beside him.

'So you'd no idea you were being staked out by the same people who followed us yesterday?' she said.

'No. They police as well?'

'Maybe. But like I said before, it's hard to tell the good guys from the bad guys at the moment.' She looked at Trevor in the mirror again. 'And I have to say the same applies to you, my friend.'

Trevor shifted his position and asked if it was safe to sit up yet. Sandra told him it would be better to stay put for a few minutes, and she waited until they got to the junction with the main road before she stopped the car to let him move into the passenger seat. He strapped himself in, and she heard a strange sound that was somewhere between a gurgle and a growl.

'Christ,' she said. 'Is that you or the dog?'

'I've hardly eaten a thing in two days. I don't suppose we could—'

'No, I don't suppose we could.'

Sandra tightened her grip on the steering wheel. My God but he'd got some nerve. First he dumps you at some crappy little roadside diner – which, by the way, involved you in a shitload of time, trouble and expense to get back to the festival and pick up your car – and now he reckons he can try it on again. Well have I got news for you, Trevor boy.

'The thing I don't get...' he began.

Oh yeah? And what would that be, Mastermind?

'*One* of the things I don't get is how you knew where I was. I mean, I know the police have a whole load of technology and stuff, but...'

Sandra didn't feel much like answering or getting into technical details about automatic numberplate recognition, but he'd probably just keep on at her till she did. 'Let's just say I have some useful contacts. When I called this particular one, there were already two APBs out on you, so I—'

'Two?'

'Yup.'

'I don't understand. Why would the police put out *two* APBs?'

'I didn't say the police were behind both of them, now did I?'

Sandra kept her eyes fixed on the road ahead, but she could sense that Trevor was staring at her, waiting for her to continue with an explanation. She decided to make him work for it.

'Well?' said Trevor eventually. 'So who put out the other one?'

'The thing is, this contact of mine is a pal, right? But even he couldn't tell me the answer to that.'

'Couldn't or wouldn't?'

Sandra shrugged. 'What's the difference? It all comes down to the same thing.'

'And what's that exactly?'

'Think about it. Somebody with the authority – but who's not the police – puts out an APB, but no-one's supposed to know who that somebody is. In fact, it's a big *secret*,' she said with heavy emphasis on the last word.

She looked across at Trevor's expressionless face and realised the penny still hadn't dropped.

'Secret Service would be my guess,' she said and turned her attention back to the road.

'Secret Service?' Trevor laughed. 'What, MI5 and all that?'

'Probably.'

'And why would the Secret Service be interested in *me* for God's sake?'

'You were the one who told me your van used to belong to James Bond,' she said and hummed the first few notes of the 007 theme tune.

Ever since she'd spoken to her contact and begun to suspect that MI5 might be involved, Sandra had developed serious misgivings about the true significance of the package she'd been hired to collect and deliver. Of course, she'd assumed from the very first that there had to be something not entirely legal about the whole setup. No-one's going to pay out two thousand pounds when a courier service could do exactly the same thing for a pittance – unless there was something dodgy going on. But operating on the edge of the law – or sometimes just outside it – was often part of the job as far as she was concerned, and the money had been too good to turn down. MI5, on the other hand, was an entirely different matter. Jesus, they only ever got interested if it was something to do with national security or terrorism. That kind of stuff.

Then there was the issue of the cigarette packets. She had grilled Trevor about those back at the campsite, but he'd been so adamant that they were all he'd found in the Jiffy bag, she'd been inclined to believe him. But even when she'd carried out a pretty thorough search of the van, she couldn't be a hundred per cent certain he was telling the truth, and she wasn't about to take any chances. She didn't know much about her clients, but she'd formed the distinct impression that they weren't the kind of people who would take failure lightly. If any shit was going to hit the fan when she dropped off the package, she wanted Trevor there as her human shield. Not surprisingly, he'd dug his heels in at first, insisting that he'd simply made a huge mistake and almost pleading with her to just take the Jiffy bag and leave him behind, but Sandra's gun had soon convinced him that this was not an option.

She'd also been more than curious to know why the police had picked him up, but she'd decided that her priority was to get the package to Sheffield as instructed. She'd told the guy on the phone it would take her about two hours to get there, and she was already running late. Quizzing Trevor about the police could wait till they were on the road, and now seemed like as good a time as any.

He was gazing out of the side window, his arms folded tightly across his chest.

'This business with the police,' she said. 'You want to tell me what that's all about?'

'Not particularly.'

Oh great. He'd gone sulky on her again. There was always the gun of course. That would loosen his tongue quick enough, but it'd be tricky to drive and aim at the same time, and stopping the car would waste valuable minutes. Not that she was in the mood right now, but maybe it was worth a crack with the good cop approach, and if push came to shove, she could even cross her fingers and promise him an all-you-can-eat at the next services they came to.

'You never know,' she said, injecting a caring, agony auntish tone into her voice. 'I might be able to help. I've got some pretty important friends in the Force.'

Okay, she had one, and he wasn't that important either, but Trevor didn't need to know that. Whatever,

155

the little white lie seemed to do the trick, and he launched into his story without any further prompting. Perhaps he was stupid enough to believe she really would help, or perhaps he just wanted to get it off his chest. But she didn't much care why he opened up so easily. The important thing was that she got the information she wanted.

He told her how his wife, Imelda, had disappeared more than eighteen months ago and hadn't been seen since. There'd been an investigation at the time, but it had been abandoned after only a couple of weeks, and he'd heard nothing more about it until the police knocked on his van door at eight o'clock that morning.

'So they've re-opened the case?' said Sandra.

'Because my dear batty old mother told them I'd murdered her.'

'Your wife?'

He explained how his mother had never made any secret of the fact that his older brother, Derek, was always her blue-eyed boy, and when he'd died in a car accident eight years ago, she'd seemed to blame Trevor for his death even though she hadn't said it in so many words. Perhaps that was why she'd developed the absurd notion that he'd murdered Imelda – some kind of bizarre transference thing.

'The cops don't seem to think it's an absurd notion,' said Sandra, relieved that the police's interest in Trevor appeared to have no connection with the job in hand.

'Maybe they have to follow these things up as a matter of… routine. Maybe they don't realise quite how batty she really is.'

'Well they let you go, so presumably they must think you're innocent.'

'Who knows?' said Trevor. 'We didn't actually get that far.'

'What do you mean?'

He told her how another officer had interrupted the interview to tell one of the detectives there was an urgent message for him, and he'd left the room.

'A few minutes later, he came back and said I could go.'

'Just like that?' Sandra frowned but kept her eyes on the road ahead. 'No explanation?'

Trevor shook his head. 'He didn't give me one, and I didn't ask. All I cared about was getting the hell out of there before he changed his mind.'

'Hmm.' Sandra's relief of a few seconds earlier was in danger of spontaneously combusting.

'What's that supposed to mean?'

'Sounds like MI5 again,' she said. 'I can't think why else the police would go to all that trouble and then suddenly release you for no apparent reason.'

'MI5 told them to?'

Sandra responded with a shrug and tooted her horn at the back of a battered old truck which was weaving in front of her and spewing out clouds of black smoke from its exhaust. Aroused from her sleep, Milly sat up on the back seat, her eyes darting this way and that as if trying to locate the source of any new stimulus. Trevor twisted round in his seat and stroked the top of her head a few times before resuming his position of staring out of the side window, his face an unhealthy shade of pale grey, rather like the colour of snow as it's just beginning to turn to slush.

29

MacFarland lay on the double bed, propped up with a couple of pillows, reading *Guns and Ammo*. He held the magazine in his right hand while he flexed the fingers of his left. His face contorted from the occasional stabs of pain, but at least the blood had stopped seeping through the heavy bandage.

When he realised he had read the same sentence four times, he looked up at the source of his distraction. The voice from the enormous television screen on the opposite wall had reached an almost deafening level of hysteria, and MacFarland watched as three horses galloped towards the finishing line with barely a length between them. Seconds later, the commentator shrieked out the news that Cosmic Dancer had won by a short head.

'Any good?' said MacFarland without taking his eyes off the screen.

''Fraid not,' said the man lying in a similar position on the other double bed. 'Fourth.' He dropped his folded newspaper onto the bed and replaced the cap on his pen.

'Ye ever win?'

'I have my moments.'

'Yeah?'

'Mostly when I get a tipoff that the race has been rigged.'

'That happen often?'

'Not often enough,' the other man said and stood up from the bed. 'You fancy something from the mini-bar?'

'Aye, may as well,' said MacFarland and turned towards the man that most people knew as Delia.

He had earned the nickname not just because his surname was Smith but because of his background in accountancy and his reputation as one of the best in the business when it came to cooking the books. He was several years older than MacFarland and, like most of his countrymen, fiercely proud of his Welsh roots. Even so, he spoke without any trace of an accent except on the few occasions when he seriously lost his temper. MacFarland had learned a long time ago that if you ever heard him utter the word "boyo", it was time to take cover.

'Vodka? Scotch? Gin?' said Delia, crouching down to examine the contents of the mini-bar.

'Giz a beer,' said MacFarland. 'I'd best keep a clear heid in case anyone actually turns up.'

Delia handed him a can and opened one himself. He looked at his watch and sat down on the edge of his bed. 'She should be here any time now.'

'Aye, well, the way things have gone the last coupla days, I'll believe that when I see it.' MacFarland gulped down half of his can of beer and belched loudly.

Delia winced. 'That's the trouble with you Scots. No finesse.'

'At least we dinnae have sheep-shaggin' as our national sport.'

'No, just swilling huge amounts of booze and scoffing deep-fried Mars bars till they're coming out of your ears.'

MacFarland laughed and was about to come back with a remark about how Offa's Dyke got its name when there was a loud rattling sound.

Both men snapped their heads round towards the vibrating door handle. They looked back at each other as the rattling stopped and was replaced by an insistent knocking.

'Right on cue,' said Delia.

The knocking was repeated but with an even greater sense of urgency.

'Bit bloody pushy, ain't she?' said MacFarland and took up a position to one side of the door so he wouldn't be seen by their visitor, the butt of his gun clasped between both hands.

Delia unlocked the door and eased it open a few inches. He peered through the gap and then immediately jumped backwards. 'Bloody hell,' he said, snatching the door open to its full extent.

MacFarland tensed both of his elbows and flicked off the gun's safety catch with his thumb.

'What the fuck is this for?' Harry Vincent strode into the room, holding out a laminated "Do Not Disturb" sign. 'You two been at it or what?'

'He's not my type,' said Delia and closed the door.

MacFarland relaxed his stance as soon as he recognised the voice and reset the safety catch on his gun. Harry turned and spotted him.

'Expecting trouble?' he said.

'Cannae be tae careful, boss,' said MacFarland, lowering the weapon to his side.

'Yeah? Well I wish you'd been a bit more bloody careful yesterday, 'cos maybe then I wouldn't have had to get up at the crack of sparrow fart to fly all the way over from Greece to sort out your fucking cockups.'

MacFarland tried to explain that it hadn't been entirely his fault, that Humpty was a useless waste of space, that he'd been expecting a woman to make the pickup, and that he'd had no idea Special Branch – or whoever it was – were going to get in the way. But he knew he was wasting his breath.

Harry threw his overnight bag onto the nearest bed and flopped down beside it. 'I s'pose they do room service in a gaff like this? Food on the plane was shite.'

Delia went over to a small desk in the corner of the room and fetched a menu.

Harry took it from him and flicked it open. 'You tried any of this stuff yet?'

'Had breakfast this morning, but we got an Indian takeaway last night.'

'They let you bring a Ruby Murray into a place like this?'

Delia smiled. 'We didn't exactly broadcast the fact.'

Harry looked up at him and then went back to studying the menu with a slight shake of his head. Delia returned to the desk and sat in the leather covered swivel chair while MacFarland continued to hover near the door.

''Ello. What's this then?' said Harry, bringing the menu a couple of inches closer to his face. 'Panini? That's a minge, innit?'

'You're probably thinking of punani,' said Delia.

'That'll do me then. Minge Special with chips and onion rings. They got any decent lager 'ere?'

'Dunno, boss. There's these in the wee fridge there.' MacFarland picked up his almost empty beer can from the bedside table and held it out for inspection.

'Fuck me,' said Harry. 'I 'ope you two 'aven't been layin' into the mini-bar. Costs a bloody fortune, that does.'

Delia assured him this was their first today and they'd only had a couple last night to go with the curry. Harry pointed out that all this was coming out of his own pocket and that they'd better not be taking the piss. Then he told MacFarland to make himself useful for a change and fetch him a can while he waited for a proper pint to be sent up with the food. Taking the phone from its mounting on the wall next to the bed, he placed an order for three Panini Specials with chips and onion rings and three pints of Stella.

'Cheers, Jock,' he said with a leering grin and popped the ring-pull under MacFarland's nose when he handed him a can of beer.

Harry knew how much he hated being called Jock – or, for that matter, Scotchboy or Porridge or Haggis-knob – but he apparently got some kind of kick out of humiliating him whenever and wherever possible. Oddly enough, he never once called him Jimmy, but that was probably because Jimmy happened to be his real name.

Why the man seemed to despise him quite so much had always been a mystery to MacFarland, and he often wondered why Harry had employed him in the first place or why he was still on the payroll after all these years. All right, so yesterday wasn't the first time he'd cocked up, but he wasn't the only one. Even Delia – Mr Efficiency himself – had dropped the odd bollock now and again, and as for Humpty Numpty, well, the man was a walking disaster area. But Harry never seemed to get on Humpty's case like he was always getting on his.

It wasn't as if he was particularly anti-Scottish either. There'd been other Scots on the team from time to time, and Harry had never had a problem with any of them. Nor had he ever called them Jock or Mars Bar or Glenfiddick. Always their real names. Okay, if any of them screwed up, then he'd totally lose it and threaten them with all kinds of stuff – usually involving the removal of some body part or other – but then it'd all be over and there'd be plenty of back slapping and drinks all round.

He'd never been like that with MacFarland. Not even when he'd done a really good job on something. Christ, if it hadn't been for him, Harry would be doing fifteen to twenty right now instead of swanning around some bloody villa in Greece necking ouzo all day long. Who was it who'd got hold of the substitute body and been mostly responsible for setting up the whole car bomb thing? Jimmy MacFarland. That's who. But what thanks had he got? Cheers, Jock. That was it. No more and no less than if he'd handed him a can of beer from the mini-bar like he had just now. Cheers, Jock.

He snorted at the thought of it and put his own can to his mouth.

'Jesus, Deep-fried, ain't you got a bloody 'andkerchief?'

'Sorry, boss.' MacFarland's mind was elsewhere, and his response was as automatic and emotionless as a mind-the-gap announcement. What was it they said about dishes and revenge?

Harry's mobile phone rang. He took it from his jacket pocket and checked the display before answering.

'Where are you now?' he said.

... 'Where's that? Italy?'

... 'Oh, right.'

... 'Yeah, I guessed you might. What did they say?'

... 'Okay, send an email back and tell 'em they'll get the address when I'm ready to give 'em the address. All right?'

... 'And listen. Soon as you've sent it, get yerself back on the bike and put in some serious miles, yeah?'

... 'You too. – And don't get done for speeding, right?'

Harry clicked off the phone and returned it to his pocket. 'At least there's somebody I can trust not to make a complete bollocks of what I ask 'em to do,' he said, eyeballing MacFarland. 'Still, he *is* my nephew, so I s'pose it must be in his blood.'

Delia raised a quizzical eyebrow, and Harry took the hint.

'Some place in Italy,' he said. 'Been getting some rather pissed off emails from our benefactors about why we didn't leave the address details in the locker. Good fucking question, wouldn't you say?'

MacFarland avoided Harry's malevolent stare and took himself off into the bathroom. He didn't really need a piss. He just wanted out of Harry's company for a few minutes in case the temptation to deck the bastard became too overwhelming. He unzipped and gazed blankly at the gleaming white tiles as he waited for the flow.

Then it came to him. Revenge is a dish best served cold. That was it. He wasn't really sure what it meant, but right now it sounded pretty good.

* * *

At the first knock, MacFarland grabbed his gun and took up position beside the door again. At the second, Delia opened it by a few inches.

'I'm Sandra Gray. I think you're expecting me.'

'Who's that with you?' said Delia.

'My... associate. Trevor Hawkins.'

'Let 'em in for Christ's sake, Delia,' said Harry from the bed.

Delia opened the door wider and stepped back. Even from behind, MacFarland knew it was them.

'Well well, I was kinda hoping it would be youse two,' he said.

They turned to face him, and he relished the way both pairs of eyes popped at the sight of his gun.

Harry swung his feet onto the floor and sat on the edge of the bed. 'Do the honours, Delia, if you would.'

Delia relieved Sandra of her shoulder bag and took out a large padded envelope. 'Looks like it's been opened, Harry.'

Harry took it from him and examined the seal. 'Well?'

'Of course not,' said Sandra with a smile of such simpering innocence that MacFarland itched to remove it.

Harry nodded at Delia, and he emptied the rest of the shoulder bag's contents onto the bed.

MacFarland edged closer whilst keeping his gun and one eye trained on Trevor and Sandra. He fixed his other eye on the small mountain of lipsticks, mascara, hairbrushes, pens, tampons, notepads and a variety of other items as Delia picked through them and removed a mobile phone, a dictaphone and a Heckler and Koch semi-automatic.

'That's mine,' he said, taking the gun from Delia and dropping his other weapon onto the bed.

Then he spotted a small black aerosol canister which Delia's rummaging had brought to the surface of the heap. He snatched it up and inspected the label.

'Pepper spray?' he said and shifted his focus back to Sandra. 'Is this what ye damn near blinded me with?'

She held his gaze but didn't respond.

MacFarland felt the surge of adrenaline, which in turn caused his injured hand to throb. 'Oh am I goin' tae have some fun with youse two,' he said as he began a one-handed but none too gentle body search.

What was it again? Revenge is a dish best served cold. Oh yes.

30

Harry Vincent went over to the leather swivel chair and sat down. He flipped open the Jiffy bag and emptied six cigarette packets onto the desk. Breaking the seal on the first packet, he pulled out a small bundle of banknotes and passed it to Delia to count.

From where he sat, next to Sandra on the foot of the nearest bed, Trevor could see it was some kind of foreign currency, but he couldn't tell which.

Harry took another roll of notes from the second packet and again handed it to Delia. Trevor leaned forward to get a better view, and he was pretty sure that each note was worth a thousand something-or-others. He tried to keep up with Delia's counting. Thirty-five? Forty maybe? Bloody hell, if there was the same amount in each packet, all together there must be... two hundred and forty thousand whatevers.

Harry must have noticed the intensity of Trevor's interest. 'Quarter of a million Swiss francs,' he said, ripping the cellophane wrapper from the next packet. 'Thousand Swiss francs is one of the highest value notes around, so you can fit a lot of dosh into a small space, see.' He gave a beaming smile and tapped the cigarette packet as if he was doing a commercial.

It wasn't until he got to the fifth packet that Trevor became aware of the mattress vibrating beneath him, and he glanced down to see that Sandra's knee was jigging up and down like a piston. Okay, so this wasn't the most relaxing of situations to be in, but she seemed to be even more agitated than he was – and getting increasingly so. By the time Harry opened the last of the cigarette packets, her knee was almost a blur.

'Well now,' said Harry. 'And what 'ave we 'ere?'

He pointed the open end of the packet towards them.

'Cigarettes?' said Sandra. 'But no thanks. I'm trying to quit.'

'Wiseguy, eh?'

Blimey, thought Trevor, these people really did say things like that.

Harry crushed the cigarette packet in his meaty fist and dropped the mangled mess of cardboard, tobacco and paper to the floor. 'So where is it?'

Trevor turned to Sandra, as eager to hear her answer as Harry was, but she said nothing.

'All right, Sporran,' said Harry. 'On yer go.'

The Scottish guy moved towards the bed, turning his gun to hold it by the barrel. Trevor had no idea which of them he intended to hit, but by rights it ought to be Sandra. After all, it was her that had maced the guy and smashed his hand, not him. He watched the upward trajectory of the pistol butt and then screwed his eyes tight shut.

'It's nothing to do with me,' he spluttered. 'I don't know where it is.'

'Is that right?' said Harry.

When the anticipated burst of pain failed to materialise, Trevor slid one eye open to see Harry was holding his palm up to MacFarland, who lowered the gun to his side, his face twisted into a mixture of intense disappointment and unrelieved rage.

Trevor nudged Sandra in the ribs. 'Tell him, will you?'

The pause that followed seemed interminable, but finally she spoke. 'I kept back some of the money as a kind of... insurance.'

167

'Against what?' said Harry.

'Against whatever it was I might walk into here.' She looked up at MacFarland with a wry grin. 'Turns out I was right.'

'So 'ow did you know it wasn't just cigs in the packets? I mean, that's why we got 'em to put the money in sealed fag packets in the first place. In case prying little eyes like yours got tempted to 'ave a peek inside the Jiffy bag.'

Sandra laughed. 'Yeah, like I'm gonna believe you paid me two grand to pick up and deliver half a dozen packets of fags.'

This was turning out to be even more of a nightmare than Trevor had expected. As if it wasn't bad enough that the Scottish guy already seemed intent on inflicting some serious physical pain, she also had to go and nick a load of their money. What had possessed her to open one of the packets anyway? And when did she have the opportunity to do it without him noticing? Must have been when she'd stopped to let him out for a pee at the side of the road. But where'd she got the replacement pack from?

'But you 'ad instructions not to open the Jiffy bag, never mind what was inside it,' said Harry and looked up at Delia as if for confirmation. Delia nodded.

'Look,' said Sandra. 'My instructions were to pick up a package from a locker and then wait till I was told where to deliver it. Nobody said anything about handing it over to Rob Roy here.'

Harry shot Delia a look. 'That true?'

'Covering our options, Harry,' he said. 'I reckoned the sooner we had hold of the money, the better. But if that didn't work out—'

'As it didn't.'

'If that didn't work out, we'd just revert to Plan A and get her to deliver the package here.'

'Well,' said Sandra, 'if you'd let me in on your little change of plan, I might not have had to do quite so much damage to Mr MacPsycho.'

Trevor wondered if it was such a good idea to antagonise the Scottish guy any more than necessary, and judging by the narrowed eyes and the clenching jaw muscles, he was probably right.

'Okay, I'm not gonna ask you again,' said Harry. 'Where's the rest of it?'

'Safe.'

'*In* a safe or *somewhere* safe?'

'The latter.'

'Listen, sweetheart, don't piss me about or my Scotch friend will 'ave to show you the error of your ways.'

MacFarland smirked, and he tapped the butt of the gun onto the palm of his bandaged hand. He seemed about to repeat the action, but the smirk was instantly transformed into a wince.

'It's in my car.'

'Which is… ?'

'A Peugeot 206.'

Harry slammed his fist onto the desk. 'You know bloody well what I mean. Where's the fucking car?'

'Outside.'

'Oh for—' He turned away and gave an imperious wave of the hand in MacFarland's general direction. 'All right, Porridge, get on with it.'

The look of pleasure on MacFarland's face was even more intense than before. He raised the gun to shoulder height once again and brought the butt crashing down towards an area just behind Sandra's left ear. But there was no sudden halt, no sound of metal against bone. Instead, the pistol continued on its rapid arc through the air as she threw herself sideways from the bed and onto the floor.

She rolled onto her front and hauled herself up onto

her knees. 'Outside in the street... is what I meant... Hundred yards or so...' The fall had winded her, and her words came in staccato bursts.

Harry stared into her eyes for several seconds, but Sandra didn't so much as blink.

'Okay,' he said eventually. 'Kiltboy will keep you company.'

MacFarland rubbed his thigh where the butt of his gun had made enough of a connection to cause a minor bruise. He too was breathing hard, but not as the result of any physical exertion. The rise and fall of his chest were more reminiscent of the rumblings of a volcano just before it erupted.

Sandra got to her feet, and Trevor followed suit.

'And where d'you think you're goin'?' said Harry.

Trevor hadn't believed for one moment that they would let him go with them but decided it was worth a try, however half-hearted. If the sarcasm in Harry's tone wasn't enough, the look on his face left him in no doubt he would be staying exactly where he was for the foreseeable future.

'Er... sorry. I didn't think you needed me any more.' As soon as the words were out of his mouth, Trevor realised how ridiculous they sounded and wasn't in the least surprised by the reaction. He flinched inwardly as his peripheral vision told him that even Sandra was unable to suppress a giggle.

As for Harry, his laughter almost amounted to a guffaw as he swivelled back and forth in his chair. 'You 'ear that, Delia? He reckons we don't need 'im any more. – Feeling unwanted, are yer?'

The laugh lines on Harry's face, accentuated as they were by the depth of his tan, morphed into a frown as he compressed his features into an exaggerated pout. But no sooner had it appeared than this too was replaced by yet another expression. This one bore no trace of humour whatsoever.

Trevor sank back down onto the foot of the bed.

'You can be *my* insurance,' said Harry. 'Just in case your lady friend decides to do a runner or something.'

If he hadn't been on the verge of crapping himself, Trevor might have laughed at the absurdity of this remark. The man had clearly misinterpreted their relationship. If Sandra saw an opportunity to get the hell out of this mess, she'd grab it without a second thought. What did she care if they beat him to a pulp and left him for dead? But to be fair to her, he knew he'd do exactly the same himself. He decided, however, that there was nothing to be gained by pointing out his worthlessness as a hostage. Instead, he kept his mouth shut and watched MacFarland beckon Sandra towards the door and then follow her out of the room, snatching his jacket from a peg as he went and draping it over his gun hand.

When they had gone, Trevor stared down at the carpet between his feet and, not for the first time, wondered how this would all end. He was certain now that some degree of physical pain was almost inevitable and could only hope that whatever damage they did to him wouldn't be permanent. – Permanent? What was he thinking of? These were the sort of people who probably didn't give a shit whether they put a bullet in your kneecap or in your brain. And that's about as permanent as it gets.

'Bloody Nora.'

'What you say?' said Harry.

Trevor raised his head and met Harry's gaze, oblivious to the fact that he had spoken out loud. 'Pardon?'

'You said something.'

'Did I?' Trevor noticed the whiteness of the man's knuckles as he gripped the arms of the swivel chair. 'Er... bloody Nora, I think it was.'

'Bloody what?'

'Nora?'

'You 'ear that, Delia?' said Harry and rotated his chair a few degrees in his direction. 'I think our friend 'ere must be a bit posh.'

'Oh yes?' said Delia, who was standing by the window, staring down at the outside world.

'Bloody Nora, vicar, but it would be simply splendid if you'd care to partake of another of these rather delicious cucumber sandwiches, what.'

It was a rubbish attempt at an upper-class accent, but Trevor decided not to mention it and resumed his detailed study of the carpet pile.

Harry drained his can of beer. 'Anything 'appening out there?'

'Can't really see from here,' said Delia without turning round.

'What you lookin' at then? Tottie, I s'pose.'

'As if.'

'We got this young Greek lad does odd jobs for us at the villa now and again. Cleans the pool and stuff. I might even fancy him myself if I was, you know... that way inclined. You'll have to come out some time.'

Trevor was too absorbed in the all-too-vivid images of his own painful and bloody demise to have registered much of what had just been said, but Harry's sudden burst of laughter shook him back into the reality of the present.

'Come out?' he was saying. 'Bit bloody late for that eh, Delia.'

Trevor had no idea what the joke was, and if the lack of reaction was anything to go by, Delia hadn't got it either – or at least hadn't found it particularly funny.

Harry's laughter subsided like a punctured balloon, and he crushed the empty beer can in his fist. 'Any more of these in there?' he said, nodding in the direction of the mini-bar.

Delia either had eyes in the back of his head or the crunching metallic sound was enough to convey what Harry was asking. 'Dunno, Harry. Probably.'

There was a brief pause as Harry seemed to be considering a response, but he said nothing and went over to the mini-bar to investigate for himself. He took out a can and cracked open the ring-pull.

'Where's this food then?' he said. 'I'm bloody starving.'

No sooner had he spoken the words than there was a knock at the door. For the first time in several minutes, Delia turned his attention away from the window and caught Harry's eye.

'Who is it?' Harry called out.

'Room service,' came the barely audible response.

Harry looked down at Trevor and put a finger to his lips. He then used the same finger to make a slashing movement across his throat. 'Got me?' he said and picked up the gun that MacFarland had left on the bed. He sat back down on the swivel chair and placed the pistol on the desk, covering it with the room service menu.

Delia made his way to the door and, as before, opened it a few inches and peered through the gap.

'You order room service, sir?'

The voice was clearer now, and Trevor picked up the strong foreign accent. Delia stepped back, and a two-tiered trolley entered the room followed by a sallow featured young man in a blue and grey uniform. He wheeled the trolley over to the desk, and Trevor caught a tongue-tingling whiff of onions, chips and hot bread, which gave his badly deprived stomach the gastric equivalent of a hardon.

Harry held up his hand. 'Just leave it all where it is.'

The waiter looked at him and then down at the first of

the three covered plates which he had begun to transfer from the trolley to the desk. 'You no want me to—?'

'What's the matter with you? Don't you understand fucking English?'

The expression on the waiter's face was a cross between indignation and bewilderment as he put the food back on the trolley and pulled himself upright. He showed no sign of leaving, however, and it was clear to Trevor that he was expecting a tip. Harry either didn't notice or didn't care. He merely reached over to the trolley and picked up the nearest of the three pints of lager. He held the glass up to the light and was about to take a drink when he stopped and squinted up at the young waiter. 'You still 'ere?'

The waiter opened his mouth to speak, but no words came. Instead, he turned abruptly and walked towards the still open door. As soon as he began to move, Trevor jumped to his feet and hurried to intercept him before he left the room.

'Just a minute,' he said and pulled out his wallet.

The waiter accepted the five pound note that Trevor held out to him with a broad grin and a slight bow of the head. 'Thank you, sir. Most kind.' He thrust the money into his jacket pocket and was about to continue on his way when Trevor laid a gentle hand on his shoulder.

'Hang on a sec and I'll come with you. I need to get going myself.' He flashed an unconvincing smile at Delia, who had not moved since he'd let the waiter into the room, and then at Harry. 'Sorry I can't stop for lunch. Maybe some other time.'

Trevor was surprised at how confident and natural he thought he sounded, whilst he was all too aware of the Japanese drumming troupe striking up inside his chest once again. The rhythm intensified as he saw the crimson flood into Harry's cheeks and his eyes narrow to the merest of slits. But the pounding reached a crescendo when he noticed a hand ease itself under the room service menu on the desk.

'Surely you don't have to rush off quite so soon?' Harry said through lips so tightly drawn they were almost invisible.

'Places to go. People to kill— I mean, see,' said Trevor, his concrete smile already beginning to crumble. 'You know how it is, Harry mate.'

'Oh I do indeed. I do indeed.'

The sight of movement under the menu convinced Trevor it was well past time for him to make his exit, and with a hollow sounding 'See you then, guys. Don't do anything I wouldn't do' over his shoulder, he strode out of the room with the waiter immediately behind him.

31

From the moment they'd left the hotel room, Sandra had considered every possible means of escape that presented itself but dismissed each one almost as soon as it occurred to her. MacFarland and his gun were always just too close behind her, and now and then she even felt the hard point of the muzzle in the small of her back. At first, she had thought her best opportunity would be in the hotel foyer or the street outside, where there should be enough people around to deter the guy from actually pulling the trigger. But she wasn't at all sure this would be the case. His undisguised lust for revenge might well be acute enough to blind him to the presence of witnesses, however many there might be. Come to think of it, he was very probably the type who wouldn't much care if the odd bystander stopped a bullet or two in the process. She couldn't even rely on his sense of logic telling him he had to keep her alive at least until she'd shown him where her car was parked.

As it turned out, the hotel foyer was almost deserted, and the Sunday lunchtime street was only sparsely populated with pedestrians. For want of any better ideas, Sandra made a vague attempt at playing for time. When they reached the pavement at the bottom of the hotel steps, she stopped and looked back and forth along the road.

'Now where the hell did I leave it?' she said, scratching her head for good measure and with almost as much exaggerated theatricality as a Stan Laurel impersonator.

She was enjoying winding the guy up but wondered if this might not be her best strategy when she felt the heat of his breath in her ear and caught a whiff of stale beer as he said, 'Listen, hen, I'm nae even gonna count tae three.'

'Maths not your strong point, eh?' The beginnings of a smile were short lived as the gun barrel caught her somewhere in the region of her right kidney.

The flash of pain persuaded her there was little to be gained from the smartarse approach, and she was about to set off down the pavement when an elderly man with a thin grey moustache and a checked cap stopped in front of her and said, 'You're looking a bit lost, love. Can I help at all?'

The smile reappeared and now spread unhindered across her face. 'That's very kind of you. I'm actually trying to get to er... the er... bus station.'

'Happens I'm going that way meself,' said the man, beaming back at her. 'Come on and I'll show you the way.'

As he began to turn, Sandra felt a firm hand on her shoulder.

'Ye know, darlin',' said MacFarland. 'I think I must have left ma wallet back in the hotel.'

Sandra was momentarily struck by how much venom someone could inject into the word "darling". 'Oh dear,' she said. 'Well never mind, darling. Perhaps you could catch us up.'

She felt the fingertips dig into the flesh of her shoulder and thought she heard the faint click of the gun's safety catch.

'I dinnae think so, pet.'

The man in the cap looked mildly puzzled but gave them directions to the bus station and then went on his way with a cheery wave.

This time, the gun barrel scored a direct hit on her kidney, and Sandra bit her lip to stop herself from crying out. Again, she smelt the warm, beery breath as MacFarland lowered his mouth to her ear and said, 'Ye tired o' living or wha'?'

Another violent prod in the back gave her sufficient motivation to start walking, but after thirty or so, she spotted a boy of about eleven or twelve running towards them with a skateboard under his arm. She offered up a silent prayer that his plastic helmet and the protective pads on his elbows and knees would prevent him coming to any real harm from what she was about to do, and when he drew level with them, she edged her foot to the side and made the lightest of contacts with his right ankle. The kid staggered and dropped his skateboard, his arms flailing through the air as he fought an instinctive and desperate battle against the forces of gravity. But the speed of his momentum and Sandra's accuracy meant that there could only be one winner, and he sprawled onto the pavement in an awkward tangle of limbs.

MacFarland had no time to react before Sandra threw herself down on her knees next to the boy's contorted body.

'You okay, kid?' she said, carefully turning him onto his side and then onto his back. She examined him for any sign of blood or serious damage and was relieved that there didn't seem to be anything obvious. The vacancy of his stare was worrying though, and she tried to remember her First Aid lessons and what you were supposed to do to treat concussion.

Just then, however, the boy's eyelids flickered, and it was as if a light had been switched back on inside his head. Sandra noticed the tears that were beginning to form and felt a wave of guilt.

'You hurt anywhere?' she said.

He blinked again. 'Don't think so.' He groaned as he

attempted to push himself up into a sitting position, and Sandra told him to stay where he was for a few more minutes till he got his breath back.

She looked up at MacFarland and tried to ignore the intensity of the rage that glared back at her. 'Here, give me that,' she said and reached out towards the jacket which was still draped over his arm.

'Bloody comedian now, are we?'

'I need it to support his head.'

'Aye, right,' he said with a snort of derision.

A small group of people had begun to gather by now, and a smartly dressed woman with a poodle rounded on him with a look of disbelief. 'Come on,' she said. 'Give her the jacket.'

She too stretched out a hand towards it, and MacFarland took a step back. 'Listen, hen, why don't ye just piss off and mind yir own bloody business? Okay?'

He seemed faintly amused by the woman's open mouthed look of horror and then gestured to Sandra with his covered gun hand. 'Right, ye. That's enough o' the Florence Nightingales.'

She realised she had no choice but to follow him, although first she needed to accomplish the main purpose of her plan. Another woman among the group of spectators handed her a thick woollen cardigan, and she rolled it into an elongated ball and eased it underneath the boy's head. As she leaned over him, she kept her back to MacFarland and made sure he couldn't see her face or hear the words she whispered into the lad's ear. 'I'm in big trouble. As soon as I've gone, get someone to call the police.'

The blankness of the boy's expression made her doubt that he'd understood her or grasped what she wanted him to do, but she got to her feet, MacFarland's pistol jabbing her repeatedly in the lower back as she walked away. 'One more wee trick like that and yir gone. Ye get me?' he said. 'Oh and dinnae think I give a shite if some other poor bastard gets taken out in the process, 'cos I don't.'

So she'd been right about his total lack of scruples, and she knew she was wasting her breath when she reminded him that this was a public street and it was broad daylight so the likelihood of him getting away with it was pretty slim. – She'd contemplated using the phrase "scot free" but had decided against it.

She heard the now familiar snort of laughter and then: 'Aye, but that's the beauty of it though. Public place? Broad daylight? Nobody's expecting a shootin'. They'll just think it's a car backfirin', and whoever sees ye drop will just think ye fainted or somethin'. By the time someone actually notices the blood, I'll be well on ma way.'

Sandra had to admit to herself that he might well be right, so she decided not to give him any more reasons to carry out his threat – for now at least – and they walked on in silence until they arrived at her car.

'This is it,' she said, regretting that she hadn't had the foresight to have stashed a spare gun or even a can of mace in the glove compartment.

Inside the car, Milly had seriously overheated and was panting heavily even though they had left all of the windows slightly open. As soon as she spotted Sandra though, she began to perform the canine equivalent of a triple Salchow with double backflip.

'What ye daein'?' MacFarland said when Sandra's hand moved towards her jacket pocket.

'Key?' she said. 'I need it to get into the car? – Anyway, you frisked me back at the hotel if you remember.'

'Okay, get on wi' it.' He watched closely as Sandra reached inside her pocket.

Her fingertips grazed the leather fob of the car key

before she withdrew her hand, and she made sure he could see her empty palm. She tried the other pockets in her jacket and then in her trousers, feigning an increase in frustration after each unsuccessful search.

'Oops,' she said when there were no more pockets to explore. 'Seems I must have left it back at the hotel.'

'Yir kiddin' me, right?'

Sandra noticed a slight movement of his gun hand under the jacket and stretched her arms out to the side. 'You can always frisk me again if you don't believe me.'

MacFarland's eyes darted up and down the street. 'Put yir bloody arms doon, will ye?'

She did as she was told, the irony not lost on her that he seemed reluctant to be seen feeling her up in public even though he clearly had few qualms about shooting her dead on the spot. It also occurred to her that now he knew where the car was, he had no further need to keep her alive. She knew it was a gamble, but if the key ploy worked, she thought that even he would probably opt for the relative privacy of the hotel room before he blew her brains out. If that was the case, she'd be safe for a little while longer at least, and during that time a better means of escape might actually present itself.

He seemed to be hesitating about what to do for the best, so Sandra gave him a gentle verbal prod. 'Now that I think about it, I'm pretty sure it was in my bag.'

MacFarland continued to dither, probably playing some version of Kim's Game where he was trying to remember whether he'd seen the key amongst the heap of her belongings on the bed.

'Phone a friend?' said Sandra, feeling now that whatever revenge he intended to exact couldn't get any worse, so she may as well derive the maximum pleasure from winding him up.

Her remark seemed to jolt him into making up his mind. 'Just shut yir damn hole and get moving,' he said, and she felt the jab of the pistol, this time in the region of her left kidney.

When they approached the spot where she had tripped the young lad with the skateboard, Sandra was glad to see that both he and the small crowd had disappeared. She had neither heard nor seen any sign of an ambulance, so she assumed that any injury the boy had sustained must have been slight. On the other hand, there was still no wailing police siren either or even so much as a beat copper to indicate the kid had done as she had asked.

* * *

Trevor was beginning to think the lift door was never going to close when a dull click and a soft whirring sound reassured him that he was mistaken. It couldn't have happened a moment too soon because the guy they called Delia was almost on them. That was strange though, Trevor thought. Delia had only been a few yards behind them when he and the waiter had left the hotel room. It would have taken very little extra effort to have caught up with them even before they'd reached the lift, never mind got into it, hit the button and waited for the door to close. It was almost as if the guy had deliberately dragged his heels.

'Your friends no nice people, eh?'

Trevor turned to the waiter at his side and was struck by the sadness which seemed to be indelibly etched into his black-brown eyes. 'You could say that,' he said. 'But I certainly wouldn't describe them as friends. In fact, they're very bad people indeed.'

'Heh. Tell me about it. That fat son of a beach who treat me like piece of shit? I like to kick his goddamn arse.' He feigned spitting on the floor and added, 'Putka!'

'Putka?'

'It mean lady's baby tunnel in Bulgarian,' the waiter said with evident delight.

'Ah, I see,' said Trevor.

'Very useful word if ever you come in my country.'

Judging by the waiter's earnest expression, Trevor realised the remark was merely a linguistic slip of the tongue rather than a deliberate double entendre. 'I'll bear it in mind,' he said.

Seconds later, a robotic female voice with an American accent announced that they had arrived at 'Ground floor and reception', and the lift door slid open. Trevor paused only to thank the young waiter and then hurried off across the thinly populated foyer. He glanced around him as he went, and particularly towards the foot of the main stairs, in case Delia had discovered a sudden burst of energy and raced into the reception area ahead of him. Apparently, he hadn't. He was nowhere to be seen.

The Japanese drummers were still pounding away inside Trevor's chest, but the rhythm was more mellow now, the beat less strident than before. He was within five or six yards of the exit, and only a short distance beyond lay his escape from the sheer hell of the last couple of days, not to mention the prospect of his first proper food since lunchtime on Friday. Oh yes, as soon as he was through the door, all he had to do was—

At that precise moment, whoever was conducting his internal percussionists must have suddenly decided to up the tempo and simultaneously bring in the gong and cymbal players too. Sandra was on the other side of the revolving glass door, and MacFarland was right behind her.

Trevor's instincts screamed at him to leave the fighting to someone else and stick with the fleeing option, but he had no time to act. Sandra was already through and was bracing her back against the door, trapping MacFarland in the next compartment.

'Quick,' she said. 'Get me one of those.'

He followed her nod to the half dozen umbrellas in a tall metal bin beside the door. He grabbed one and held it out to her.

'Shove it in the gap.'

Again, Trevor followed the direction of her eyes and saw that the crack between the edge of the revolving door and the outer casing was widening. He bent low and put his shoulder to the glass. The addition of even his minimal strength slowly reduced the opening, and the moment it became little more than a narrow slit, he rammed the umbrella in.

He stood upright, and Sandra stepped away from the door, both looking to see if the plan had worked. MacFarland was heaving alternate shoulders at the glass with such force that the entire structure seemed to shudder on its mountings. Trevor couldn't make out exactly what he was saying, but he didn't have to be a lip reader to get the gist. The venomous glare of unbridled malevolence was a bit of a giveaway.

The umbrella was already working its way loose.

'Time we weren't here, I think,' said Sandra.

She blew an exaggerated kiss at MacFarland, but neither she nor Trevor waited to see if he responded in kind. They headed out of the more traditional door to the side of the revolving one and clattered down the steps to the pavement.

As they ran, Trevor glanced repeatedly over his shoulder and prayed for all he was worth that MacFarland was in as bad a condition as he looked.

32

MacFarland slumped down on a wooden bench which was almost opposite the hotel and tried to decide what the hell to do next. His chest heaved as he gasped for breath, and he massaged his throbbing right foot. All that running and the bastards had still got away. He'd been within five yards of the Peugeot when he'd heard the engine burst into life and then the shriek of tyres as they'd fought for traction on the tarmac. He'd been inches from grabbing the door handle on the passenger side when the car leapt away from him, a rear wheel jolting over his foot in the process.

He hadn't even noticed the pain to begin with. He'd been too busy aiming his gun. But when he'd caught sight of the dog jumping about on the back seat, he'd lowered the weapon to his side. It wasn't that he was getting soft or anything, he'd kept telling himself as he'd hobbled back up the street towards the hotel, shafts of pain blazing up his leg with every other step. Shit no. He wouldn't have hesitated if he'd had a clear shot at either of the two *people* who had caused him so much grief, so why should he give a damn about some mongrel mutt? No, the thing was, he'd known he'd probably only have time to fire once, and what was the point of wasting a bullet on the dog? That wasn't going to stop them, was it?

Of course, the dog issue wouldn't form part of his explanation to Harry, but he felt he had to work the thing through in his head to convince himself he wasn't losing his touch. So what was he going to say to Harry? The guy didn't need any more reason to despise him, and this latest little incident would be more than enough to tip him over the edge completely. This wasn't the kind of business where you could just walk in and offer an apology and a letter of resignation. Shit, it wasn't even the kind of business where you'd just get fired. Harry had a reputation to maintain, and part of that reputation included doing some pretty unpleasant stuff to people who'd pissed him off.

He remembered one occasion when Harry's driver was a few minutes late picking him up from some club in Soho, which made him late for an important appointment, and Harry had the poor sod's little finger taken off with a pair of secateurs. 'Ten bloody minutes I had to wait,' Harry had said at the time. 'Maybe you'll remember that in future when you wanna count to ten and can only get up to nine.'

One thing was certain. It wouldn't be just his little finger Harry would cut off once he knew the bitch had got away with his money. But what was the wimpy guy doing on his own in the hotel foyer? Surely Harry wouldn't have let him go before he had the rest of the cash?

'Mind if I have a sit?'

MacFarland barely registered that someone was talking to him but looked up to see an old man with a tanned and cracked face eyeing the vacant space on the bench beside him. His long straggling beard was almost entirely white except for the dark brown stain of his moustache, and he wore a rainbow coloured woollen hat and a filthy tweed overcoat tied at the waist with string.

'Suit yirself, pal,' said MacFarland. 'Free bloody country.'

He clocked the unmistakable stink of cheap wine and stale tobacco as the old man flopped down next to him

186

with a groan. MacFarland edged away from him slightly and tried even harder to control his rasping breath so as not to inhale too deeply.

'Not sure you're right about that, old boy, if you don't mind me saying so.'

'Eh?' MacFarland was shocked into taking notice by the old man's voice and turned towards him. The middle-class, educated tones just didn't match up with the tramplike appearance.

'What you were saying about this being a free country. Not if my own experience is anything to go by. Of course, it might be totally different in Scotland but, sad to relate, I have only rarely ventured further north than the delightful county of Durham.' He pulled a half empty bottle of red wine from an inside pocket of his overcoat. 'I take it from your accent that it is from Scotland that you yourself originally hail?'

Glesga,' said MacFarland, wondering whether the guy really was English or from some other planet altogether.

'Ah, Glasgow. European City of Culture 1990 and home to the Old Firm of Celtic and Rangers football clubs,' the tramp said and took a modest sip from the wine bottle. 'And to which of these two fine exponents of the beautiful game do you yourself pledge your allegiance?'

MacFarland took a moment to work out exactly what he was being asked. 'Celtic,' he said, surprised to find himself engaging at all with this pissed-up old scadge. It wasn't that long ago that he and his mates used to patrol the streets of his hometown on the lookout for a loser exactly like this to kick seven sorts of shit out of. 'Ye ken a bit about fitba then?'

The old man smiled. 'You may find this hard to believe, looking at me now, but many years ago I actually had a trial for Oldham Athletic.'

'Oh aye?'

'Not quite good enough though apparently. Story of my life in a way.' He took a long drink from the wine bottle and then offered it to MacFarland.

He held up the palm of his bandaged hand. 'No for me, pal.'

'Been in the wars, I see.'

MacFarland glanced down at the bandage and flexed his fingers. 'Aye, ye could say that. But it's ma bloody foot that's killin' me right now.'

The old man watched as he bent to massage it. 'Like me to take a look at it, dear boy?' he said and then laughed at MacFarland's bewildered expression. 'Don't worry. I'm not a foot fetishist. I used to be a doctor at one time.'

'Oh aye?'

The tramp laughed again. 'Only goes to show you can't judge a book by its cover, eh?'

It was true that MacFarland had had enough trouble picturing this scruffy old wino running out onto the pitch at Oldham Athletic in full kit, but the whole white coat and stethoscope thing? Nah.

'And in answer to your unspoken question, I was struck off in my prime, so to speak.'

'Oh aye?'

'The demon drink, I'm afraid,' said the tramp and flicked the neck of the wine bottle with his fingernail. 'Of course, I wasn't the only one who was somewhat over-fond of the sauce. I just happened to get caught being squiffy on the job a few times too many. That and the fact that most of the top bods couldn't bear the sight of me. Truth is, I never have got on very well with authority figures.'

MacFarland snorted. 'Huh. Tell me about it.'

'Spot of bother with your… employers, eh?'

'Ye could say that, aye.'

The old man finished off the wine and dropped the

empty bottle into a waste bin at his end of the bench before pulling a full one from inside his overcoat. 'Care to share the gory details?'

'Some other time mebbe,' said MacFarland, wincing from the fire which shot up his leg as he levered himself up into a standing position.

'Something I said, dear boy?'

'Nae, yir fine. Have tae be on ma way is all.'

'The aforementioned employer, eh?'

MacFarland's eyes narrowed as he watched the tramp take a corkscrew from another pocket in his overcoat and open the fresh bottle of wine. There was something about this guy that bothered him. Not the stories about football or all the doctor stuff. They were harmless enough even if they were – as he suspected – a load of bollocks. No, it was more a feeling that he seemed a little too... over friendly. And why had he turned up when he did? Why hadn't he gone to one of the other vacant benches? Hell, he thought, maybe the old bugger just liked to chat and he happened to be the nearest victim. Anyway, he'd got more important things to worry about right now, like telling Harry Vincent how he'd cocked up yet again.

'You sure you don't want me to take a look at that foot?' said the tramp when MacFarland tried to put weight on it and gasped with the pain.

'It'll be fine. Just a wee bruise, I expect.'

The old man raised the bottle as if he were proposing a toast. 'Oh well. Here's to a complete and speedy recovery. Nice to meet you, Mr... Sorry, I didn't catch your name.'

'MacFarland. Jimmy.'

'Julian Bracewell, at your service.'

He tipped the bottle to his mouth and drank deeply. MacFarland turned and half hopped, half limped his way across the street to the hotel. He hoisted himself up the steps, relying heavily on the handrail for support, and was heading for the revolving door when he suddenly changed direction and made for the more conventional door instead. The moment he took hold of the handle, he thought he heard someone shout, 'And don't forget to give my regards to Harry.'

He spun round, but the tramp had vanished.

33

When Delia got back to the room, Harry was still sitting at the desk, munching on a panini. He swivelled his chair to face him and dabbed at his mouth with a napkin, his expression negating any need to put the question into words.

Delia shrugged. 'Sorry, Harry. He was already on his way down in the lift, and by the time I got down the stairs, he'd disappeared.'

'Oh for f—' Harry slammed his fist down onto the desk with such force that everything on it jumped, including the gun. 'So where's MacFarland?'

Delia's shrug was even more emphatic. 'Didn't see him.'

Harry heaved himself out of the chair and stomped over to the window. 'I 'ave to say, I'm not undisappointed, Delia,' he said, looking down at the street below. 'I mean, I expect the Scotch git and all the other muppets to fuck up, but not you. You, I thought I could rely on.'

'What can I say, Harry? The little sod was just too quick for me. I'm not as young—'

'Yeah, yeah,' said Harry with a curt wave of the hand. 'He's not that important anyway. But if Porridge Boy loses the tart as well, I'm twenty-five grand down the toilet.'

He returned his attention to scouring the street for any sign of MacFarland and the woman, and Delia wandered over to the room service trolley and picked up one of the two remaining pints of lager. He took a sip and then removed the aluminium lid from one of the plates. He eyed the panini, chips and onion rings with suspicion and tried a chip. As he'd suspected, it was stone cold.

''Ang on a minute. What the…?'

At the sound of Harry's voice, Delia replaced the lid over the food and looked up. Harry had his right cheek pressed against the window and was wiping his condensed breath from the glass with his sleeve. He seemed to be straining to get a better view of something which was on the edge of his range of vision.

'He's only sat on a bench 'avin' a good old chat with some bloody tramp,' said Harry, his voice distorted by the pressure of the glass on the side of his mouth.

'Who? Mac?' Delia joined Harry at the window and pushed his own face against the glass, scanning the area outside until he spotted the bench in question.

* * *

'Where the fuck 'ave you been?' said Harry when MacFarland hobbled into the room. 'More to the point, where's the tart with my twenty-five grand?'

MacFarland hopped to the nearest bed and slumped, his face contorted in pain as he massaged his foot. 'She got away. Sorry, boss.'

'What's the matter with your foot?' said Delia.

'Stupid bitch ran over it.'

'Never mind his bloody foot. Just tell me she didn't get away with my money.'

'Believe me, boss. I only wish I could.'

'Jesus wept,' said Harry and slapped his palm hard against his forehead. 'So you wanna tell me how a big tough Glaswegian hardman like you managed to get shafted by some bloody tart – and an unarmed bloody tart at that?'

MacFarland opened his mouth to speak, but Harry motioned him to silence. 'And while you're at it, you might want to put some serious thought into givin' me one good reason why I shouldn't separate you from your precious meat and two veg with a fucking chainsaw.'

By the time Harry finished the sentence, his voice had increased in volume to such an extent that he was screaming like a jet engine on full thrust. His face had turned a vivid shade of crimson, and every visible vein seemed to have more than doubled in size.

MacFarland swallowed. 'Thing is, boss,' he said, 'it wasnae just her. The wee bawbag was there too. I couldnae figure out why ye'd let him go.'

Delia couldn't remember ever having seen Harry flustered before – or even mildly embarrassed – so his reaction on this occasion was one to be treasured in the memory. He transformed the beginnings of a smirk into a cough as Harry said, 'Never mind that. Just... just get on with it.'

Taking a deep breath, MacFarland explained how he'd gone with the woman to her car and about the tricks she'd used to try and escape. When they'd got to the car, he'd kept his gun on her while she'd opened the glove compartment, which is where she'd said the money was. The next thing he knew, the dog tried to take a chunk out of him and—

'Dog? What dog?'

'She had a dog in the back o' the car. Big bastard too. Teeth like ye've never seen.' He went on to describe in some detail how the dog had launched itself at him and the woman had used the distraction to grab a pistol from the glove box. By then, the dog had MacFarland's gun arm clamped between its massive jaws, so the weapon was useless. With his free hand he'd knocked the dog unconscious with an uppercut and, at exactly the same time, lashed out with his foot and sent the woman's gun flying. But just when he'd thought he'd got the situation back under control, he'd felt a heavy blow to the back of his head. 'I must've been out for a coupla seconds because when I came to, the bastards were driving off. That's when they ran over ma bloody foot.'

As if to reinforce the point, he bent down to give it a rub, although Delia suspected this was simply a sham to avoid Harry's piercing stare. There was a lengthy pause, the only sound coming from Harry cracking his knuckles, one... by one... by one...

'So 'ow d'you know it was our bloke that jumped yer?' Harry said at last.

'Sorry, boss?'

'Well, you say you got whacked from behind. So 'ow come you knew who it was?'

Delia noticed MacFarland become even more attentive to his latest injury. Christ, Harry might be a loud-mouthed, uneducated slob, but he wasn't stupid. He couldn't fail to see that the guy was lying his arse off. A dangerous game to play when you're up against the likes of Harry Vincent, he thought. A very dangerous game indeed.

'Er... I saw him in the car. Aye. When they drove off like,' MacFarland blurted out eventually.

With slow deliberation, Harry picked up the gun from the desk and tapped the tip of the barrel against his front teeth. 'Okay, so what about this dog? This hound of the fucking Baskervilles.'

'Aye, big bastard it was.'

'And it 'ad yer by the arm, you say.'

'Tae right, boss. Hurt like buggery.' He moved his foot-massaging hand and gingerly laid the palm onto his forearm.

Harry nodded towards the arm. 'Roll it up then, 'Aggis.'

'Uh?'

194

'The sleeve. I wanna 'ave a butchers at this nasty dog bite of yours. I mean, you can't be too careful with dog bites. Tet'nus. Gangrene. Rabies even. You might need medical attention.' Harry's face twisted into a leering grin, and his eyes were those of a predator that knew it had its prey trapped and totally at its mercy. 'You see how much I care about yer.'

'Thing is, I dinnae think it actually broke the skin 'cos I—'

Harry's grin vanished, and he whipped the gun round to point it at MacFarland's forehead. 'Roll – up – your – fucking – sleeve.'

MacFarland stole an imploring glance at Delia, but there was nothing he could do to prevent the inevitable.

'Whassa matter? You want Delia to do it for yer?'

MacFarland's hand slid down his arm towards the button on his shirt cuff. 'Ye know anyone called Julian Bracewell?' he said quietly.

'What?' Harry's expression instantly changed to that of prey rather than predator, and all trace of colour flooded from his cheeks.

'I think that was the name anyways,' said MacFarland, who seemed to be making very little progress unbuttoning his sleeve.

'Julian Bracewell?'

'Aye. He said tae give ye his regards.'

'When?'

'Just now. I'd sat down on a wee bench outside tae rest ma foot for a minute, and this soap dodgin' auld wino comes up and…'

His voice tailed away as Harry got to his feet and dropped the gun onto the desk before slowly making his way over to the window. MacFarland gave up all pretence at fiddling with his shirt button and seemed to have a sudden flash of inspiration.

'Hey, wait a wee second,' he said. 'Julian Bracewell. I

thought the name was familiar. But I thought he was deid.'

'Well he's either a fucking ghost or I was sadly misinformed about 'is very timely demise.' Harry had his back to them and his voice sounded muffled. 'Either way, it seems as if our Mr Bracewell's come back to haunt me, and if that's the case, we could well find ourselves in some seriously deep shit in the very near future.'

34

She lay on her back on the rear seat of the Peugeot, her legs wide apart, writhing and squirming and occasionally letting out a soft moan of pleasure.

'At least someone seems happy,' said Sandra, glancing in the rear-view mirror.

Trevor screwed his head round to see that Milly was indeed exhibiting every physical manifestation of a dog who was beside herself with ecstasy. She'd treated them both to an impressive display of acrobatics when they'd first returned to the car, but by the time they'd reached the outskirts of the city, her unrestrained joy had given way to a rather less energetic demonstration of contented bliss. They were on the road again, which meant that the reunion was not a temporary one. More than that, they were on their way to some new destination which would no doubt be abundant with fresh sights and smells and, with a bit of luck, a mouthwatering array of ground-level snacks.

Soon after they'd made their escape, Sandra had quizzed Trevor about how he'd managed to get away from Harry, and he'd told her the whole story, adding that he'd been surprised the Delia guy hadn't caught up with him before the revolving door incident.

He'd asked her about the cigarette packets, and it turned out he'd been right that she'd opened one of them while he was having a pee at the side of the road, but that didn't explain where she'd got the replacement pack from.

'Like I told Harry,' she'd said. 'I quit smoking. Six months, one week and four days ago to be precise. Never really thought I'd hack it, so I always made sure I had some with me. Still do. Silk Cut blue label. Not quite the same as Harry's purple of course but close enough.'

'Yeah, until he opened the bloody thing,' Trevor had said.

Since then – and up until the moment that Sandra commented on Milly's antics on the back seat – the two of them had barely exchanged more than a few words. Sandra had been concentrating on finding her way out of the city as quickly as possible but without damaging any innocent pedestrians, and Trevor had simply stared through the windscreen in a daze of catatonic stupor. His mind had gone into rewind and then fast forward, freeze-framing intermittently as he struggled to make sense of the last couple of days, and especially the last hour or so. It wasn't that long ago that his only excitement in life was sitting down in front of the TV on a Saturday night to check the lottery results or finding there was fifty per cent off frozen peas at his local supermarket.

He tried to tell himself this was precisely why he'd finally decided to jack in his mind-numbingly tedious job at Dreamhome Megastores, buy himself a camper van and set off in search of adventure. In hindsight, though, being held at gunpoint and threatened with extreme acts of violence – not to mention being accused of murder and chased by the Secret Service – wasn't exactly the sort of adventure he'd had in mind.

He remembered having hummed a few bars of *Born To Be Wild* just before the van had broken down but couldn't recall anything from the lyrics that seemed particularly life-threatening. Hitting the open road and seeing where it took you. All pretty harmless really. And he very much doubted that the kind of adventure-seeking Steppenwolf were singing about involved ending up rotting in some prison for the rest of your life or some psychopath depriving you of your kneecaps or an unnatural and very bloody death.

He'd always thought that spending day after endless day advising ungrateful members of the public about the respective merits of different brands of drain rod was a living hell, but recent experience had taught him that hell was perhaps not a finite concept after all. There seemed to be *degrees* of suffering so that hell was more like a continuum where Satan's eternal fires increased in intensity between working in a DIY superstore and being subjected to all the nonsense that had happened to him since he'd broken the lid of the toilet cistern at the hotel in York.

'You want me to drop you somewhere?' said Sandra.

The question was straightforward enough on the face of it, but Trevor's brain wrestled with the words as if trying to evaluate their true meaning.

'You're letting me go?' he said eventually, sensing there might be some kind of trap for the unwary in what she'd asked.

Sandra shrugged. 'You're not exactly my prisoner.'

'Not any more, you mean.'

'That was then. The situation's different now.'

Trevor pondered this statement and decided that the situation had certainly changed, but for the worse rather than for the better. This was even truer in her case than his. It was Sandra who still had a chunk of Harry's cash, so it stood to reason that it would be her that the psychos would be after, not him. And if MI5 really was involved, this whole business with Harry and the money was most likely to be the reason for their interest. No, all he had to worry about was that the police were probably still wanting to pin Imelda's murder on him so, all in all, his most logical course of action would be to get as far away from Sandra as he could and sooner rather than later. At

199

least then he might be able to get some much needed solids into the gaping black hole which was where his stomach used to be.

'Where are you heading anyway?' he said.

'Bristol,' said Sandra. 'Which reminds me. Have you still got the card with the address on it?'

Trevor rummaged in the pocket of his fleece and pulled out the two index cards. He looked at them both and returned the card with the locker details to his pocket.

'You actually going to this Cabot Tower place then?' he said, scanning the address on the second card.

'That's the plan.'

'Why?'

'Call it professional curiosity if you like. And I also want to know what I've let myself in for if MI5 come knocking on my door.'

Trevor grunted. 'Well you know what curiosity did, don't you?'

She gave him a broad smile. 'But then again, I'm not a cat.'

'Which also means you don't have nine lives either,' said Trevor, studying her profile as she turned her attention back to the road. He hadn't really looked at her this closely before, but now that he did, he saw that she was really quite attractive in a no-oil-painting kind of way. Her blonde hair was an inch or so too short to be shoulder length and was obviously dyed, but the colour was tastefully understated and looked as if it had been professionally done. Despite the variety of mascaras and lipsticks which had been tipped out of her bag at the hotel, she seemed to wear a minimal amount of makeup, although this might have been simply because she'd had little opportunity to add any in the last few hours. Even so, to Trevor's eye, she had no need to enhance her already prominent cheekbones or the naturally rosy tint of the complexion beneath them.

His eyes flicked upwards when she glanced back at him again, and he pretended to be examining some minor defect in the roof lining directly above her head.

'So do you want me to drop you off or not?' she said.

Trevor chose to answer the question with one of his own. 'What do you expect to find when you get there anyway?'

'Hard to say.'

'Are you always this cryptic?'

'Only when I don't want to commit myself to a straight answer and especially when I'm distracted.'

Trevor noticed she was taking a particularly keen interest in the rear-view mirror and started to turn in his seat.

'Don't,' said Sandra, putting a hand on his arm. 'Don't do anything to attract their attention.'

'Oh God, it's not the Scottish bloke, is it?'

'Nope. It's the boys in blue this time. Been behind us for nearly five minutes now. Maybe it's just coincidence.'

Trevor gave a nervous laugh. 'Yeah. Course it is.'

'There's one way to find out.'

Sandra flicked on the indicator and took the next turning on the left.

'Well?' said Trevor after a few seconds, fighting the urge to look round and see for himself.

'So far, so g— Shit.'

'They're still behind?'

'Seems like it really is us they're after.'

'Oh terrific. Now what?'

'First, we wait and see if they pull us over. If not, we keep going and hope they get bored. There's no way we can outrun them, and I certainly can't see the petrol trick working this time. I'm already down to a quarter of a tank.'

Trevor squinted into the wing mirror on his side of the car, but the angle was too acute to see anything. He folded his arms and felt the pounding vibration from inside his chest. He closed his eyes and lowered his head as if in prayer, but it wasn't praying in the strict sense of the word. Rather, he was concentrating hard on wishing the police car would simply disappear – a wish that wasn't addressed to anyone or anything in particular. He'd tried the "Oh Lord, if you make X happen, I'll devote the rest of my life to your service" gambit too many times in the past to know that God wasn't easily fooled.

'Oops.'

Trevor's eyes snapped open at the sound of Sandra's voice, and a split second later he heard the wail of a siren. He watched in dismay as the police car drew level and the cop in the passenger seat jabbed his finger at them.

'I think he wants us to pull over,' said Sandra, acknowledging the policeman's gesture with a cheery wave.

The cop car pulled in front of them, a bank of blue lights flashing on its roof, and after about fifty yards it turned off the road into a lay-by. Sandra followed, brought the Peugeot to a halt behind it and switched off the engine.

'Of course,' she said as they sat and waited for the cops to get out of their car, 'it's probably you they're after.'

'Oh thanks,' said Trevor with a sarcastic grin.

'Well think about it. Okay, so I've got a bunch of gangster headcases who would be more than keen to have my arse on a plate – and maybe MI5 as well – but as for the Old Bill, I think that's down to you, my friend. After all, you're the wife murderer, not me.'

Trevor rounded on her, his eyes blazing. 'Listen. How

many more times do I have to—'

'Shut up. They're coming,' said Sandra, once again placing a firm hand on his arm. 'Leave this to me, and don't say a bloody word.'

'Oh right, so you can drop me in the shit and be off on your merry little way.'

This time, Sandra punched him hard just above the elbow. Trevor winced, and then his whole body tensed as he watched the two police officers walk slowly towards them – one male and one female. He eased himself down in his seat and pulled up the hood of his fleece.

'Jesus, Trevor,' said Sandra out of the corner of her mouth. 'What did I say about not drawing attention to yourself?'

The male officer carried a clipboard and began making a cursory inspection of the outside of the car while his partner bent down to peer in through Sandra's open window. 'Afternoon, madam... Sir.'

Trevor would have preferred not to have made eye contact with her but decided that continuing to stare straight ahead through the windscreen might be construed as highly suspicious. She smiled warmly at them, but he guessed this was probably a mask they learned to put on during the first day of basic training.

By now, Milly had leapt to her feet on the back seat and was panting enthusiastically at the policewoman, simultaneously depositing large gobbets of saliva onto Sandra's shoulder.

'Nice dog,' said the officer. 'Yours is it?'

'Mine,' said Trevor, producing his own false smile and just managing to suppress a sigh of irritation.

'Anything wrong, officer?' said Sandra with a look of innocent congeniality that made Trevor wonder whether all three of them were taking part in some kind of charity Smile-athon. If it had been a competition, he would have lost there and then as the quivering grin vanished from his face altogether, and he braced himself for the response.

35

As far as MacFarland was aware, there was no logical explanation for Harry's aversion to travelling or his particular reluctance to go anywhere by road, which bordered on the phobic. He had never been involved in anything even approaching a serious car accident, and as for his own "death", it hadn't actually been him that was in the car when it exploded.

But whatever the reason for his pathological fear of cars, buses, taxis or any other mode of transportation by road, the outcome was that he was now fast asleep in a First Class carriage of the 15.50 from Sheffield to Bristol, his head lolled back and his gaping mouth periodically erupting in an explosion of volcanic snoring. MacFarland and Delia sat opposite him, Delia staring out of the window at the blur of the countryside and MacFarland staring at Harry and wondering how even he could look quite so innocent when he was asleep.

Being a tight-arse, Harry had bought tickets for Second Class, but when they'd boarded the train, it was heaving with pissed-up football supporters. They had presumably spent the night in whatever northern town they'd been to the previous day, and judging by the state of them and the mountains of empty cans, most seemed to have been swilling beer solidly for twenty-four hours or more. Happy-drunk would have been irritating enough, but this lot were boiling over with alcohol fuelled aggression, which made them louder and even more annoying. MacFarland could only assume that whichever club they supported had taken a severe hammering.

Soon after the train had pulled out of the station, Harry's rocketing blood pressure appeared to add several decibels to the volume he achieved in making himself heard over the din, and he had issued a general warning as to what he was going to do to 'you bunch of shitheads if you don't shut the fuck up'. The threat seemed to have had the desired effect as a sudden and eerie silence had descended over the entire carriage, but almost immediately, three shaven-headed cave trolls with as many piercings as tattoos sauntered over to where they were sitting. The biggest of them had opened his mouth to speak but had instantly closed it again when MacFarland eased his jacket back to reveal the butt of his shoulder-holstered gun.

'Now fuck off and let me get some kip,' Harry had said when the three window-lickers backed sheepishly away.

He'd settled back in his seat and closed his eyes but had opened them again after less than a minute when the noise in the carriage had risen to an even higher level than before. MacFarland hadn't been sure exactly what Harry had in mind when he'd given him the nod and begun to lever himself to his feet, but it was probably going to result in some serious shedding of blood – very likely their own included. With almost precision timing, however, a ticket inspector had appeared at the far end of the carriage and started battling her way through the mass of staggering bodies.

''Scuse me, darlin',' Harry had said as soon as she was within shouting range. 'Can't you do something about this lot? I mean, I didn't pay good money to 'ave to put up with this sort of shit.'

The inspector had shrugged and said, 'They lost five one apparently' as if this was a perfectly valid reason for doing nothing at all to try and restore some kind of order.

Harry had smashed his fist down onto the arm of his seat and was presumably about to give her a mouthful when the inspector pre-empted him by saying, 'Of course, you'd be much better off in First Class. It's only ten pounds each to upgrade at weekends.'

Tight-arse or not, Harry hadn't hesitated before reaching for his wallet. At first, though, he'd only asked for two upgrades, telling MacFarland he could stay where he was as he seemed quite at home here amongst his own kind. But then he'd changed his mind and forked out the extra tenner with the explanation that 'Useless twat as you are, if Bracewell really is on my tail, I want you with me twenty-four seven from now on.'

They had left the hotel in a hurry, partly because Harry wanted to get down to Bristol as quickly as possible, but mainly because he didn't want Julian Bracewell paying them a visit. MacFarland had never seen Harry in such a state of anxiety, and it had shown no sign of abating as they had driven the short distance to the railway station. He had been constantly alert to anyone or anything that struck him as being in the least unusual and paid the utmost attention to any vehicle which stayed behind them for more than a few seconds. Only now in the comfort of the sparsely populated First Class carriage did his lolling head and the sound of his baritone snoring indicate that, for the time being at least, he felt safe from whatever Julian Bracewell had in mind for him.

'Ladies and gentlemen, CrossCountry trains would like to apologise for the delay. This is due to essential engineering works on the line.'

It may have been the shrill, distorted tone of the announcement over the tannoy or the absence of the train's soporific motion that shook Harry from his slumbering, but he spluttered awake with the same look of anxiety as before.

'Wha—? What's 'appened?' he said, scanning his immediate surroundings for any sign of danger.

'We've stopped,' said MacFarland.

'No shit.' Harry's voice was thick with sarcasm as he looked out of the window at the static view of fields and hedges stretching into the far distance. 'How long we been 'ere?'

'Five or six minutes,' said Delia without diverting his attention from the same snapshot of rural England. 'Engineering works apparently.'

'Bloody country's gone to the dogs if you ask me. That's why I got out in the first place.'

It was all MacFarland could do to stifle a hoot of laughter. Surely even Harry couldn't delude himself that the real reason for his self-imposed exile was that he'd had no desire to spend most of the rest of his life in jail. He wondered if it might also have had something to do with getting away from Bracewell, but that didn't make sense because, at the time, Harry'd believed he was already dead. Now he came to think about Bracewell, MacFarland realised he knew a fair bit of the story but not all the details. Maybe he should do a bit of homework in case he did show up again and was as dangerous as Harry thought.

'So ye wanna tell us about this Bracewell guy, boss?' he said.

Ninety-nine times out of a hundred, Harry would have treated any question of MacFarland's with contempt and told him to mind his own business. On this occasion, however, he seemed to actively welcome the invitation to tell all as if giving voice to the cause of his fear might have some kind of therapeutic effect. Whatever the reason, he launched into his story and began by explaining that he and Bracewell had once been the heads of two rival gangs operating in the same area of south London. The mutual animosity between them had eventually reached a peak with a particularly bloody spate of violence which culminated in the death of one of Bracewell's men. A few days later, when both gangs had turned up to rob the same security van at exactly the same time, Harry and Bracewell decided that enough was enough. Both had agreed they were committing a disproportionate amount of their resources to fighting each other when they should be getting on with the real business of stealing other people's money.

After a series of arguments over a suitable venue that would be equally acceptable to both of them, Harry Vincent and Julian Bracewell had finally sat down together in the back room of a seedy little nightclub in a neutral part of the city to try and thrash out the terms for some sort of truce. Any idea that there could be a positive outcome to the meeting had seemed doomed from the start as the two men spent the first hour or so hurling abuse, recriminations and threats at each other. However, about halfway down the second bottle of Chivas Regal, the atmosphere slowly began to mellow, and there was even the occasional manifestation of mutual respect. By about five in the morning, it was as if they had been soulmates since childhood with never so much as a harsh word between them. By six, a deal had been struck and cemented with handshakes, backslaps and – much to the amazement of everyone present – a prolonged and almost tearful hug. From now on, the two gangs would amalgamate into one with Harry and Bracewell as joint bosses, and everything they made would be put into a pool and split fifty-fifty.

Harry paused at this point in his story and laughed. 'Dozy twat must've thought I was born yesterday.'

A beaming grin continued to illuminate his face as he told Delia and MacFarland how he'd never had the slightest intention of doing a deal with Bracewell. On the contrary, his only motivation for agreeing to the meeting in the first place was because he'd seen it as the perfect opportunity to 'get the little bastard out from under my feet for good an' all.'

It turned out that, unlike Harry, Bracewell liked to go on a job himself every now and then, partly because he missed the heart-pumping buzz of frontline action and partly because he believed it was good for the morale of his men. Harry made some crack about Napoleon fucking Bonaparte and then went on to relate how the first target of the newly formed joint venture was a smalltown bank near Croydon. Maybe he'd seen it as some kind of historic and defining moment in his criminal career, but Bracewell had made it crystal clear from the outset that he wasn't going to be left sitting in some bar on the day of the heist.

'Cops were all over 'em the minute they stepped through the fucking door,' said Harry and sat back in his seat with a look of smug self-satisfaction.

'Ye shopped him?' MacFarland couldn't believe what he was hearing.

Harry seemed to have little difficulty in reading the expression on his face. 'And don't give me that honour amongst thieves bollocks. That bastard 'ad been crossin' me for years. A bullet through the brain would've been far too quick.'

'But wasnae that what happened?'

Before Harry could reply, a steward rattled her trolley to a halt in the aisle next to them and offered a choice of "complimentary hot and cold drinks". Each of them ordered a coffee and then watched in silence as she poured the steaming black liquid into three cardboard beakers. She deposited half a dozen plastic pots of cream and milk on the table with a handful of sugar sachets and set off with her trolley to the next set of occupied seats.

'I dunno 'ow he managed it, but he got bail,' said Harry as soon as she was out of earshot, 'and while he was out, he topped 'imself. Blew his own 'ead off with a sawnoff apparently. Word was, not even his own mum could've identified 'im. Dental records weren't much use either, so they say. Daft prat didn't open his gob properly and blasted the crap out of most of his teeth as well as his brains.'

'Jeez,' said MacFarland and produced a low soft whistle through his own relatively sound teeth. 'Ye reckon he did the same as ye then? Faked his ain death, I mean.'

Harry slowly clapped his hands together in mock applause. 'You 'ear that, Delia? MacEinstein 'ere thinks Bracewell might've faked it.'

Delia, who had continued to stare out of the carriage window throughout Harry's story, now turned to him and gave him the grin of amusement he seemed to be expecting. 'Could be,' he said. 'Could well be.'

'Still, it seems like we've given him the slip for now,' said MacFarland, ignoring Harry's snide remark. 'Anyways, him turning up like that might be just a... coincidence. Mebbe he's nae after ye at all.'

The beaker of coffee was within a couple of inches of Harry's mouth. He paused it and lowered it gradually back down onto the table, fixing MacFarland with an icy glare. 'You know, 'Aggis, if you 'ad shit for brains, it'd be a major fuckin' improvement.'

Perhaps he had been too busy laying into MacFarland to notice the steady increase in the volume of the train's engines, but Harry chose exactly the wrong moment to raise the beaker to his mouth again. He was about to take a sip when the train suddenly lurched forward, jolting the carriage to one side and then the other.

'Jesus Christ,' he said as hot coffee spilt down his chin and over the back of his hand. He slammed the cup down on the table, spilling even more over his hand, and snatched a handkerchief from his trouser pocket.

MacFarland smiled to himself as he watched Harry start to clean himself up.

* * *

Julian Bracewell studied his face in the mirror for a few seconds before taking hold of one side of his beard where it began next to his right ear. Grasping it firmly between forefinger and thumb, his features contorted as he carefully peeled it from his skin, the glue setting up a stubborn and somewhat painful resistance.

Once he had completely removed the beard, he reached towards the moustache, but the movement was abruptly interrupted. He threw out his arm and slapped his palm against the wall of the toilet compartment to steady himself as the train lurched forward with a shuddering jolt to one side and then the other.

36

'Bingo,' said Maggie Swann as she breezed into the tiny office that had been allocated to them at the local police station.

DS Logan was half lying, half sitting on the thinnest of cord carpets, his shoulders against the peeling cream paint of the wall and his jacket rolled into a makeshift pillow behind his head. The servings of steak and kidney pie at the pub had been generous in the extreme, and he should probably have stuck to two pints of Pheasant Plucker, but they had slipped down so easily he hadn't been able to resist a third. Besides, he'd only been halfway through the second pint when they'd heard that Hawkins had disappeared into the police surveillance equivalent of a black hole. Until they could pick up his trail again, there wasn't much they could do except wait, so staying sober and alert had suddenly become less of a priority.

If the soporific effects of the food and the beer hadn't been enough, the stuffy heat of their temporary office back at the station had made him even more desperate for sleep, although the hardness of the floor had rendered anything more than a fitful doze utterly out of the question. But he had no intention of letting Swann know that she hadn't woken him from the deepest of slumbers.

'This had better be good,' he said, his tone of voice laced with irritability as he slid open the lid of one eye and slowly focused on the sheet of paper that DC Swann was waving in front of his face.

'Like all your Christmases come at once.'

Logan peeled open his other eyelid. 'Don't tell me I've been retired early on a Chief Constable's pension?'

'In your dreams.'

'Dreams, constable, are commonly held to be the preserve of those who are fortunate enough to be allowed to sleep. As your highly developed sleuthing abilities will no doubt inform you, that happy state can no longer be applied to myself.'

'Didn't wake you, did I, sarge?'

The sarcasm was undisguised, but he was too tired and jaded to think up a wittily scathing response. Instead, he simply grunted and waited for the inevitable explanation.

'APB,' she said after less than a moment's pause and brandished the piece of paper again. 'Seems we might have caught up with our Mr Hawkins at last.'

Logan sat forward, groaning as the stiffness in his joints reminded him of just how hard the floor had been. He remained in this position for several seconds before hauling himself to his feet and listened attentively while Swann fed him the details. She told him how a patrol car had pulled a Peugeot 206 for having a defective brake light but had let the driver off with a warning.

'Anyway,' she went on, 'it turns out that one of the plods thought the passenger was behaving a bit suspiciously and checked out the APB notices in the patrol car. And like I said, bingo.'

'Hawkins?'

'Yep.'

'Thank God for a uniform with a brain,' said Logan. 'So if Hawkins was the passenger, who was driving? The dog?'

Swann glanced at the paper. 'Er... woman called Sandra Gray. I checked her out, and she's listed as a private investigator.'

'Curiouser and curiouser,' said Logan, raising a

bemused eyebrow.

'Maybe he's taken her on to try and prove his innocence.'

Logan looked doubtful. 'He was bloody quick off the mark then. Where were they when the plods pulled them over?'

'Just outside Derby, heading south,' said Swann. 'But better than that, the uniforms asked them where they were making for. – Bristol.'

'They might have been lying of course.'

'True, but it doesn't much matter now we've got the details of the car. We have the technology, as they say.'

'And so do the spooks,' said Logan, hurriedly packing his briefcase.

* * *

The particular spooks that DS Logan had in mind were, at that precise moment, doing about a hundred and ten miles per hour in the southbound fast lane of the M6 motorway. Patterson checked his safety belt was securely fastened for the umpteenth time and tried to convince himself that gripping the edges of his seat so that his knuckles showed white might help save him in the event of an accident. He wasn't exactly a nervous passenger, but he became distinctly nauseous at anything over seventy miles an hour. Driving at high speeds was sometimes a necessity in this job though, so he just had to grit his teeth and put up with it whenever the occasion arose. This was one such occasion, and he was grateful it was Statham behind the wheel and not some hothead rookie who fancied himself as the next Sebastian Vettel. He had consistently excelled at every driving course the Service had sent him on and had never once been involved in anything more than a minor bump.

Even so, Patterson's intense anxiety meant that he

couldn't help offering unwelcome and unnecessary words of advice at annoyingly frequent intervals. He seemed particularly fond of shouting 'Careful!' or 'Watch out!' whenever a slower vehicle was blocking their path and Statham raced up to within three feet of its rear bumper, flashing his headlights until it got out of their way.

'Do you have to get quite so close?' he said when Statham's latest victim – a silver BMW convertible – gradually eased over into the middle lane. The driver's obvious reluctance to give way had perhaps been compounded by Statham having added several blasts of the horn to his repertoire of intimidation techniques.

'Sorry,' he said, taking his hand from the steering wheel just long enough to return the BMW driver's single finger salute as he accelerated past. 'I thought we were in a hurry.'

'All I'm saying is that...' Patterson lost the will to finish the sentence. 'Oh never mind.'

They drove on in silence for several minutes, and both men stared straight ahead through the insect spattered windscreen.

'You're not still being cranky about that bacon sandwich this morning, are you?' Statham said eventually.

'Oh for goodness' sake,' said Patterson with more than a hint of petulance. 'It may have escaped your notice, Colin, but this whole operation has been an unmitigated bloody disaster right from the start. We've shelled out a hundred and fifty thousand quid of taxpayers' money for an address we still don't have. I've spent the last God knows how many hours twiddling my thumbs because two of the most incompetent agents in the Service managed to lose the pillock who actually took the money – and probably also knows what the address is. And, to cap it all, I've got the top brass all over me, wanting to know what the hell is going on, and some jumped-up Al Capone wannabe telling me he hasn't got the money and the whole deal's off until he has. And you think I'm being "cranky" because of some bloody undercooked bacon sandwich?'

Statham did his best to placate him by pointing out that they'd finally got a result from the APB and at least they were back on track again, so things could be a lot worse. But Patterson barely heard him. He was far too preoccupied with the rear end of a dark green Range Rover which loomed ever larger as they hurtled towards it.

'Watch out!' shouted Patterson, his knuckles glowing whiter than ever on the edges of his seat.

37

Quarter-pounders, half-pounders, cheeseburgers, chilliburgers, veggieburgers, nuggety things in batter – the pictures themselves looked almost good enough to eat. Trevor wiped his mouth with the back of one hand and steadied himself against the counter with the other.

'Hello, sir. And what can I get you today?'

Trevor's gaze drifted downwards from the photograph of an apple pie that was topped with a small tower of what looked like shaving foam, past the cherry red baseball cap and the enormous zit on the lad's forehead to the slab-lensed glasses and the eager piggy eyes beyond them.

He shook his head and tried to focus. 'Uh?'

'What can I *get* you, sir?'

'Erm, do you take Swiss francs?'

'Pardon me?'

'Like this,' said Trevor and painstakingly smoothed out a thousand franc note on the counter. 'Sorry, I haven't got anything smaller.'

Piggy Eyes's laugh was more like a whinny. 'It's not that, sir. It's just that we don't—'

'How much for a piggy sandwich?'

'Sir?'

'Bacon. – *Bacon* sandwich. Oink oink?'

It was as if his tongue had been taken over by some alien being. He could hear the words that came out of his mouth, but he seemed to have no control at all over what those words might be. The only drugs he'd ever taken were the sort you bought at Boots, but he would hazard a guess that this must be what it felt like when you were stoned. Not just the verbal thing but the slow motion wave machine inside your head and the feeling that someone else was operating all your limbs with lengths of floppy elastic.

Concentrate, Trevor. You need to get a grip before someone calls the manager – or the police even. He grabbed at the overhanging lip of the counter to stop himself from falling.

'You feeling all right, sir?'

Again, Trevor shook his head in an attempt to clear his hunger-addled brain but immediately realised he'd failed when his mouth began to move and he heard the words: 'I'll give you a thousand Swiss francs for one BLT and a piece of apple pie. You can even skip the cream if you want. Frank won't mind. He's Swiss anyway. He's got all the cream he can handle.'

Oh hell, that wasn't really him with the braying cackle, was it?

'I'm sorry, sir, but I'm going to have to ask you to—'

Before Piggy Eyes could finish the sentence, Trevor leaned towards him across the counter and, with a conspiratorial wink, whispered, 'We've got a gun, you know.'

'Ah, so this is where you've been hiding, is it?'

The woman's voice was familiar and so too was the firm grip on his arm. He turned to face her.

'Come along now,' said Sandra. 'The coach is waiting, and everyone wants to get back for their tea.'

Coach? What coach? What was she on about? And why was she talking to him like he was a three-year-old?

'I do hope he hasn't caused you any bother.'

Trevor followed the direction of her sickly grin, which appeared to be targeted on Piggy Eyes's Vesuvius of a pimple.

'Well, er, no. I suppose, er...'

Even from where he stood in his own not-quite-so-parallel universe, Trevor could tell that the lad was struggling to come up with the appropriate corporate-approved response, and he was struck with a sudden and largely genuine pity for the poor kid. But the 'Have a nice day?' Piggy Eyes eventually opted for lost him every one of the sympathy votes he'd just notched up, especially as he made it sound more like a question than an imperative. And as for the accompanying stab at a mission statement smile, well...

'Chop chop then, Mr McMurphy. Shake a leg,' said Sandra, snatching up the thousand franc note from the counter.

Her grasp tightened around his arm, and he felt himself being half dragged towards the exit.

'Shouldn't be allowed out if you ask me,' he heard somebody in the queue say as they passed.

Outside in the car park, Sandra let go of his arm and rounded on him with an expression that was entirely unsuited to her carer's act of a few short moments ago.

'Are you completely bloody insane?' she said. '"We've got a gun, you know".'

Trevor could remember saying it, but he was sure he hadn't used such a whiney voice.

'I couldn't help it,' he said. 'I'm delirious from lack of food. It's like I was having some kind of mini breakdown. Like someone else was saying the words and there was nothing I could do about it.'

'Oh gimme a break.'

'It's true. And if you hadn't left your purse back at the hotel—'

'I didn't *leave* it. It was *taken* from me if you recall.'

'Whatever,' said Trevor, warming to his theme and suddenly aware that the fresh air seemed to have brought him back down to Planet Earth – for now at least. 'And if I hadn't had to spend a small fortune on van repairs and extortionate hotel rooms, I would've had more than enough cash on me to buy eight zillion whopper-cheesy-chilli-veggie-nugget-burgers and still have had enough left for three quarters of a ton of apple pie with or without squirty-foamy-cream.'

'Finished?'

'No. How much of my tenner did you spend on petrol?'

'All of it.'

'All of it?' Trevor felt decidedly faint.

'We need to get to Bristol, don't we?'

'*You* do. At this rate, I'll have died of starvation long before we—'

'Oh don't be such a baby,' said Sandra, reaching into her jacket pocket. 'Here.'

Trevor caught his breath and stared down at the King Size Mars bar in her hand. 'What's that?'

'What's it look like?'

The juices began to flow inside Trevor's mouth, and he gulped them back. 'But I thought you said—'

'Found a few coppers down the back of the seat in the car and a bit more under the mats.'

Trevor wanted to kiss her, but he wouldn't have been able to take his eyes off the Mars bar long enough to aim straight. Besides, it was a pretty safe bet that she'd slap him.

'I was going to say we'd split it fifty fifty,' she said, 'but it seems your need is far greater than mine. I don't want you pegging out on me just yet.'

A variety of protestations flashed through Trevor's mind, and he knew full well that the eventual 'Oh no, I wouldn't dream of it' sounded limp and utterly unconvincing.

'Just eat the bloody thing, will you?'

He wrenched his attention away from the Mars bar to

check out her expression. Yep. Definitely pissy. His fingertips reached out and made contact with the wrapper, and this seemed to trigger a slight thaw in her features.

'In any case,' she said. 'I need to shed some weight.'

'No you don't.'

Trevor blurted the words out before he had given them due care and attention, and he couldn't even blame the alien being for taking over his tongue this time. For once, Sandra seemed at a loss for a response, and she put a hand to her face and glanced over her shoulder as if startled by a sudden noise behind her. That wasn't a... blush, was it?

'Come on,' she said. 'Time we weren't here.'

38

Apart from the fitted cupboards, cooker and refrigerator in the kitchen area of the open plan living room, the apartment was almost entirely devoid of furniture except for a wing-backed armchair with wooden arms and legs, upholstered in faded gold Dralon, which looked like it had recently been retrieved from a skip. It was in almost the exact centre of the room, facing towards a wide, aluminium-framed window set into the wall opposite the main entrance to the flat. There were no curtains, and the late afternoon sun streamed in, illuminating vast clouds of dust particles that drifted lazily through the breezeless atmosphere.

The grey-haired man in the suit who occupied the armchair would have felt the warmth of the sunshine on his pallid and wrinkled face even though he was unable to see it. Nor would he have been able to walk over to the window and open it to let in some cooler air. He could not have politely asked the man who sat on the floor beneath it to put down his Nintendo game for a moment and reach up to open it for him. The same silver duct tape that held his arms and legs firmly fixed to the chair had also been used to gag and blindfold him.

Lenny – the man with the Nintendo – had not so much as glanced in his direction for the past half hour or more, so intent was he on his game. His brow was deeply furrowed in concentration as his thumbs worked feverishly at the console, stopping abruptly every once in a while and swearing in frustration. Considerably less often, he would lift one of his thumbs from its button to punch the air with a victorious exclamation such as 'Yes!' or sometimes 'Oh yes!'

'What time is it?'

'Damn it,' said Lenny, dropping the console onto his lap. 'I was just about to get to Level Four then till you opened your pie-hole.'

Carrot's bald head protruded from a blue and yellow sleeping bag in the far corner of the room, his features almost entirely obscured by the ginger toupee, which he had pulled down over his eyes to block out the light while he tried to sleep. He wriggled a hand up through the neck of the sleeping bag and adjusted the wig to its rightful position. Then he unzipped the bag as far as his waist and sat up, rubbing his eyes with his knuckles and yawning loudly.

'As if it isn't hard enough to sleep with your constant bloody bleeping,' he said through the tail end of the yawn, 'I also have to put up with you shouting "yes" or "bugger" or "shit" every few seconds.'

'Oh pardon me for breathing.'

Carrot looked at him and stretched expansively. 'Lenny, I hate to have to tell you this, but you do sound unbelievably camp at times. You know that, don't you?'

Lenny gave him the finger and took hold of the window sill to haul himself to his feet. He pulled a face and massaged his backside with both hands. 'Jesus. Remind me to bring a cushion or something next time, will you?'

'Next time?' Carrot snorted. 'I bloody hope not.'

'It's all right for you, matey. You're not the one with the old racing injury.'

Carrot made no reply, but his eyes followed Lenny as he walked stiffly over to the kitchen area and began rummaging through the litter of empty cans, foil takeaway containers and pizza boxes on top of the breakfast bar.

'So what time *is* it then?'

Lenny checked his watch. 'Half four,' he said with the irritable tone of someone who had yet again been distracted from the job in hand. 'Don't tell me there's no bloody food left in this craphole.'

'You only just had lunch.'

'What are you? My mother?' said Lenny, continuing his fruitless search amongst the debris. 'Makes me hungry, all this hanging about.'

Carrot gave a heavy sigh. 'Have a look in my bag. There might still be a few biscuits left.'

'Holding out on me, eh?'

Lenny strode over to the small black holdall near the door of the flat's only bedroom. He crouched down and unzipped it, scouring the contents momentarily before snatching up a half-empty packet of McVitie's plain chocolate digestives.

'Happy now?' said Carrot and watched Lenny unravel the twisted neck of the packet and peer inside.

'Milk chocolate would have been better.'

Carrot called him an ungrateful little prick and told him to hand them over if he didn't want them.

Lenny teased out a biscuit between forefinger and thumb. His features instantly pinched into a scowl of disdain. 'Ah, Jeez.'

'Now what?'

'They're bloody melted.'

'Oh, for f— Well, put them in the fridge or something.'

Lenny was holding the biscuit up to his face, turning it this way and that as if trying to decide whether it was fit for human consumption in its present state. 'Don't be a twat,' he said. 'There's no electricity, remember?'

Carrot sucked air in through his teeth as a prelude to launching into a tirade of abuse, but he was interrupted by the ringing of a mobile phone – *his* mobile phone. He swallowed back the first of the insults that had already begun to form on his tongue and told Lenny to pass him the phone. 'It's in my bag.'

For some unaccountable reason, Lenny transferred the still untasted biscuit from his right hand to his left and licked the goo of molten chocolate from his fingertips before delving into the holdall once again. He tossed the phone to Carrot, who fumbled the catch so that it bounced off his chest and onto his lap. The tinny sound of Michael Jackson's *Beat It* came to an abrupt end as Carrot pressed the answer button and put the mobile to his ear. Almost immediately, his palm flew to the crown of his toupee as if a sudden gust of wind had threatened to whisk it from his head.

'It's Harry.' He mouthed the words silently at Lenny and then: 'He's here... in England.'

Lenny responded to each unspoken statement with a frown and shaped his own lips into an inaudible 'What?' His mouth still open from the second 'What?', he apparently decided this was as good a time as any and took a large bite out of the chocolate digestive. As he began to chew, a look of satisfaction spread across his face, and he nodded to himself as though pleasantly surprised that the taste was far better than he'd anticipated. From then on, he took little or no interest in Carrot's phone conversation.

Carrot, on the other hand, had no option but to listen to Harry Vincent's expletive-strewn monologue. So shocked had he been to hear his boss's voice that he hadn't even smiled to himself at Harry's opening line of 'I'm on a train'. This was then followed by a brief explanation as to why he'd had to fly all the way over from fucking Greece to sort out their fucking cockups and the announcement that he'd be at the flat himself in the next couple of hours or so.

Towards the end of the "conversation", Carrot became aware that Lenny was slowly circling the armchair in the centre of the room whilst steadily munching biscuit after biscuit and occasionally licking his fingers. At first, he seemed to take only a passing interest in the occupant of the chair, but Carrot grew increasingly concerned as Lenny's circling brought him closer and closer to their captive with each rotation. Not only that, but his passing interest in the man gradually transformed into attentive curiosity and then into concentrated study. By the time Carrot ended the call, Lenny had stopped circling altogether and was stooping over the guy in the chair and gently patting both of his cheeks between the palms of his hands.

'What's up?' said Carrot, wrestling himself out of the sleeping bag.

'Not sure,' said Lenny without turning. 'I think he might be dead.'

Three paces brought Carrot to Lenny's side. The guy certainly didn't look too good. His complexion was a bluish shade of grey, and the complete absence of movement from his chest was a worrying indication that he had stopped breathing.

'We need to get a look at his eyes,' said Lenny and took hold of one end of the duct tape that obscured them.

Carrot shot out a hand and grabbed his arm before he could peel back the tape. 'Hang on. Hang on. If he's still alive and you take the tape off, he'll be able to identify us later. That's the whole point of the blindfold.'

'Yeah, I see what you mean,' said Lenny, letting go of the duct tape. He pulled himself up to his full five foot two inches and tweaked his chin as if giving the dilemma some serious deliberation. 'How about the gag? At least that'll tell us if he's breathing or not. If he shouts out, we'll know he's still alive and we can slap it straight back on again.'

The length of tape came away with a sharp screeching sound as Carrot tore it from across the man's mouth. There was no cry of pain even though the stickiness of the tape must have taken a considerable amount of four-day-old facial hair along with it. This was not an encouraging sign, Carrot realised, and he bent his ear close to the man's mouth.

'Well?' said Lenny.

'Can't hear a thing. You got a mirror?'

'What?'

'A mirror. You hold it up to his face, and it clouds up if he's breathing.'

'No, I haven't. Have you?'

'No.'

'There's one in the bathroom,' said Lenny after a moment's contemplation.

Carrot slowly turned his head to look up at him and pointed out that the bathroom mirror was not only about three foot square, but it was also screwed to the wall, so unless he had a screwdriver in his pocket, the idea was a non-starter. He didn't even bother to respond when Lenny said something about mountains and Mohammed and suggested they could carry the guy into the bathroom, chair 'n' all, and hold him up to the mirror instead.

He shifted his ear downwards to the man's chest but could detect no sign of life there either. He stood upright and absent-mindedly adjusted his toupee, suddenly aware that Lenny had left his side and was once again sifting through the litter of empty food containers on the breakfast bar.

'For Christ's sake, Lenny. Don't you think we've got more important things to think about than your bloody stomach?'

Lenny ignored the remark but came back from the kitchen area, polishing the base of a tinfoil takeaway carton with his sleeve. 'Here,' he said. 'Try this.'

Carrot was forced to admit – but only to himself – that Lenny wasn't *always* quite as stupid as he looked. Taking the empty container, he caught a whiff of curry as he bent down again and held it up to the man's face. He kept it there for several seconds and then inspected the reflective base for any sign of misting. It was still just as shiny as when Lenny had handed it to him. He listened to the chest again. Nothing.

It occurred to him that the pulse might be a better indicator of life or death but instantly realised that both of the man's wrists were hidden beneath the silver duct tape which secured them to the arms of the chair. He had an idea you could also check someone's pulse in their neck, so he placed the tips of his fingers gently against the side of his throat.

'Anything?' said Lenny.

He shook his head and moved his fingertips an inch to the right.

'Maybe you should try the other side.'

'Don't be a prat,' said Carrot, but since he was hardly an expert in such matters himself he did as Lenny suggested.

'I still reckon we need to take a look at his eyes,' Lenny said when it became clear there were no apparent signs of life from either side of the neck. 'It's what they do in all those hospital shows on the telly. They pull back the eyelids and have a good look inside with some kind of torch or something.' By way of demonstration, he used his forefinger and thumb to roll back the lids of one of his own eyes and, for added authenticity, ranged the protruding eyeball in a random variety of directions.

Carrot straightened up and was about to remind him of the inherent dangers of removing the guy's blindfold when he was struck by what he considered to be an ingenious solution. 'Hang on a minute. I've got an idea,' he said and scuttled over to his holdall.

He took out two pairs of underpants, one black and one bright red, and held them aloft, a pair in each hand, with a triumphant 'Ta-daa.'

Lenny looked from one pair of briefs to the other and then back at Carrot. 'And your point is?'

'Disguises. We can use them as masks.'

There was a lengthy pause before Lenny replied. 'You out of your fucking mind?'

'They're perfectly clean,' said Carrot and held out the black pair. 'Here.'

'They might not be. Even boil washing doesn't always get rid of all the… skidmarks.' He uttered the last word with obvious distaste and added, 'You wouldn't be able to see 'em on the black ones, but they might still be there all the same.'

'Oh for God's sake. Have the red ones then.' He threw the red pair at Lenny, who dodged to the side, and the briefs came to rest on the lap of the man in the chair.

'I'm telling you, I'm not wearing either of 'em. All seems a bit pervy if you ask me.'

'Well wear a pair of your own then.'

'I haven't got any clean ones left.'

Carrot's hand flew to the crown of his toupee yet again, and he kept it there while he considered the matter. 'Okay then,' he said. 'I'll wear the bloody underpants and you stay behind him. But whatever you do, don't let him see you.'

Lenny seemed satisfied with the change of plan and positioned himself behind the chair as instructed. Carrot quickly checked that the black briefs were really as clean as he'd claimed and then removed his toupee and dropped it on top of his holdall. Pulling the waistband of the underpants down over his head, he realised that the leg holes were too far to the sides of his face and he couldn't see a thing. Not to be thwarted, however, he grasped the crotch piece and squeezed the material together into a narrow band. This had the effect of pulling the leg holes inwards towards his nose so that the openings coincided exactly with his eyes.

'What do you think?' he said, his voice slightly muffled by the cotton waistband, which completely obscured his mouth.

Lenny gave him a thumbs up and winked. 'Very nice.'

'I mean, does it work? Would you recognise me if you saw me again?'

'Only if you were wearing a pair of black underpants on your head.'

Carrot stooped over the man in the chair, and with rather more care than he had taken with the gag, he began to unpeel the silver tape blindfold. As soon as the first eye was revealed, he hesitated and sucked in a gasp of air. It was staring straight back at him, the lids stretched wide and the eyeball boggled in much the same way as Lenny's had done during his demonstration of a few minutes earlier. Unlike Lenny's, however, this particular eye showed not even the slightest flicker of movement. The pupil was unnaturally dilated, and the whiteness around it was tinged with a dirty grey.

The remainder of the tape came away with one swift tug as Carrot was impatient to see if the second eye betrayed any more indication of life than the first. It didn't. The protruding bulbousness of the eyeball, the dilation of the pupil, the greyish staining, the fixed rigidity of the stare – all were exactly the same. Carrot shifted his focus to include both of the eyes, and the combined effect made him feel even more acutely that the unflinching stare was directed specifically at him and was exuding a look of malevolent accusation. He waved the palm of his hand to and fro in front of the man's face a few times. Nothing.

'Well?' said Lenny from his position behind the chair.

'Is he dead or what?'

Carrot straightened, grateful for an excuse to transfer his attention away from the almost mesmerising gaze of the man's eyes.

'Looks like it,' he said, wrenching the underpants from his head and using them to mop the beads of sweat from his brow.

'Shit,' said Lenny and sidled round to the front of the chair to see for himself. He bent down and repeated the same action as Carrot, waving his hand in front of the man's face, and then added a few clicks of his fingers for good measure. 'Maybe we should get something with a sharp point – like a pen or something – and shove it at his face. That'd make him blink if he's still alive.'

Carrot finished wiping the perspiration from his neck and hairless head and flung the underpants towards his holdall. They landed on top of his ginger toupee. 'Do shut up,' he said. 'And stop bloody hitting him, will you?'

Lenny had resumed his cheek patting routine from before but with increased vigour so that the sound of slapping resonated off the walls of the apartment. He stopped the slapping and gave voice to the question which was suddenly uppermost in both their minds: 'So now what do we do?'

His toupee firmly back in place, Carrot was already packing his bag. 'I don't know about you, mate, but I'm gone. Harry'll be here in a couple of hours, and I don't intend to be around when he arrives and finds out our Mr Stiff has croaked. And nor do I want the filth after me for murder.' He closed the zip on his holdall and scanned the room for anything he'd left behind that might incriminate him. 'Come to think of it though, a life sentence would be a damn sight preferable to what Harry Vincent'll do if he ever catches up with us. – You coming or what?'

Lenny did his chin stroking thing again, apparently giving some serious consideration to his options. 'Prints,' he said.

'What?'

'Fingerprints. Ours. They must be all over the place.' He waved his arm aimlessly around the room to reinforce the point.

Carrot's mouth hung open for a moment before he released his grip on the holdall and let it fall to the floor. 'Bollocks,' he said and snatched the toupee from his head once more. Reaching the kitchen area in two strides, he began frantically rubbing the ginger hairpiece over the nearest work surface.

39

Milton Street was firmly ensconced in one of the seedier areas of Bristol, far away from the bistros and art galleries of the gentrified dockland area. The pavements were strewn with piles of plastic garbage sacks, many of which had been ripped open – presumably by a variety of scavenging animals – and their contents spewed into the road. Swarms of food wrappers and empty carrier bags scurried this way and that according to the fluctuations of the light summer breeze, which itself was tinged with the scent of decay and degradation.

A faint odour of stale urine and burning rubber invaded Trevor's nostrils as soon as Sandra parked the car and he wound down his window. He looked across the street at the shabby block of flats and craned his neck to peer upwards at the fifteen or so storeys with all but a few of its myriad windows firmly closed to the outside world. Lowering his gaze to ground level again, he took in the grimy glass of the aluminium-framed entrance and the faded gold lettering on the pane above the main door, which was barely decipherable as CABOT TOWER. A more brightly printed estate agent's sign was attached to a wooden post at the side of the entrance and announced that Flat 12 was TO LET – or it would have done if some wit hadn't added an "I" between the TO and the LET.

Very appropriate, thought Trevor.

Milly's olfactory sense appeared to be not in the least offended by the aroma of her new surroundings. On the contrary, she had woken from a near comatose sleep on the back seat of the car the moment Sandra had switched off the engine and was now poking her snout through the open window, sniffing the air with obvious enthusiasm.

Trevor wasn't entirely sure what he was doing here. After he'd bolted down the King Size Mars bar back at the motorway services, he'd felt better able to cope with something approaching rational thought again, and Sandra had repeated her offer to drop him off somewhere, but he had eventually declined. His mind had reeled at the barrage of contradictory advice offered by all of the competing voices inside his head, each of them determined to be heard above the others:

Where are you going to go if she does drop you off? You're totally out of cash, and you left your bank cards in the van, which is miles away. And even if you managed to hitch back, the police are probably still keeping tabs on it.

Trevor had had a vision of scores of heavily armed police officers in riot helmets descending on his camper van as soon as he turned the key in the ignition.

Get the hell away from this woman. She's trouble. You really want to be cut up into little pieces by a bunch of psychopathic gangsters?

The image of his own disembodied head rocking gently from side to side in a pool of blood and surrounded by a variety of internal organs and severed limbs had made him feel decidedly unwell.

You're the one who wanted an adventure. You're the one who wanted to do something with your life. So you want to quit the moment things start turning a bit dodgy? What are you, a man or a mouse?

He had pictured himself in his black and orange Dreamhome Megastores uniform but with the addition of enormous whiskers and huge mouselike ears, nibbling on a lump of cheese whilst sweeping up an avalanche of broken plumbing accessories in Aisle Three.

Okay, so you think this Sandra woman's attractive. So she reminds you a bit of Imelda. Get real, Trev. You seriously believe she might be interested in a loser like you? She worth getting killed for, is she?

Well of course she's not worth getting killed for, he'd replied to himself, but I have to say that I strongly resent being referred to as a loser. After all, that's one of the main reasons I set off on this trip in the first place – to prove to myself that that is precisely what I'm not.

'Besides,' he'd said aloud as if Sandra had been privy to his internal debate, 'I've got a sister in Bristol.'

Even allowing for the fact that he hadn't seen Janice since soon after Imelda's disappearance more than eighteen months ago, Trevor had been well aware that the convenience of being able to call in on his younger sibling was hardly a valid reason for putting his life in danger. The decision hadn't been simply about whether to carry on to Bristol or not. Staying in Sandra's car instead of letting her drop him off meant that he would be committing himself to an encounter with whatever might be awaiting them in Flat 12, Cabot Tower.

When he had finally told Sandra he'd decided to go with her, she hadn't seemed as surprised as he would have expected. Naturally, he'd been somewhat economical with the truth when she'd asked him his reasons, and the bit about being an ideal opportunity to visit his sister clearly hadn't washed. Even so, despite her doubts about his motives, Trevor thought he'd detected the faint trace of a smile when he'd observed her reaction in profile. Perhaps she'd been secretly pleased that she wouldn't be on her own if anything hit the fan. Okay, so maybe he wouldn't be his own first choice as an ally if things got out of hand, but she'd have to admit that it was because of him she'd escaped the clutches of Harry Vincent – for the time being anyway.

Regardless of what her true feelings had been, the result was that they were now sitting in her car opposite a shabby block of flats, inside which they would soon discover the unknown object of their quest.

'Flat Twelve, right?'

He pulled the two index cards from his jacket pocket and smoothed the worst of the creases against his thigh before reading out the address. 'Flat Twelve, Cabot Tower, Milton Street.'

'Might as well get on with it then,' said Sandra, unfastening her seatbelt.

Trevor wound up his window, and Milly withdrew her snout just in time to avoid it being trapped between the glass and the top of the frame.

'I suppose we'd better leave her here,' he said, remembering that Milly was well overdue for a pee and turning round in his seat to clip a lead to her collar.

'She can guard the car,' said Sandra. 'At least then it might still be here when we get back.'

Her use of the word "when" rather than "if" struck Trevor as encouragingly positive, and he hoped her optimism didn't turn out to be misplaced. He opened the door, and Milly hurtled across his lap and down onto the street. It was as much as he could do to keep hold of the lead and stop himself from being dragged headlong out of the car. He shouted at her and pulled back on the lead, but Milly was far too intent on investigating the nearest pile of busted rubbish sacks to take any notice.

The lead went slack as soon as they got there, and Trevor stood patiently as the dog began a detailed examination of the rotting debris in search of anything edible. While he waited, he watched Sandra go to the back of the car and open the tailgate. She leaned inside and then re-emerged a few seconds later. Slamming the tailgate shut, she sauntered over to him and held out her hand. Lying flat on her palm was a gun.

'You ever used one of these?' she said.

Trevor stared at the pistol and shook his head.

'Oh well, never mind. You'd better have this instead.'

'Is that—?' Trevor began when she held out her other hand and offered him a small black aerosol can.

'Pepper spray. It's what I used on MacFarland back at the festival. Totally illegal of course, but I have my sources,' she said with a wink and a smile.

Trevor took the spray from her and examined it briefly before thrusting it into his fleece pocket. He felt the blood drain from his face and the cold sweat begin to ooze from his pores. Whilst they'd been on the road, he had, to some extent, been able to curb his fear of what unpleasantness might lay in store for them in Bristol. But now that Sandra had produced the gun and the pepper spray, the potential danger seemed all too imminent.

'You can always change your mind, you know,' she said when she noticed him wiping his palms on the front of his fleece.

What he really wanted to say was: 'Okay then, I'll stay here with Milly and mind the car', but instead he shrugged and said, 'In for a penny.' He wasn't at all sure what he meant by it though. If it was an attempt to reassure himself with an expression of casual bravado, he had failed completely.

All this hanging about wasn't doing him any good. His imagination had too much opportunity to fuel his anxiety. He tugged at Milly's lead, but although her hunting expedition amongst the rubbish sacks had so far proved fruitless, she was not yet ready to give up the search. Trevor had other ideas, however, and he needed most of his strength to drag her back to the car.

* * *

Trevor was surprised at how hard Sandra was breathing

238

as she pressed her ear against the faded blue paintwork of the door to Flat 12. The lift had been out of order, so they'd had to take the stairs, but there had only been two flights – hardly a major climb unless you were asthmatic or seriously out of condition.

Then he became aware of the rapid rise and fall of his own chest, and the realisation struck him that, even though she was an ex-smoker, Sandra's rasping breath might have had nothing to do with any lack of fitness. It might just be that she was as scared as he was.

After listening for a few seconds, she looked at him and shook her head before bending down to put her eye to the keyhole. Almost immediately, she stood upright again and beckoned to Trevor to follow her. She took a dozen or so paces along the dank, graffiti-infested hallway and stopped.

Turning to face him, she spoke in a low murmur. 'Can't hear a thing. And there's a key in the lock, so I can't see anything either.'

'Maybe there's no-one in there,' said Trevor, knowing full well that the presence of the key tended to indicate the exact opposite.

'Now that *would* be disappointing.' Sandra smiled mischievously at him and took the gun from her jacket pocket.

Trevor swallowed hard as he watched her eject and then reinsert the ammunition magazine. As far as he was concerned, the nobody-in-the-flat scenario was by far the most popular choice on his list of possible outcomes. Not only would it mean he could feel proud of himself for not bottling out of a potentially dangerous situation, he would also be able to walk away from it with all of his body parts still intact.

'So what do we do?' he said.

'First, we do what any normal person would do.'

'Run like hell?'

'We knock.'

With that, Sandra set off back down the hallway, and Trevor followed close behind, wondering whether a simple knock on the door would achieve anything more than alerting whoever was inside to get their own guns at the ready.

She motioned to him to stand beside her against the wall on the hinged side of the door and whispered to him to take the pepper spray out of his pocket. The gun in her right hand, she reached out with her left and rapped hard. There was no response, so she knocked again. Nothing.

She took a step forward and grasped the doorknob, turning it millimetre by millimetre until Trevor heard a faint click and saw a crack of light appear. As soon as she realised the door was already unlocked, she let go of the doorknob and stood back. Nodding to Trevor to make sure he was prepared, she smacked the sole of her foot against the lower part of the door. It flew open, and both of them were inside the flat even before it reached the full extent of its hinges and started on the rebound.

There was no sudden burst of gunfire, and the only apparent occupant was sitting in an armchair in the middle of the room, the top of his head just visible above the back of the chair. Alert for any sign of movement from either of the two open doorways leading off from the main living area, Sandra raced up behind him and rammed the muzzle of her gun into the nape of his neck. His head lolled forward, and, taking a couple of steps to the side, Trevor could see that his wrists were fastened to the chair arms with silver duct tape.

Without stopping to check whether the man was dead or merely unconscious, Sandra edged towards the nearest of the open doors. Trevor hesitated as he looked over to the second doorway and took a deep breath to try and calm the enthusiastic excesses of the Japanese drummers in his chest. Then, holding the can of pepper spray outstretched in front of him, he sidled over to what seemed to him to be the gateway of hell itself.

As he drew closer, however, he recognised that it was in fact the entrance to a rather shabbily equipped bathroom. Three feet from the threshold, he came to an abrupt halt when he caught sight of a face staring back at him from the opposite wall. He aimed the aerosol and was about to press down on the button when he saw that the other guy was doing exactly the same thing. He adjusted his focus and realised he'd been on the point of macing his own reflection. The terrified eyes which studied him from the mirror above a chipped enamel sink were his. He averted his gaze, unable to bear the sight of his own fear, and as he did so, the reflected image of the open door came into view. There was no-one lurking in the shadowy corner behind it, nobody ready to pounce on him as soon as he set foot through the doorway.

By moving his head from side to side, he was able to examine every part of the bathroom in the mirror except for the bath itself. This was almost completely obscured by a yellow and white striped shower curtain which fell to within a few inches of the floor. Trevor took a step forward to bring the whole of the curtain within his direct field of vision. He narrowed his eyes and squinted hard at the mildew stained plastic, but the light was too dim to make out whether there was anyone behind it or not. Noticing there was an unshaded bulb hanging above the bath, he reached round the upright of the door frame for a switch, and his hand brushed against a nylon cord. He gave it a sharp pull, not sure if this was a good idea or not, but all it produced was a loud clicking sound.

Given the position of the light bulb, he had hoped it would instantly reveal whether anyone was standing in the bath by silhouetting their shape against the curtain – or rather, he had hoped that it wouldn't. When the expected illumination failed to materialise, Trevor knew there was only one course of action left open to him. He would simply have to bite the bullet and— Then it occurred to him that there might be a second option. He could wait until Sandra came, and she could blast hell out of the shower curtain with her gun. He was beginning to ponder the distinct advantages of this approach when the image of the Dreamhome Megastores mouseman flashed into his mind once again, but this time he was alternately chewing on a lump of cheese and a bullet.

'Oh come on, you wuss. Get on with it,' he said to himself and shook his head to clear it of the grinning rodent in the black and orange uniform.

Wishing that he hadn't watched quite so many serial killer movies, he wiped the sweat from his forehead with his sleeve and tightened his grip on the pepper spray. He reached the bath in two strides and tore open the shower curtain. Without waiting to see if anyone was behind it, he pressed down on the aerosol button and released a jet of gas in every direction. He just had time to register that there was no-one either standing or lying in the bath before his eyes closed instinctively to shield themselves from the needles of pain being fired into them by the mist of pepper spray.

'It's not bloody air freshener, you know.'

Trevor was scarcely aware of Sandra's voice from the doorway behind him and even less so of the amusement in her tone. His lungs heaved with the effort of fighting for breath, and her words were almost inaudible over the din of his relentless coughing. Nor did he hear the clatter of the aerosol can as he dropped to his knees and let it fall from his fingers into the empty bath. Supporting himself by gripping the rim of the tub with one hand, he clutched at his pumping chest with the other. He blinked repeatedly to try and cool the infernos that blazed beneath his eyelids, but it brought him little relief.

'Now you know why it's illegal,' said Sandra, and he felt her arms slide under his armpits.

'Come on,' she said. 'You need to wash some of this crap off.'

With Sandra's help and by pushing downwards on the edge of the bath, Trevor managed to get to his feet and, still half blinded, allowed himself to be guided to the wash basin. He heard the rush of water as she turned on the tap, and only then did it occur to him that he wasn't actually dead.

40

Statham turned into a narrow side street and eased the Skoda to a halt behind the unmarked police car.

'I guess this is it then,' said Patterson, opening the passenger door, his relief that the white knuckle ride was finally over immediately subsumed by a growing anxiety as to what they might be about to discover. If it was bad, his job could be at stake. If it was very bad, his life might be.

Statham followed him over to the police car, and they identified themselves to the two uniformed officers, one of whom went with them to the corner of the street and pointed out the target's Peugeot and the scruffy block of flats which they had passed about fifty yards up the road.

'Cabot Tower,' said the officer. 'That's where they went when they got out the car.'

'Any idea which flat?' said Patterson.

'Sorry, sir. Our orders were just to keep tabs on the car.'

'Fair enough.' Patterson caught Statham's look of surprise, but he knew he had little or no grounds for giving the officer a bollocking. He'd simply done what he'd been told to do and that was that. No more, no less.

'So what do we do now then?' said Statham.

'We wait.'

'For?'

'For them to come out.' Patterson looked towards the block of flats. 'I don't see we have much choice given that they could be in any one of seventy-odd apartments.

In the meantime, we need to find out how many exits there are and stick a tracker on the car. Just in case they give us the slip – again.'

He pondered the situation while Statham went back to the Skoda and opened the boot. On balance, grabbing them in the street might even be a better option than bursting into some flat where they'd no idea what to expect. How many of them were there? He doubted there'd be just the two from the Peugeot What sort of weapons had they got? He checked his watch. And where the hell were Jarvis and Coleman?

Statham came back from the car and, as if seeking Patterson's approval, held out a piece of black plastic that was about the same size and shape as a box of matches. Patterson glanced at the tracking device and nodded.

'It's a pity the car's right opposite the flats,' he said. 'We'll just have to brazen it out and hope the apartment's at the back of the building or that no-one's looking out the window.'

They set off down the litter-strewn pavement, and when they reached the Peugeot, Statham knelt down and attached the magnetic tracking device to the underside of the car. The metallic "clunk" must have woken the dog, which he'd failed to notice on the back seat, because she immediately sprang to her feet and began barking wildly at the perceived intruders through the partially open window.

He staggered backwards on his haunches and threw out a hand to stop himself falling. 'What the—'

'Still got the mutt I see,' said Patterson and scratched his head while he contemplated whether the dog's presence had any particular significance.

'You might have warned me,' said Statham, getting to his feet and brushing the dust from his trousers.

Patterson ignored the remark and scanned the

windows at the front of the apartment block. 'Don't think anybody heard.' He looked back at the dog, who seemed to take this as her cue to crank up the volume by several decibels.

'Not yet anyway,' he added and stepped off the pavement as the dog threw back her head and emitted a wolf-like howl of ear shattering proportions. 'Come on, Colin. Get a wriggle on.'

They had barely reached the middle of the road when a screech of tyres from the far end of the street stopped them in their tracks. They spun round to see a dark blue Mondeo hurtling around the corner and fishtailing this way and that as the driver fought to regain traction.

Patterson's jaw dropped as he watched the car straighten and then accelerate towards them. When it was within a few yards of where they stood, they heard the high pitched squeal of rubber against tarmac for a second time, and the car slewed sideways and came to a shuddering halt, almost blocking the entire width of the road.

'Well if it isn't Starsky and Hutch,' Patterson muttered through gritted teeth, glaring back at Jarvis and Coleman as they beamed at him through the windscreen.

Jarvis leaned his head out of the driver's window. 'All right, guv?' he said and gave him the thumbs up.

Patterson walked slowly over to the car. 'I'm surprised that's pink and not brown,' he said, pointing at Jarvis's outstretched thumb.

'Sir?' Jarvis's broad grin was instantly replaced with a look of blank incomprehension.

'Given that you seem to spend most of your time with your thumb up your bum and your brain in neutral.'

Jarvis's vacant expression remained unchanged.

'Tell me, Jarvis. Exactly what does the word "covert" mean to you, as in the phrase "covert operation"?'

'Er—'

Patterson slammed his fist down onto the roof of the car. 'Just park the bloody thing before you cause an accident.'

He stood back, and Jarvis began to manoeuvre the Mondeo towards the kerb. Once again, his eyes ranged across the windows of the apartment block to check whether anyone had been alerted by this second disturbance, but it appeared that all of the residents were either profoundly deaf or none of the flats at the front were inhabited.

'Second floor.'

'What?' Patterson turned to see that Statham was pointing towards the flats.

'Third from the left,' he said. 'Thought I saw somebody.'

Patterson grabbed his wrist and forced his arm downwards. 'Jesus, Colin, you don't have to *point*.' He looked up at the window Statham had indicated. 'Well there's nobody there now, which I must say I find quite surprising. I mean, short of parading up and down with a bloody great banner saying "Hello, we're from MI5 and we're after your arses", I don't think we could have done a better job of announcing our presence.'

'Double bluff?' said Statham with a half-hearted shrug.

'Excuse me?'

'Well if you think about it from the bad guys' point of view, they probably wouldn't take any notice. They'd be expecting the Secret Service or whoever to be a bit more... secret.'

Patterson stared at him and wondered how it was possible that he had been assigned three of the most incompetent agents in the Service to carry out an operation which was supposedly a matter of national importance. – Or maybe it wasn't. Maybe the whole thing was about setting him up to fail.

He hadn't exactly been popular with MI5's top brass ever since he'd been involved in an investigation into a suspected terrorist plot to assassinate Prince Charles some years back. Despite being a loyal patriot, Patterson had never been a big fan of certain members of the Royal Family and had happened to remark to a colleague that Prince Charles was a gormless tree-hugger with delusions of ordinariness and that his dad was a freeloading waste of space with a talent for insulting people. Unfortunately, the comment was overheard by one of the Prince's staff, who put in an official complaint questioning whether "an anti-monarchist and probable communist sympathiser" was the right sort of person to be working for the British security services.

Patterson's superiors were clearly of a similar opinion, and it was only because of the impressive inroads he'd made in a separate ongoing investigation that he wasn't sacked on the spot. But that investigation had long since been concluded, and every assignment he'd been given from that point on could have been filed under "Largely Pointless and Potentially Dangerous" or occasionally "Successful Outcome Unlikely". Perhaps his bosses had some knowledge that this current operation came into the second category – if not both – and failure would give them the perfect excuse to get rid of him once and for all.

'Sod that for a game of soldiers,' he said aloud and registered Statham's frown of bewilderment. He had no intention of explaining what he meant, so he pre-empted any enquiry by turning his back and strode towards the entrance to the flats.

'Stop dawdling, Colin,' he called over his shoulder. 'We've got work to do.'

41

Trevor's eyes still smarted from the pepper spray, but at least his vision had returned to something like normal and he no longer had to rely on Sandra to lead him around by the hand. The hacking cough had also subsided to the occasional need to clear his throat, and when he spoke, the words were accompanied by an asthmatic wheezing sound from deep inside his chest.

'So what's with... the underpants?' he rasped as he and Sandra stood gazing down at the dead man in the armchair and the pair of bright red briefs that lay in his lap.

Sandra picked them up daintily between her forefinger and thumb.

'Haven't a clue,' she said, holding them up to the light to examine them more closely. 'Maybe some sort of pervy thing. Doesn't seem to be any sign of semen, though, as far as I can tell.'

'Oh please,' said Trevor, his features contorted with repulsion.

Sandra grinned at him. 'What's the matter? Not going squeamish on me, are you?'

With that, she flicked her wrist and let go of the underpants, launching them directly at Trevor's face. He instinctively threw up his arms to defend himself, but his reactions were too slow, and the briefs landed on his shoulder. He brushed them off with the back of his hand as if he were being attacked by a swarm of hornets.

'Do you not think we could be... serious here for a

moment?' he said, stifling a coughing fit. 'I mean, we do happen to be in an empty flat with a dead bloke strapped to a chair and God-knows-who about to walk through the door at any second.'

Sandra forced the corners of her mouth downwards and frowned in a theatrical display of gravity. 'Sorry, Trevor,' she said, her voice almost masculine in pitch. 'It won't happen again. Promise.'

'You see. That's exactly what I—'

'Have a look through his pockets.'

Trevor recognised the sudden shift in her tone from sarcastic to businesslike. He understood exactly what she was asking him to do but decided he needed further confirmation. 'Pardon?'

'We need to find out who he is, don't we?'

Assuming that the question was rhetorical, he didn't reply. Besides, he was busy contemplating whether they really did need to find out the guy's identity. What did it matter? He was dead. End of story. Or perhaps it wasn't. The end of the story – or the beginning of the end – might be when the police or Harry and his cronies or some other bunch of psychopathic lunatics turned up and found them with a dead body. Why should *he* care who the bloke was? Far better that they left it a mystery and got the hell out of there.

'He's not going to bite,' said Sandra with evident impatience.

'Why don't you do it then?'

'I'm covering you.'

'From a dead man?'

'From any unexpected visitors.' Sandra waved her gun vaguely in the direction of the apartment door.

She was right of course. It wasn't as if a corpse could do him any harm as such. It was just that—

'Oh for goodness' sake,' said Sandra and reached towards the body with her gun-free hand.

'Okay, okay, I'm doing it,' said Trevor, deflecting her outstretched arm with his own and placing himself between her and the chair.

He avoided looking at the man's face and concentrated instead on the lapel of his charcoal grey jacket. Careful not to make any direct physical contact with the body itself, he slowly peeled the lapel backwards until the inside pocket was revealed.

'Expensive,' he said, more to himself than to Sandra when he spotted the Savile Row label.

He slid his fingers into the pocket and felt the edge of some kind of wallet. With all the caution of someone removing the trigger mechanism from a nuclear bomb, he eased it out and saw that it was indeed a slim, black leather wallet and had the initials G.M.Q. embossed in gold in one corner. He flipped it open. The main section contained a dozen or so banknotes, and all the other compartments were filled with an assortment of business cards and credit cards. He selected one of the latter at random.

'Mr Gerald M. Quicke,' he read aloud. 'Mean anything to you?'

Sandra shrugged. 'The Quicke and the dead? Never heard of him. See if there's something else.'

Trevor looked again, and although only the top edges of the cards were visible, he noticed that one of them was slightly different from the others. It was fractionally larger than a standard credit card, and the upper part of a gold-coloured crest seemed strangely familiar. He slipped the card from its compartment.

'Bloody Nora,' he said, almost dropping the card.

'Well?' Sandra's patience was clearly being tried to the limits.

'Gerald Montague Quicke—'

'Yes, you've said that already,' she snapped.

'—Member of Parliament for Baileyhill and

Redbridge.'

Sandra whistled softly through her teeth and pursed her lips. 'As you say, bloody Nora,' she said and took the card from him to examine it for herself.

'Right,' said Trevor, trying to sound assertive but the quaver in his voice giving him away. 'There's nothing else we can do here, so I suggest we get out before someone turns up.'

But his attempt to take control of the situation fell on deaf ears, and Sandra ignored him.

'At least that explains why MI5 are involved,' she said, looking from the photograph on the identity card to the ashen features of the man in the chair and back again as if to verify they really were one and the same.

'Oh?' said Trevor, realising that unless he walked out of the flat on his own, he'd just have to wait until Sandra was good and ready to go with him.

She nodded towards the body in the chair. 'This isn't just any old stiff. This is a Member of bloody Parliament. The duly elected representative of the good people of Baileyhill and...'

'Redbridge.'

'Whatever. You want me to draw you a picture?'

Trevor guessed his expression must have conveyed mystified bemusement, but this was far from being the case. He knew as well as she did how all of the pieces had suddenly fallen into place. Or nearly all.

'The bit I don't get though...' he said, hoping this would indicate that he understood all the rest of it and so wasn't as stupid as she seemed to think. 'The thing I can't get my head round is why Harry's mob would want to kidnap an MP. I mean, he's not even a well known one, is he? Why not go for a Cabinet Minister or one that's never got their mug off the telly?'

'No idea. But I certainly intend to find out,' said Sandra. 'Anyway, there's nothing else we can do here.

Let's go before someone shows up.'

Trevor rolled his eyes. So she had been listening to him after all. 'And what about the Honourable Member for Baileyhill and Redbridge?' he said, even though he had no desire to delay their escape a second longer than necessary.

Sandra glanced at the dead MP. 'There'll have to be a by-election, I suppose.'

'That's not what I meant,' he said. 'I'm talking about…' He tailed off when she turned towards him and he could see the smirk on her face.

'I know what you meant,' she said. 'We'll tip off the police as soon as we're clear of the place. Anonymously, of course.'

Trevor barely registered the last few words as his attention was distracted by the screech of tyres from the street outside. 'What was that?'

'Somebody in a hurry by the sound of it.'

He was already at the window, looking down on a dark blue Ford Mondeo that was slewed sideways across the middle of the road. The driver had his head out of the window, and a shortish man in a tan-coloured leather jacket seemed to be yelling at him while another guy stood watching from a couple of yards away. There was something familiar about the man in the leather jacket, but he couldn't quite place him. As he trawled his memory for some clue as to where he'd seen him before, he became aware of Milly's frantic barking from inside Sandra's car.

'Anything I should know about?' said Sandra, who had made no move to join him at the window.

Trevor was beginning to feel distinctly uneasy about what he was seeing and hearing from outside and thought that her tone seemed inappropriately nonchalant. He was about to tell her what was going on when the man who was talking to the driver suddenly slammed his fist down onto the roof of the car and took a step backwards.

'Holy shit,' said Trevor when the man's face came fully into view for the first time, and he instantly ducked down below the window sill. 'It's him.'

'Him who?' Sandra's tone was a lot less nonchalant all of a sudden.

'The guy who stopped me when I was trying to leave the festival.'

'The one you almost ran over?'

'That's the one. Er… Patterson.'

'On his own?'

Trevor shook his head and crawled to the side of the window so he could stand upright again without being seen. 'No, there's at least two others. Maybe more.'

'Anyone see you?'

'Don't think so.'

'Well that's something to be grateful for, I guess.'

From his position beside the window, Trevor strained to try to see what was happening in the street below without being spotted himself. He soon discovered that this was an almost impossible task and decided to err on the side of caution. He began to turn towards Sandra but stopped immediately when he felt something hard and cold being pressed into the back of his neck, just below the base of his skull.

42

'Useless fucking twats.'

MacFarland had seen Harry Vincent in some blisteringly foul moods before but never anything that came even close to this one. Apart from an all too brief interlude when he'd fallen asleep, Harry had spent almost the entire train journey labelling pretty much everyone as useless fucking twats – all of the other passengers who were keeping him awake with their 'constant bloody yattering'; the train company for making him spill piping hot coffee and staining his clean white shirt; the railway engineers for 'pratting about' and making him half an hour late arriving in Bristol; and of course MacFarland himself for just about everything.

The driver of the taxi they'd climbed into outside the station was another one, but this was after he'd taken exception to Harry's derogatory remark about his ethnicity and ordered them back out again before he'd even released the handbrake. Then, every taxi driver on the planet automatically became a useless fucking twat on the basis that Harry had had to wait ten more minutes until another cab was available.

In this particular instance – and on several occasions during the past hour – the twats in question were Carrot and Lenny. Ever since Harry had first called them from the train, he had repeatedly tried to phone them back but with a resounding lack of success.

'Why don't the bastards pick up?' he said in response to the incessant ringing tone as the second taxi driver ferried them through the streets of Bristol.

'Maybe there's no signal,' said the cabbie helpfully, glancing at Harry's reddening face in the rear-view mirror.

'Course there's a fucking signal, you usele…'

MacFarland smiled to himself as Harry's voice petered out. Despite his mood, it seemed that even Harry didn't relish the idea of having to stand around waiting for yet another cab.

By shifting his position slightly in his seat next to the driver, MacFarland managed to glimpse Delia's profile in the mirror. He was staring fixedly out of the side window and appeared to be lost in thought. Come to think of it, he had spent most of the journey from Sheffield doing much the same thing, gazing out of the carriage window and barely speaking unless Harry addressed him directly. Once, he had left his seat to go to the toilet but hadn't returned for several minutes. Harry had even commented on his lengthy absence and made some remark about how Delia might benefit from a good dose of Ex-Lax.

MacFarland guessed that Delia had realised long ago that the best strategy for dealing with Harry in situations like this was to say as little as possible for fear that whatever he said might set him off on yet another rant. All the same, he couldn't help wondering what was going through Delia's mind. Keeping your gob shut to avoid incurring Harry's wrath was one thing, but there was something about his body language and the faintly furrowed brow which seemed to suggest that something was troubling him. Maybe he was anxious about what they might find when they got to the flat, or maybe he was just mentally going through the runners and riders for tomorrow's big race at Haydock Park or wherever.

Then again, Delia's behaviour had struck him as particularly odd when they'd stepped off the train at

Temple Meads Station. He'd been strangely agitated and had looked repeatedly up and down the platform as if he was trying to spot someone he knew amongst the throng of disembarking passengers.

'How much further?' said Harry from the back seat of the taxi as he pressed the redial button yet again and held the mobile phone to his ear.

'Not far,' said the driver, gently revving the engine while he waited for a traffic light to turn to green.

Harry leaned forward a few inches. 'That's not what I asked you,' he said quietly but in a tone that was heavy with menace. 'How – many – minutes?'

The cabbie eyeballed him briefly in the mirror. 'Dunno. Ten? Five maybe if the traffic's not too bad and we don't get too many more red lights.'

Harry slumped back into his seat, clicked the cancel button on his phone and tossed it onto the space between him and Delia. 'Useless fucking twats.'

This time, the driver glared at him in the mirror. 'What you say?'

'It's okay, pal,' said MacFarland, deciding that an immediate diplomatic intervention was called for. 'He wasnae talking to ye.'

'And you can fuck off an' all, 'Aggis Bollocks.'

* * *

Once they'd spotted the dark glasses and the white stick, most of the people in the queue for taxis outside the station were insistent that he should go in front of them.

How quaint, he thought. Almost restores one's faith in human nature.

But Julian Bracewell had no intention of getting too close to the head of the queue until he saw Harry and his companions were safely aboard a taxi of their own. As soon as this was accomplished, however, he became rather more proactive in getting himself to the front of the line, tapping his white stick loudly on the pavement to attract the attention of anyone who had so far failed to notice his disability. A young Nordic-looking man with an enormous rucksack helped him into a cab that had been five cars behind Harry's, but even though these had already driven off, Harry's hadn't moved an inch.

'Where to, guv?' said the cabbie.

'Milton Street, please. Cabot Tower.'

The cabbie clocked him in the mirror. 'You sure about that, guv?'

'Oh absolutely.'

The driver pulled away from the taxi rank, and Bracewell was surprised to see the passenger and rear doors of Harry's cab suddenly open and all three men getting back out again.

What's he playing at now? he wondered, but quickly decided that arriving at the flat before them was probably not such a bad thing after all.

* * *

Logan stamped on the brake pedal and gave a long blast on the horn. The taxi had pulled straight out of the station car park and directly in front of them.

'Bloody taxis,' he said. 'Idiot wasn't even looking.'

'We could always pull him over, sarge.' Maggie Swann wasn't entirely serious, but she had a vague notion that Logan might actually take her up on the suggestion if only to vent some of the anger that was threatening to resurface once again.

He'd been perfectly upbeat when they'd first set off for Bristol, almost to the point of being uncharacteristically chirpy. But that was when they'd had some solid information to go on – the news that their quarry had finally been spotted, the vehicle he was in and even where he was heading. Since then, however, they'd had no reports about his current whereabouts. Not a dickybird. Logan was convinced this was because MI5 had put a block on anyone getting updates but themselves.

'Seems like they don't trust us,' he'd said after yet another failed attempt to prise the information out of one of his many inside contacts.

Swann had pointed out that this was hardly surprising since they had totally ignored the spooks' order to drop the Trevor Hawkins enquiry altogether. This was when Logan had lost it completely and yelled at her that she was a brainless slapper and he'd see to it personally that she'd be back on the beat the minute this whole sorry business was over and done with. She had responded by telling him he was a sexist, arrogant narcissist with delusions of grandeur and the detective skills of a myopic jellyfish. After trading a series of increasingly inventive insults, they had lapsed into a sulky silence which lasted all the way from Junction 16 of the M6 motorway to just beyond Junction 7 of the M5.

During this period, Swann had occupied herself with recalling each of the occasions when DS Logan had said or done something that had made her want to commit various acts of GBH, most of which were directed at a specific part of his anatomy. But there were just far too many to remember them all.

From time to time, she had also found herself mulling over the facts of the current investigation – such as they were – and what the hell they were going to do when they finally got to Bristol. It was at one such moment that an idea had occurred to her, and she had reached round and grabbed Trevor Hawkins's case file from the back seat of the car.

She had flipped it open on her lap, aware that Logan was watching her out of the corner of his eye whilst studiously pretending to be taking no interest whatsoever in what she was doing. She'd flicked through the scant few pages to a photocopy of the notes she'd made during their interview with Trevor's mother, and her eyes had flashed across the barely legible scribblings until she'd found the particular passage she'd been looking for.

'That's *it*,' she'd said, jabbing a finger at the relevant section on the page.

Logan hadn't given the slightest indication that he'd even heard her speak, but the twitching muscles on the side of his face had betrayed him.

'Oh for God's sake,' she'd said, 'can't you stop sulking just for a minute?'

'I am *not* sulking. I am simply concentrating on driving.'

'Fine. So you won't want me to distract you by telling you my idea then.'

'Huh.' Logan had managed to pack all the teenage angst of a pubescent schoolboy into that one syllable.

Swann had slammed the folder shut and stared out of the side window while she'd waited for the inevitable.

'Well?' Logan had said after a silence of no more than thirty seconds.

'Well what?'

'This brilliant idea of yours. You gonna tell me or not?'

'I thought you didn't want me to distract you from your driving.' She could play the sulky card as well as him any day of the week.

'Oh for f— Look, just tell me, okay?'

'Trevor Hawkins has a sister,' Swann had said with more than a hint of triumph in her voice.

'Remarkable.'

'And guess where she lives.'

'How the hell should I know? The Mull of Kintyre?'

She had milked the pause for as long as she'd dared.

'Bristol.'

Logan had countered the pause with one of his own. 'Interesting.'

Interesting? *Interesting*? Was that the best she was going to get?

'And do we have an address?'

Apparently it was.

'Not yet,' she'd said. 'But it won't exactly be hard to find out.'

Logan had smiled for the first time in quite some while, but since they'd reached the outskirts of Bristol, the tension had returned with a vengeance. The order from MI5 couldn't have been clearer, so even if Hawkins was at his sister's place, what were they going to do about it?

One thing was certain as far as Swann was concerned. Telling Logan to drop a case was almost guaranteed to make him want to pursue it all the harder, and she was being dragged along in the wake of his pigheadedness. It definitely wasn't going to do much for her chances of promotion. – Hell, disobeying a direct order from MI5 was probably even a sacking offence.

43

Until the day before, Trevor's experience of firearms had been almost non-existent, but he had little doubt that the cold, hard object which he now felt being pressed into the back of his neck was the muzzle of a gun.

'What's going on?' he said as the drummers in his chest begin to limber up.

'You're my hostage.'

'Pardon?'

'Look,' said Sandra, 'for all we know, this Patterson guy might already be on his way up here, and I for one have no intention of being caught in a flat with a dead MP who's been strapped to a chair.'

Trevor could appreciate the logic of this statement but still had no idea what she was proposing. He didn't have to wait long for an explanation.

'We have to get out of here sharpish,' said Sandra. 'The lift's not working, and there's only one lot of stairs. Even if there's a fire escape, you can bet your life he'll have that covered as well as every other way out of the building.'

The light finally began to dawn in Trevor's mind, and he turned to face her, assuming he was no longer in imminent danger of having his brains blown out. 'So you're suggesting we *pretend* you've taken me hostage and you're going to shoot me if anyone tries to stop us.'

'Precisely,' she said and lowered the gun to her side.

'But we don't even know for certain who this Patterson is. Okay, so he might be Secret Service, but he might just as easily be one of the bad guys. Either way, he might not give a toss whether you shoot me or not.'

Sandra shrugged. 'I guess that's a risk we're going to have to take.'

'We?'

'For goodness' sake, Trevor, I'm not *actually* going to shoot you whatever happens.'

'Well that's very reassuring, I must say,' said Trevor, and then another thought occurred to him. 'But *they* might.'

Sandra rolled her eyes and sighed heavily. 'Will you please just stop with the arguing and start looking scared?'

Scared could be tricky, thought Trevor. On the other hand, pants-pissingly terrified would be a doddle. He looked down as she jammed the barrel of the gun into his ribs with what he considered to be an unnecessary excess of force.

'You sure the safety catch is on?' he said.

Sandra grabbed him by the arm and marched him towards the door of the flat.

* * *

They were both surprised not to come across Patterson or anyone else on their way down the stairs, but as soon as they reached the ground floor they spotted him standing just inside the main entrance talking to a man in a blue denim jacket. Sandra raised her gun and pressed the muzzle against the side of Trevor's head, making sure the weapon was clearly visible to Patterson. With her other hand, she held him firmly by the hood of his fleece.

'Don't even think about it,' she shouted when the two men instantly thrust their hands inside their jackets.

They froze and then obeyed Sandra's barked

instruction to put their hands in the air and keep them where she could see them.

'Now move away from the door,' she said with a sideways nod of her head.

The man in the denim jacket started to move but stopped again when he realised that Patterson had stayed exactly where he was.

'How do we know you're not bluffing?' Patterson said.

'Try me,' said Sandra and pushed the gun barrel harder against Trevor's cheekbone.

Trevor managed to stop himself saying 'Ow! That hurt!' and simply winced instead. He was determined to play his part in convincing Patterson that Sandra meant business, and if the pounding of the taiko drummers in his chest and the unpleasant gurgling sensation in his bowel area were anything to go by, he was doing a pretty good job of looking terrified.

'You want me to count to three?' said Sandra when Patterson continued to stand his ground, and she gave Trevor another jab with the gun.

'I do wish you'd stop doing that,' he wanted to say, but he decided to save his complaints for later – if there was going to be a "later" of course. The likelihood that he would be having any kind of conversation with anyone in the future diminished dramatically when he heard her say 'One' and Patterson failed to move so much as a muscle.

'Two.'

Oh bloody Nora. Trevor closed his eyes and braced himself. Surely she wasn't going to go back on her promise. What would she have to gain? Patterson or his mate – or probably both – would take her out a nanosecond after she pulled the trigger.

'Thr—'

'Okay, okay, but I don't know how far you think

you'll get.'

Trevor opened one eye and then the other as Patterson finished speaking, and he felt a tidal wave of relief flood through his body.

'Far enough,' said Sandra and released her grip on Trevor's fleece long enough to point at the wall that was furthest from the entrance. 'Over there. Shift it.'

There was a moment's pause, but then Patterson moved slowly in the direction she'd indicated. His companion followed, and all the while both men kept Sandra unblinkingly in their sight. Once they had reached the wall, she told them to turn and face it and place their palms against it as far up as they could reach.

'Now spread 'em,' she said.

'What?' said Patterson, turning his head slightly away from the wall.

'Come on, guys,' said Sandra. 'I'm sure you know the drill.'

Patterson muttered something that Trevor couldn't quite catch, but both men took a step back and positioned their feet about a yard apart.

'You see? That wasn't so difficult, was it? And I'm sure I don't have to emphasise the fact that I'll have no hesitation in blowing this bloke's brains out if I even *think* you're coming after me.'

She winked at Trevor and released the pressure of the gun against the side of his head as they made their way to the exit. He opened the glass door, and they looked up and down the street for any sign of Patterson's other pals. There was no-one in evidence, so they quickly crossed the road to Sandra's Peugeot with frequent backward glances towards the flats.

By the time they got to it, Milly was already performing her acrobatic routine and barking wildly. They made their way round to the far side of the car, and Trevor climbed in behind the steering wheel whilst having to use considerable force to push Milly over onto the passenger seat. Sandra ducked down as she made out the shapes of four men through the glass entrance to the apartment block.

'Now what?' said Trevor when she had clambered into the back of the car and handed him the keys.

'First of all, just get us out of here.'

He started the engine, and the Peugeot lurched forward as the clutch reacted very differently from the one in his van. But by the time they reached the end of the street and he randomly decided to turn left, he'd pretty much got the hang of it.

'We could do with somewhere we can lay low for a while,' said Sandra, looking through the back window of the car to make sure they weren't being followed. 'Somewhere we won't be disturbed while we make one or two phone calls.'

Trevor glimpsed the back of her head in the rear-view mirror and then her face as she turned towards him.

'Where exactly does your sister live?' she said.

* * *

As soon as Trevor and Sandra had left the building, Patterson had radioed Jarvis and Coleman and told them to leave their posts at the fire escape and the emergency exit at the back and get their arses round to the entrance hall. They had arrived within seconds, and the four men watched as the white Peugeot lurched off up the road. All of them had their guns drawn, but Patterson had given the order that no-one should fire unless he told them to. In the end, though, he'd decided it was just too risky. He still had no idea who this Trevor Hawkins was, and maybe he was totally innocent. If so, he certainly didn't want to be held responsible for the guy having his head blown off. Besides, the tracking device on the car meant they could keep tabs on them and do the necessary when the conditions were more favourable.

'Let's just hope the bloody tracker's working,' he said when they stepped through the door and saw the car turn left at the top of the street.

'No reason why it shouldn't,' said Statham. 'Those things are usually pretty reliable.'

Patterson turned to him with a world weary expression and a tone of voice to match. 'That's what they said about the Titanic.'

'Anyway,' he went on, 'instead of standing around gassing, I suggest we get on and put your optimism to the test.'

He was about to tell Jarvis and Coleman to stay where they were and keep an eye out for anyone who looked even vaguely suspicious when a silver-coloured taxi pulled up on the opposite side of the street. All four watched in silence as the driver got out and opened the rear door that was nearest to them and then went to the back of the car and lifted the boot. The passenger emerged, wearing dark glasses and carrying a long white stick, and felt his way along the side of the taxi while the cabbie took a small brown suitcase from the boot and slammed the lid shut.

Taking him by the arm, the cabbie guided him onto the pavement and set the suitcase down next to him. The blind man pulled a wallet from the inside pocket of his jacket and handed the driver a couple of banknotes. After a brief exchange of words, the cabbie got back into the car and drove off.

With his wallet still in his hand, the passenger raised his sunglasses so that they perched on top of his head and looked up at the block of flats. Then he removed a small piece of paper from the wallet and studied it for a moment. Returning his glasses to the bridge of his nose, he picked up the suitcase and started to cross the road.

As he went, he glanced repeatedly up the street in the direction from which he'd just arrived and occasionally tapped his long white stick on the ground in front of him.

Jarvis and Statham were partially blocking the doorway and stepped to the side as the man approached.

'Thank you,' he said and pushed open the glass door.

Patterson immediately began to give Jarvis and Coleman their instructions, and only Statham continued to watch the blind man as he crossed the entrance hall and pressed the button for the lift.

'Something very odd about that bloke,' he said.

Patterson broke off from what he was saying to the other two. 'What?'

'The way he took off his dark glasses and looked up at the flats for a start. And I'm bloody sure he was reading something on that bit of paper he took out of his wallet. If you ask me, he's no more blind than I am.'

All four of them peered through the glass as the man prodded at the lift button once again, and Patterson realised that immediate action was called for when he saw him turn away from the lift and head towards the stairs.

'Right, Jarvis,' he said, 'you get after him and see which flat he goes to. Coleman, you go and fetch whatever surveillance gear you've got with you. I don't want you two barging in on anything yet, so get yourselves into an adjoining flat and just listen in for now till we know what's going on.'

'Okay, guv,' said Coleman and hurried off towards his car.

Jarvis waited until his quarry had disappeared from view up the stairs and then set off in pursuit.

'I only wish I had a bit more faith in those two,' said Patterson with a slight shake of the head. 'Come on then, Colin. Let's find out if that bloody tracker really is working.'

44

They climbed the short flight of steps to the bright red door at the top, and Trevor rapped three times with the heavy brass knocker. Moments later, the door was opened by a woman in a blue pirate-style headscarf, paint spattered T-shirt and jeans that were torn at the knees. She was wiping her hands on a grubby piece of rag, and Trevor caught a strong whiff of white spirit.

'All right, Janice?' he said as Milly shot past her into the house.

'Well, look what the cat dragged in,' she said.

'Sorry I didn't let you know I was coming.'

His sister shrugged. 'You'll just have to take me as you find me, that's all. I'm in the middle of decorating.'

'So I see,' said Trevor, taking the rag from her and wiping a smear of lime green paint from the tip of her nose. He handed the rag back to her and noticed she was looking beyond his right shoulder. 'Oh yes, this is a er... friend of mine. Sandra.'

Sandra stepped forward and held out her hand.

'Best not,' said Janice with a warm smile and indicated the streaks of paint on her palms. 'Nice to meet you though.'

She flashed Trevor a look, and the question in her eyes was unmistakable, but the exact nature of his relationship with Sandra was none of her business, so he ignored her.

'Any chance of a cup of tea?' he said and hoped the unspoken "and maybe a sandwich and a bit of cake" would be taken as read.

Janice ushered them into the hallway, the floor of which was covered with a variety of old bedsheets. A pair of aluminium stepladders stood against the wall she was painting, and an open five-litre can of emulsion lay on its side close to the bottom rung, its contents still adding to the spreading puddle of lime green paint.

'Bloody hell,' said Janice and grabbed the almost empty paint tin to set it upright. 'That dog of yours is a sodding menace.'

'How do you know it was Milly?' said Trevor, who feared the worst and therefore failed miserably in his attempt to sound indignant.

By way of reply, his sister pointed at the trail of lime green paw prints which led from the scene of the crime and continued on through the open doorway on the left.

'Ah,' said Trevor and followed the trail into the lounge, praying that the hall carpet under the bedsheets wasn't the same shade of pale beige.

'Oh Christ,' he heard Janice say from behind him. 'It's gone right through. Beige bloody carpet as well.'

Trevor flinched and easily resisted the temptation to tell her she could have bought some waterproof dustsheets from Dreamhome Megastores for just a few quid. Instead, his eyes tracked the paw prints across the spacious living room. He gained a modicum of relief when he saw that the intensity of the green gradually decreased until the trail vanished altogether immediately in front of the settee on which Milly was now lying. She was on her back with her legs in the air and Trevor's nephew, Josh, was stroking her chest.

'Hey, Josh. How's it going?'

The boy brushed a hank of black hair from his forehead and looked up from the television, which was blaring away from the corner of the room next to the window.

'Hi, Uncle Trevor,' he said with a broad grin. 'Cool thanks.'

'Rovers or City?' said Trevor, nodding towards Josh's red and white football shirt.

His nephew glanced down as if to verify what he was actually wearing, and his smile widened. 'City of course.'

'Expensive, aren't they?'

Josh briefly eyed the shirt once again. 'Dunno. Mum gave it me for my birthday.'

'Oh, right. Yeah, I'm sorry I missed the party.' Trevor remembered that the lad had turned ten back in February, but despite being very fond of him, he'd been at quite a low ebb at the time and decided he couldn't face a houseful of shrieking kids.

''Sokay,' said Josh and then suddenly sat upright from his slouching position at the end of the settee. 'Hello.'

Trevor turned to see that Sandra had entered the room and was staring at the trail of paw prints across the carpet.

'Hi,' she said and then switched her attention back to the splodges of paint. 'I think you'd better get a cloth or something before your sister sees this.'

'Too bloody late,' said Janice as she appeared in the doorway. 'And get the damn dog off the sofa, Josh. – Now.'

With obvious reluctance, the boy half pushed and half slid Milly onto the floor, which was no easy task as she seemed equally reluctant to relinquish her state of perfect bliss on the settee.

'She your girlfriend?'

It took Trevor a moment to register that his nephew was talking to him, and he felt the heat blast into his cheeks.

'What?' he said and instantly regretted the nervous laugh which probably sounded more like a coquettish giggle. 'Oh no, no. Just a er… friend. That's all. We er—'

He decided to shut up before he made more of a blushing idiot of himself than he had already and stole a look at Sandra. She was gazing down at her feet, and from the angle of her face it was impossible to tell whether she was smiling or frowning. His mind raced to find something to say which would divert attention from the unwelcome topic in hand, but his mental floundering was mercifully interrupted by a loud knock at the front door.

'Oh great. Why don't we all have a bloody party?' said Janice and thrust the paint sodden rag at her brother. 'Here. Make yourself useful for once.'

He took the rag and surveyed the lime green marks on the carpet. 'I think this'll make it worse if anything.'

Janice clasped a hand to her forehead. 'Jesus, Trevor, I know all men are useless, but you—'

'Have you got a clean one we could use?' said Sandra.

Janice was momentarily fazed by the interruption to her tirade. 'Er… should be one under the sink in the kitchen.'

Trevor was out of the lounge before his sister had even finished the sentence, and he reached the kitchen at the far end of the hallway just as she was opening the front door. He made straight for the cupboard under the sink but froze as he crouched down to open it.

'Sorry to bother you, madam, but we're looking for a Mr Trevor Hawkins.'

It was a man's voice and one which was instantly familiar.

'And you are?' Janice's tone sounded polite but curt.

There was the briefest of pauses before the man spoke again. 'Detective Sergeant Logan, Metropolitan Police.'

Trevor shot upright like a popped champagne cork. Shit, he thought. How the hell did *he* get here?

'Police?' said Janice. 'What's it about?'

272

That's it, sis. Keep him talking while I make my escape.

Escape? *Escape*? What in God's name was he thinking of? But even as the absurdity of the notion occurred to him, he scanned the small, neatly kept back garden through the window above the sink. It was surrounded by a tall wooden fence with a door set into the furthest corner.

'I suppose you'd better come in then,' he heard Janice say.

Trevor realised it was now or never and hesitated only long enough to consider the predicament that Sandra might be in. It's not her they're after though, is it? It's me they want.

And thus having satisfied his conscience, he was out of the back door and across the garden in a matter of seconds. He reached for the black metal handle on the gate but froze once again when he saw the latch rise slowly of its own accord. He stepped back as the gate opened inwards, and straight away he recognised the smartly dressed young woman who stood before him.

'Going somewhere, Mr Hawkins?' she said.

45

Having decided to take Jarvis and Coleman's car because it was nearer, Patterson now sat hunched forward in the passenger seat of the stationary blue Mondeo, his arms straight down by his sides and his forehead resting on the top of the dashboard.

'Why me? Oh God, why me?' he muttered every so often and at the same time raised and lowered his brow against the warm stickiness of the vinyl.

'You all right?' said Statham without diverting his gaze from the small notebook computer propped against the steering wheel in front of him.

Patterson rolled his head sideways and stared at him. 'If your definition of all right is that I am quite content to be in charge of an operation which has turned into the most monumental cockup in the entire history of the Secret Service, then my answer would have to be no, Colin, I am anything but bloody all right. In fact, if you want the honest truth, I am seriously considering the advantages of taking my gun out and ending it all right here and right now.'

'Could be worse,' said Statham, pointing at the flashing red dot in the centre of the computer screen. 'I mean, at least the tracking device is working.'

'Oh well, everything's all just tickety-boo then, isn't it?' said Patterson, his forehead reacquainting itself with the dashboard. 'There is, however, one teensy tiny problem which may have escaped your attention though. And that is that the teensy tiny device you so expertly attached to their car appears to be in the same frigging place opposite the block of flats.'

There was a pause, and he could hear Statham tapping some buttons on the computer keyboard. 'Hmm,' he said at last. 'Bit of a conundrum that.'

'Conundrum, he says. Conundrum.' Patterson's snort of laughter was more like a demonic cackle, and his head-banging intensified before he suddenly threw himself backwards in his seat and addressed himself to the roof of the car. 'It's not a conundrum. It's a typical Colin Statham bollock-dropping balls-up. That's what it is. Plain and simple.'

'Oh come on. I don't see why I should take all the blame.'

Patterson rounded on him. 'Well forgive me if I'm wrong here, but I seem to remember you were the one who was supposed to fix the tracker under the car. Now, assuming that your box of tricks there isn't telling a great big porky, I can only guess that you didn't do it properly and the little bugger is currently lying at the side of the road and bleeping merrily away to itself.'

'It was the dog.'

'The what?'

'The dog. All that barking and stuff distracted me. If you'd warned me that there—'

'Oh I see. So it was all my fault, was it?' Patterson folded his arms across his chest and turned away to look out of the side window, barely registering the taxi which pulled up in front of the block of flats or the three men who got out of it.

'I'm not saying that. It's just—'

Statham was interrupted for a second time when the onboard radio hissed and crackled into life: 'Hello? Jarvis here. Come in, guv. Are you there?'

Patterson took no notice and continued to stare out of the window.

'You want me to get that?' said Statham.

'Laurel and Hardy reporting the latest bloody disaster? Help yourself.'

Statham took the microphone from its mounting on the dashboard. Then he closed his eyes and listened while Jarvis recounted how he had followed the blind man to Flat 12 on the second floor. One of the apartments next to it was unoccupied, and he and Coleman had broken in and set up the surveillance gear. They'd only got audio, but they hadn't heard any voices yet, so it was more than likely the guy was on his own in there.

'Where are you anyway? You caught up with the Peugeot yet?'

Statham leaned forward and spoke into the microphone in little more than a whisper. 'Er... not as such, no.'

'Don't tell me the tracker didn't work. Jeez, the guv'nor must have— Hang on a minute. There's something...'

Jarvis's voice tailed off into a barrage of radio static but returned a few seconds later. 'Seems like he's got company. Two or three of 'em by the sound of it.'

This was surely too much of a coincidence, thought Patterson. It must be the three men who'd got out of the taxi just now. Come to think of it, there'd been something shifty about the way they'd looked up and down the street before they'd disappeared into the flats. And the fattish bloke in the black overcoat. He knew him from somewhere, he was almost certain of it.

He threw open the car door. 'Come on, Colin. We might be about to salvage something from this unholy mess after all.'

* * *

276

MacFarland wasn't in the least surprised that Julian Bracewell was already in the flat, nor that he was pointing a gun at them as they came through the door. Harry's tanned complexion, on the other hand, turned a pale shade of grey.

'Well, well. Julian Bracewell as I live and breathe.'

MacFarland couldn't be certain, but he thought he detected a hint of a tremor in Harry's voice. He stared at the man he had first met as a tramp outside the hotel in Sheffield only a few hours earlier. Clean shaven now and looking twenty years younger, he was half perched on the narrow window sill at the opposite end of the room, dressed in a dark blue suit and red tie. Eyeing Bracewell's gun, he contemplated reaching for his own but instantly abandoned the idea as not only a futile gesture but very probably a suicidal one.

'I must say you appear to be in remarkably good health for someone who's supposed to be dead, old boy,' said Bracewell, raising and lowering his gun in Harry's direction like it was some kind of long distance body scanner.

'Not lookin' so bad yerself in the circumstances.'

'Can't complain, Harry. Can't complain. But speaking of the dead, would this chappie here have anything to do with you by any chance?'

Bracewell nodded towards the armchair in the middle of the room, only the back of which was visible to Harry and the others.

'Dead? What the fuck are you talkin' about?' Harry seemed to have forgotten about the gun that was being aimed at him, and he strode over to the armchair. 'Jesus Christ. What did you do to 'im?'

'Nothing to do with me, old boy. He was like that when I got here.'

'And where the hell are Carrot and Lenny?' Harry's eyes darted around the flat as if he thought they might be hiding somewhere.

'Who?'

'The two muppets who were supposed to be lookin' after 'im.'

'Just me and the stiff I'm afraid,' Bracewell said with a shrug. 'Can't get the staff these days, eh, Harry? Present company excepted of course.'

MacFarland felt awkward at the wink and the beaming grin that was directed at him, uncertain whether to return the smile or not.

'How's the old war wound by the way?' Bracewell waved the barrel of his gun at MacFarland's feet.

'Aye, well,' he said, looking down at his injured foot, which still shot a bolt of pain up his leg whenever he put weight on it. 'I guess it's nae so bad now, ta very much. Mind you, I have tae—'

'Oh shut up, 'Aggis,' Harry interrupted, his face contorted with contempt. 'Nobody gives a toss about your bleedin' foot.'

Bracewell's smile vanished instantly, and he whipped the gun round to aim it at Harry's chest. 'I beg your pardon, old boy, but I do believe *I* was expressing an interest in our Scottish friend's podiatric wellbeing.'

'Whoa, whoa, whoa,' said Harry with a forced laugh, throwing his hands in the air in mock surrender. 'Let's not get hasty, shall we?'

There was a lengthy silence as Bracewell glared at him, all traces of feigned good humour now entirely obscured beneath a mask of sheer loathing. 'No, no. I think it would be best if you keep them where they are,' he said when Harry made to lower his arms.

MacFarland watched Bracewell screw a silencer onto the barrel of his gun, and his whole body tensed when he heard the faint click of the safety catch. He wondered again whether he should risk making a grab for his own weapon, but it was almost as if Bracewell had read his mind.

'I wouldn't advise it, dear boy,' he said without diverting his attention from Harry. 'We wouldn't want to ruin the English-Scottish *entente cordiale*, now would we? In fact, perhaps this might be an opportune moment to relieve you of temptation. – Delia, if you'd be so kind?'

MacFarland's immediate confusion intensified when he turned to see Delia coming towards him and gesturing at him to raise his hands. He did as he was told, and Delia reached inside his jacket and removed the gun from his shoulder holster. MacFarland studied his face the whole time for some kind of clue, but all he got was a half grin that seemed more like a facial shrug of apology. Okay, so maybe this explained his strange behaviour on the train and then later on the station platform, but why Bracewell? What was the connection?

He watched Delia cross the floor to the window, giving Harry the widest possible berth as he went. When he got there, Bracewell rested his free hand on his shoulder and, in return, Delia kissed him lightly on the cheek.

Bloody hell. So that was it.

'Fuck me,' said Harry, whose mouth had hung open in silent horror from the moment he had witnessed Delia's betrayal.

'I'd really rather not, old boy, if it's all the same to you. Besides, I'm very much a one-man man nowadays, aren't I, Michael?' Bracewell said with an impish smile and moved his hand from Delia's shoulder to his waist.

Although still in a state of shock himself, MacFarland found the look of disgust on Harry's face highly entertaining and in any other circumstance would have been hard pressed to have stifled a snigger. Despite his obvious revulsion, Harry seemed to have no such inhibition, but there was no trace of amusement in his scornful laughter.

'Michael? *Michael*? Fucking Judas, more like. Or maybe that should be Judy, eh? I've been bloody good to you, I 'ave. Scabby little cocksucker.'

'You see, Harry, it's exactly that kind of—'

It was the first time Delia had uttered a word since they'd entered the flat, but Harry wasn't about to let him get any further. In fact, he ignored him altogether and turned his attention on Bracewell instead.

'And since when 'ave you been a knob jockey? Still, I s'pose I should've known with a name like Joooolian and that poncey fuckin' accent of yours.' Then a thought seemed to occur to him, and his eyes blazed like a shark's in a feeding frenzy. 'Hey, maybe you developed a liking for takin' it up the arse ever since I screwed you over that Croydon job.'

Even though MacFarland had been half expecting it, he still flinched at the dull pinging sound and the flash from Bracewell's silenced gun.

46

Convincing DS Logan about the dead body in the flat had not been easy. From the moment Swann had brought Trevor back into the living room, he had been intent on one course of action alone – to continue questioning him about Imelda's disappearance. He had completely ignored Trevor and Sandra's protestations, and it was only when Sandra had told him the man was a Member of Parliament that he had begun to hesitate. Then she had shown him the MP's identity card, and the hesitation had turned into a full scale pause, at the end of which he had instructed Swann to make some enquiries.

She had made a couple of calls, but there had been no reports of a missing MP. Logan had seemed satisfied that Trevor and Sandra had invented the whole ridiculous story and asked them what the hell they'd expected to gain from it. But before they could answer, Swann had pointed out that the absence of any reports didn't really prove anything one way or the other.

'Maybe he hasn't been gone long enough for anyone to have noticed,' she had said. 'Besides, if what these two say is true, it would certainly explain why the spooks have got their oar in.'

Now here's a guy who doesn't like his authority being undermined, Trevor had thought as he'd caught the look of thunder which Logan directed at his colleague. But any tirade that might have followed was nipped in the bud when Sandra had launched into the briefest of explanations as to what had led them to their discovery of the dead MP.

After she'd finished, Logan had crossed the floor of the living room and stared out of the window in silence for several seconds. Then he had turned and pointed his finger at Trevor.

'And you needn't think this is going to get you off a murder charge,' he'd said. 'As soon as we get there and find out you've been pulling my pisser, I'm nicking the pair of you for wasting police time. That'll do for starters anyway.'

'As soon as *we* get there?' Trevor had repeated.

Logan's laugh had sounded more like an elongated grunt. 'You don't think I'm going to let you out of my sight after the merry little dance you've been leading me already, do you?'

Trevor's sister had been adamant that there was no way he was leaving his vandal of a dog behind, and although Logan had been equally resistant to taking her with them, Milly was now wedged between Trevor and Sandra on the back seat of the car as they sped through the streets of Bristol.

47

There was little doubt that the favourite colour of Flat 13's absent occupant was a particularly gaudy shade of purple. Every surface that could be painted purple had been – not only the doors, walls and ceiling, but tables, chairs and even the casing of the television in the corner of the room. The carpet was almost exactly the same colour, and anything unpaintable, like the two-seater settee and the single armchair, was covered in purple fabric.

'God almighty,' said Patterson when Coleman had let him and Statham into the apartment. 'It's enough to send you blind. – And speaking of which, what's our friend with the white stick been up to since his chums arrived?'

Jarvis was sitting on one of the purple wooden chairs at the side of the room, wearing a pair of headphones. These were attached to a black box on his lap, and this in turn was connected to a small square of plastic fixed to the wall. He lifted the headphones clear of his right ear and half turned towards Patterson. 'Bit hard to tell without a visual, guv, but I'm pretty sure there's a stiff in there.'

'A stiff?'

'A dead body, guv.'

Patterson rolled his eyes. 'Yes, I do know what a stiff is, thank you. Any idea who it is?'

'Dunno,' said Jarvis with a shake of his head. 'Seems like he'd already croaked when the blind guy arrived. One of them's called Julian Bracewell and then there's a

Harry and a bloke with a heavy Scottish accent. Oh yes, and somebody called Delia.'

'Delia?' Patterson thought back to the three people who had emerged from the taxi a few minutes earlier. He was sure that all of them were men. And what about this Julian Bracewell? He told Coleman to run a check on him, although he wondered whether there was much point. If, as he suspected, the dead body belonged to Gerald Quicke MP, then the whole job was screwed anyway.

'Hang on a sec.' Jarvis adjusted the headphones so that both ears were covered once again and frowned in concentration.

'What is it?' said Patterson, guessing from Jarvis's expression that he was hearing something that wasn't going to be good news.

Jarvis held up his hand to motion him to silence. 'Sounds like there's a bit of an argy-bargy going on... Cockney-sounding bloke – I think that's Harry – calling somebody a Judas... Something about a— Agh, Jesus!'

He snatched the headphones off and dropped them to the floor before clasping his hands to his ears and rubbing them vigorously. Even without the aid of a listening device, the wall was thin enough for Patterson and the others to be in no doubt as to the sound which had almost deafened him. It was a man screaming in pain.

'What the hell was that?' said Statham.

'Not exactly sure, but I think there might have been a shot,' said Jarvis, still massaging his damaged ears. 'Gun with a silencer maybe.'

Out of the corner of his eye, Patterson was aware that Statham was looking at him, apparently waiting for a decision about what they should do next. He considered his options, but there seemed to be remarkably few. Their main reason for being here at all was to ensure the safety of the kidnapped MP, but it seemed more than likely they had already failed on that score. They could always burst into the flat and grab whoever was still alive in there, but at least one of them had a gun – perhaps they all did – so the risk to him and his men was not inconsiderable. Besides, what would be the point when he knew that the case would never come to trial?

His instructions had been unequivocal in that respect. Whatever the outcome, not a single detail of the operation could ever be made public. A general election was looming, and the government's standing in the opinion polls was already causing alarm bells to ring in the corridors of power. A recent string of scandals involving some of the higher ranking party members had been particularly damaging, so the last thing the PM wanted right now was another one. If the media got even the faintest whiff of what Quicke had been up to and why he'd been kidnapped, the consequences would be disastrous. Not only that, but if it became known that the government had agreed to pay the ransom, its frequently repeated mantra never to give in to terrorist demands or any other form of blackmail would be ridiculed as a sham of the highest order.

Oh bollocks, thought Patterson, realising that he was getting nowhere with his decision-making process, and he began instead to calculate the kind of pension he might be entitled to if he took early retirement. But his financial musings were short lived.

'You're not gonna believe this,' said Coleman when he ended the call on his mobile phone.

'Don't piss about,' Patterson snapped. 'Just tell me what you've got.'

'Well, assuming it's the same Julian Bracewell, he actually died four years ago.' He paused for a reaction, but all he got was a raised eyebrow and a look of impatience, so he cleared his throat and carried on. 'Bit of a bad lad apparently. Head of some gang in South London. Armed robbery mostly. In fact, he was out on bail over a bank job when he snuffed it.'

'Bail?'

'Yeah, *I* thought that was a bit weird. Anyway, before he croaked – when he was being questioned, like – he tried to put someone else in the frame. Er...' Coleman glanced at his notebook. 'Name of Harry Vincent.'

Patterson felt as if his frontal lobe had been poked with a cattle prod. Harry Vincent. Of course. He knew he'd recognised him from somewhere when he'd seen him get out of the taxi but hadn't been able to put a name to him until now. He hadn't even twigged when Jarvis had said one of the men in the flat was called Harry. Patterson remembered him from his Flying Squad days before he'd joined MI5. Everyone knew what a nasty little bastard he was, but there'd never been enough solid evidence to pin anything on him. Even when they'd tried to manufacture the evidence, Vincent could afford to hire the most expensive lawyers in the country to make sure he wriggled away scot free every time. The last Patterson had heard was a couple of years or so ago when the police had finally been able to put together a case which was not only likely to stick but which would also have put him away for a very long time. Unfortunately, though, Vincent had been blown to pieces in a car explosion before they'd been able to run him to ground. At least, that was the story at the time.

'So what do we do now?'

This time, it was Statham who cut short his deliberations. Patterson stared at him as if he was struggling to remember who he was.

'Do?' he said at last. 'I'm really not sure what we *can* do.'

'But if they're starting to shoot people, shouldn't we be—'

'Look,' said Patterson. 'It seems a pretty safe bet that this MP we were supposed to keep alive has already shuffled off his mortal coil, and what's more, there are two dead men in there who appear to be very much in the land of the living. No, we listen and wait and see what happens. With a bit of luck they might all end up killing each other and save us the bother.'

Statham opened his mouth to speak but was interrupted by a loud knocking on the door of the flat. Of the four men, only Jarvis did not turn instantly towards it. His eardrums having recovered sufficiently, the headphones were now back in place, and all he could hear were the sounds from the next door apartment.

48

Harry pitched sideways when the bullet hit, and instinct made him throw out his hands to break his fall. One of them caught the top of the armchair, and he brought it crashing down on its back with the dead MP still attached.

'Ah, don't they make a lovely couple,' said Bracewell, clearly enjoying the sight of Harry sprawled on the floor next to the upturned corpse and clutching at the still-smoking hole in his foot.

'What the fuck d'you do that for?' said Harry through teeth clamped shut from the pain.

'Let's just say I'm not at all keen on your attitude towards the gay community, old boy.'

MacFarland laughed. Harry's complete lack of sympathy for the injury to his own foot made the scene especially comical. Harry screwed his head round to glare up at him, his face twisted into a fusion of agony and rage. Whatever happened from that moment on, MacFarland realised he was suddenly out of a job. What else did he have to lose?

'Looks like you've really shot yirself in the foot this time,' he said.

'You're a dead man, Scotchboy,' Harry snarled as he dragged himself into a sitting position with his back against the side of the armchair, blood now running freely from the hole in his tan-coloured brogue.

'Perhaps you should have stayed in Greece,' said Bracewell. 'In fact, I can't for the life of me understand why this MP chappie was so important that you felt the need to come back at all.'

'Thought your little bum-chum there would've told yer all about it,' said Harry and grunted as he struggled to untie his blood-soaked shoelace.

'Michael told me all I needed to know for my purposes of course, but not the… nitty-gritty, so to speak.'

'What d'you care anyway?'

Bracewell shrugged. 'Shall we say… professional curiosity?'

'Well yer know what you can do with that, don'tcha?' Harry said, finally releasing his shoe and tossing it weakly in Bracewell's direction. ''Cept a fucking shirt lifter like you would probably enjoy it.'

'Our wee deid MP here stitched ye up good and proper, didn't he, Harry?' said MacFarland. 'And nobody messes wi' the great Harry Vincent, do they, eh?'

'Oh do tell, dear boy,' said Bracewell.

MacFarland needed no further encouragement to add the insult of humiliation to his ex-employer's physical injury and explained how Harry had bribed the MP about a year ago to 'do him a wee favour'. As well as his less-than-legal enterprises, Harry also had his podgy little fingers in some rather more legitimate business pies and even had his own construction company. When he heard there was a major government contract in the offing, he'd decided to try and tip the balance his way, and that's when he nobbled Gerald Quicke.

The MP had been on holiday in Greece when Harry met him by chance in one of his local watering holes. A fair few sherbets later, Quicke had started bragging how he could influence which way the decision went when it came to awarding the contract. What Harry didn't know was that Quicke was so far down the greasy pole, he wouldn't even have had a say in what brand of bog roll they used in the House of Commons toilets, never mind influencing who got what contract. But Harry was taken in by all the guy's blether and decided that bunging him fifty grand would be a sound business investment.

Of course, when it was announced that some other company had got the job, Harry did his nut. And when it turned out that Quicke had done bugger all to fight Harry's corner, the writing was already on the wall.

'Ah, I see. A simple matter of revenge then,' said Bracewell. 'One can only assume that our recently departed dishonourable member had no idea who he was dealing with or what he might be capable of.'

'Should've just 'ad the little bastard wasted, but I wanted me money back, didn't I? Plus an extra hundred k for seriously pissing me off.'

'Punitive damages, eh?'

'If you like,' said Harry, who by now had removed his sock and was using it to try and stem the flow of blood.

'Still, I suppose one could say you've had your cake and eaten it too,' said Bracewell, nodding towards the body of the MP in the overturned armchair.

'Yeah, all except for a fucking 'ole in me foot and the twenty-five grand that bitch and 'er boyfriend waltzed off with.'

'Oh?' said Bracewell, raising an eyebrow at Delia.

'Bit of a long story,' said Delia. 'I'll tell you later.'

'But do I take it that the remainder of Mr Vincent's ill-gotten gains is in safe keeping?'

'Of course,' said Delia with a smile, and he pointed to the briefcase he'd left just inside the door when they'd first entered the flat.

Bracewell beamed back at him and patted him softly on the cheek. 'Well then, I do believe our business here is concluded. – Shall we?'

He ostentatiously held out his arm, crooked at the

elbow, and Delia slipped his own arm through the gap. MacFarland couldn't believe what he was seeing. Not the gay thing. He didn't give a flying fart about all that stuff as long as nobody tried it on with him. No, it looked like they were just going to mince off into the sunset and that would be that. Surely Bracewell wasn't going to leave Harry alive. That was the whole point, wasn't it? And what were they planning to do with *him*?

The two men stopped when they reached the armchair, and Bracewell looked down at Harry's contorted features. 'Goodbye, old chap,' he said. 'I won't say *au revoir* as I very much doubt I shall ever have the misfortune of seeing you again.'

Harry stared up at him with defiant loathing, but his expression switched abruptly to one of surprise when he saw his nemesis slip the still silenced gun into his pocket. 'Whassup, Julian? Lost yer bottle?'

'Not at all, dear boy. I simply decided that killing you wouldn't be nearly as much fun as leaving you to be found next to the body of the profoundly dead Member for Wherever-on-the-Wold. Even if you somehow manage to squirm your way out of this one, I have every confidence that our mutual friends in the constabulary have a rather long list of reasons why you should spend the rest of your days as a guest of Her Majesty.'

Harry hawked and spat, but the distance was too great, and the gobbet of phlegm landed harmlessly on the floor. Bracewell tutted and was about to continue on his way out of the flat when Delia held him back.

'You don't think he'll be able to get out of here before the police arrive, do you?'

'Hmm,' said Bracewell, scratching his chin and frowning. 'Good point.'

The words were barely out of his mouth when he whipped the gun back out of his pocket and shot Harry through his other foot.

'Fuuuuuuuuuucccckkkk!'

Bracewell slowly unscrewed the silencer from his gun and squinted as he watched Harry writhing on the ground and clutching his newly wounded foot. 'You know, Harry, despite your age and the fact that you could do with losing more than a few pounds around the tummy area, that tan of yours is going to make you awfully popular in the prison showers. Toodle pip, old boy.'

So saying, he set off towards the door with Delia at his side, and MacFarland fixed his eyes on the gun which Bracewell had not yet returned to his pocket. He'd often wondered what it felt like to be on the wrong end of a bullet, and it was well on the cards he was about to find out. Aye well, as long as it wasn't the stomach. – Oh Jeez, no. Not in the stomach.

'You okay, Mac?'

'Uh?' He'd caught sight of Delia stooping to pick up his briefcase on the edge of his vision, but his focus stayed pinned to Bracewell's gun.

'I said are you—' Delia began again but broke off when he realised the reason for MacFarland's distraction. 'Julian.'

Bracewell must have clocked the reproachful tone in Delia's voice because he instantly looked at his gun as if he was surprised to find it was still in his hand.

'I say. Sorry, old boy,' he said, thrusting the pistol back into his pocket. 'You didn't think I was going to— Oh dear, that really would have buggered our little *entente cordiale*, wouldn't it?'

'Listen, Mac,' said Delia, placing a hand on MacFarland's shoulder. 'I wouldn't hang around here if I were you. I'll be giving the police a bell as soon as we're clear.'

'Dinnae worry, pal. I'm just gonna say ma goodbyes and I'm away,' he said with an exaggerated wink.

Delia turned to go and then hesitated. 'Give me a call,' he said. 'We might have something for you if you're interested.'

'Aye? – Well, cheers. I may just take ye up on that.'

As soon as Bracewell and Delia had gone, MacFarland strode over to where Harry was thrashing about on the floor and gave him a hefty kick in the nuts.

'And there's one from Haggis Bollocks,' he said, 'but ye can call me James Dougal MacFarland.'

49

Patterson and Statham watched in silence as Coleman opened the apartment door, both of them with their hands inside their jackets, grasping the butts of their guns. Over his shoulder, they could see two uniformed police officers.

'Evening, sir,' said the taller of the two. 'I wonder if I could ask you a few questions.'

'What about?'

'I think it might be better if we discussed this inside, sir, if you don't mind.'

Coleman looked back at Patterson, who rolled his eyes and then indicated with a nod that he should let them in. He moved to the side, and the officers stepped into the flat. Patterson could now see from the markings on their sweaters that the taller one was a sergeant and the other a constable.

'Quite a little party you've got going on here,' said the sergeant, scanning the room and its occupants. 'Even got your own DJ, I see.'

Patterson followed his gaze to where Jarvis still sat next to the wall with his back to them, apparently listening so intently through the headphones that he was oblivious to the arrival of their uninvited guests.

'What is it you want exactly?' he said, making no attempt to disguise his irritation.

The sergeant was clearly not happy about being spoken to in this way and curled his upper lip like a recalcitrant teenager. 'You the tenant here, are you, sir?

Or perhaps one of your… companions?' He uttered the word as if it was the verbal equivalent of dog shit that he had just discovered on the sole of his shoe.

'No, but—'

'I thought not.'

The speed of the interruption and the smug grin with which it was delivered were unambiguous. The sergeant already knew full well that they were intruders.

'You see, sir,' he went on, 'we've had a report from a neighbour that she saw two men entering the flat even though the *legitimate* tenant is away on a fortnight's holiday in Majorcal.'

Despite his annoyance, Patterson couldn't help but smile at the bizarre habit Bristolians had of adding an "L" to words which ended in a vowel. Then, with all the superficial politeness he could muster, he explained who they were and why it had been necessary to break into the flat, keeping the details to the barest minimum. The sergeant, however, was not to be deprived of his moment of glory quite so easily. Even when Patterson and the others showed him their identification, he remained steadfastly unconvinced and expressed his doubts that the ID cards were genuine. Patterson offered to give him the numbers of half a dozen contacts he could call who would verify that they were who they said they were, but he wasn't buying this either.

'And how do I know *they're* who you say they are?' he said. 'I'll make my own enquiries, thank you very much.'

Several minutes then passed while the constable made a variety of calls over his radio. All the while, Patterson paced back and forth, occasionally pausing to check whether Jarvis had picked up anything of importance, but there was little that he didn't know already. Although he still had no plan as to how to proceed with the operation, he fervently hoped that the pompous jobsworth of a sergeant would soon get his confirmation and bugger off out of the way.

'Jesus!' said Jarvis, once again throwing down the headphones and clutching at his ears.

The cry of pain from the next-door apartment was even louder than the previous one, and Jarvis was certain he'd heard a gunshot this time.

'Gunshot?' said the sergeant with an anxious glance at his partner, who had just ended yet another call and was clipping his radio back onto the shoulder of his sweater.

'Seems like they really are MI5, sarge,' said the constable.

'Never mind that now. If there's people shooting in there, we need to investigate.'

The sergeant was almost at the door when Patterson whipped out his gun. 'One more step and there'll be shooting in here too.'

'Now listen here…' The sergeant's words tailed away as he turned to see the pistol aimed at his head.

'The pair of you. Over by the window.' Patterson waved his gun towards the far end of the room and rather enjoyed the look of shock on the sergeant's face and his spluttering protestations as the two uniforms did as they were told.

'I think someone's leaving, guv,' said Jarvis, his headphones back in position.

'Coleman, keep an eye on these two. Colin, you come with me.' Patterson led the way to the door, still without any particular plan in mind but instinctively aware that he should at least check out the situation.

When Jarvis informed him that all he could hear was someone groaning, he decided that any risk was now minimal, and he opened the door as silently as possible. Craning his neck forward, he peered into the corridor. At the far end, a man with a ponytail was hurriedly limping towards the top of the stairs, and even from behind, he was fairly sure it was the Scottish guy that Statham had chased after at the festival the day before.

The second he'd disappeared down the stairs, Patterson edged his way out into the hallway. The door of Number 12 was closed, so he motioned to Statham to open it. He took a deep breath and stretched his gun out in front of him, the butt clasped between both hands.

50

DS Logan marched along the hallway with Sandra at his side. Trevor followed a couple of paces behind with Milly on a lead, and DC Swann brought up the rear. The door of Flat 12 was already open and so was the door of the apartment just beyond it. Sandra hung back as Logan swept inside with such apparent nonchalance that Trevor could only assume he still didn't believe their story about the dead MP and had chosen to ignore their warnings about the potential danger.

'Who the bloody hell are you?'

Trevor recognised the voice. He joined Sandra in the doorway and saw that Patterson was pointing a gun at Logan's chest.

'Well, well,' said Patterson, swinging his pistol in Sandra and Trevor's direction. 'And if it isn't our little friends from Baader-Meinhof. Decided not to blow his brains out after all, eh?'

'DS Logan, Metropolitan Police,' Logan said in answer to Patterson's original question. 'And you are?'

There was a pause as Patterson appeared to compose himself, but the anger in his voice was plain to hear when he finally spoke. 'Forgive me if I'm mistaken, but I thought you were told to keep out from under my feet.'

Trevor watched the light dawn on Logan's face. 'Ah, so you'd be MI5 then,' said the detective and nodded towards the overturned armchair. 'And this would be the dead MP, would it?'

'What do you know about—'

'Are one of you useless twats gonna get me a fucking ambulance or what?'

The words which interrupted Patterson were uttered through gritted teeth from behind the armchair, and Trevor edged sideways to see if his suspicions were correct. They were. It was Harry, sitting in a puddle of blood with his knees drawn up under his chin and clutching his shins.

'And who's this then?' said Logan, who had also shifted his position to see who had spoken.

'None of your business,' said Patterson.

'None of my business? I'm stood here in a flat with a gun pointed at me, a dead Member of Parliament and some bloke who's been shot in the foot…' Logan leaned forward to take a closer look. '…Feet. And you tell me it's none of my business?'

Trevor began to feel like he was watching a tennis match as he looked from Logan to Patterson and back again while the two men spent the next few minutes trading threats and insults. So intent were they on their argument, he even wondered if he might be able to slip away unnoticed. He quickly dismissed the idea, however, when a glance over his shoulder told him that DC Swann was still in the doorway, and he was also aware that Patterson's pal in the denim jacket was keeping half an eye on him from his position by the window at the far end of the apartment. At that particular moment, he appeared to be talking into his sleeve, although he was too far away for Trevor to make out anything intelligible. He transferred his attention back to Patterson and Logan, both of whom looked as if they were about to throw down their racquets and storm off the court.

'What you don't seem to understand,' Logan was saying, 'is that I've got a murder investigation on my hands here.'

'And I haven't?' said Patterson, waving his gun towards the corpse in the overturned armchair.

''Scuse me, guv.'

Patterson rounded on his colleague with an expression that reminded Trevor of John McEnroe when he'd just been foot-faulted on match point. 'What *is* it, Statham?'

'Jarvis wants to know if we need any help.'

'Not unless he's exceptionally skilled in communicating with the terminally stupid, no.'

'Righto. And he also says the plods have had a call to investigate an anonymous tipoff about a murder in Flat 12.'

'This very one in fact,' said Patterson with heavy sarcasm.

'Uh-huh.'

'Oh terrific. So much for covert bloody operations. I don't know why we don't just send out invitations.'

'And send for a fucking ambulance while you're at it. I'm bleedin' to death 'ere.'

Trevor had almost forgotten about Harry, his constant moans and groans having merged into the background some time ago.

Patterson ignored him. 'Tell the plods to report back that they've checked it out and there's nothing doing. False alarm.'

Logan began to splutter his dissent, but Patterson ignored him too. Instead, he wiped a weary palm across his face and stared down at the floor. After several seconds, he looked up. 'Listen, Hogan, I'll tell you what I'll do—'

'Logan.'

'Yes, yes,' said Patterson with a dismissive wave of the hand. 'Now, whilst I would dearly love to take these two for a long walk off a short pier somewhere, I'm prepared to make you a deal.'

Trevor was in no doubt as to who he meant by "these

two", although he wasn't at all convinced he was going to like Patterson's alternative proposal any more than the short pier one. He gave Sandra a fleeting look to gauge her reaction, but there was none.

'You can have your wife murderer and his girlfriend,' Patterson continued, 'so long as you all bugger off right now and forget everything you've seen or heard. No dead MP. No Harry Vincent. No nothing. Okay?'

I suppose it could be worse, Trevor thought, the heat rising in his cheeks as he heard Sandra referred to as his girlfriend for the second time in less than an hour. It was pretty clear now that Patterson really was MI5 and that he was seriously pissed off with him and Sandra. He had no idea what he really meant by the short pier thing, but he was sure it wouldn't have been pleasant, so escaping his clutches was definitely the preferred option. The same went for Harry in spades. Trevor was very well aware of what *he* would do if he got his hands on them, but judging by his current state, it seemed unlikely that this particularly gory scenario would ever be played out. That just left Logan and the murder thing. Yeah, *just*.

DS Logan was putting up a variety of objections to Patterson's offer and firing off a host of questions, but Patterson was having none of it. Trevor had already sussed Logan as the sort of person who hated anyone getting the better of him when they were back at Janice's, but he guessed this was simply a show of bravado before he eventually backed down. He did, and he was partway through his not-at-all-happy-about-this-but capitulation speech when there was a loud bleeping sound from somewhere in the kitchen area.

Statham hurried over from the window and flipped open the lid of a small notebook computer which was lying on top of the breakfast bar.

'Oops,' he said. 'Seems like the boss wants a word.'

Patterson sighed and looked up at the ceiling. 'Oh

Christ, that's all I need. – Tell her I'm busy and find out what she wants. In fact, don't let her know I'm here at all. – And use the earpiece. I don't want all this lot listening in.'

Statham fished in his pocket and took out a thin black lead, inserting one end into the notebook and the other into his ear. He pressed a button and leaned forward to peer at the screen, supporting himself with both hands on the edge of the work surface. 'Evening, ma'am.'

'Are you listening to me?' said Logan, breaking off from his speech when he realised that Patterson's attention was now exclusively devoted to Statham and the back of the notebook screen.

'No. So shut up.'

The expression of stunned rage on Logan's mug was a joy to behold. Trevor had no reason to favour either of these two men over the other, but Logan was the one who reminded him most of the playground bullies he'd had to suffer in his childhood, and it was always good to see one of those bastards get their comeuppance. He smiled to himself as the image of the enormous dog from the *Tom and Jerry* cartoons superimposed itself onto Logan's face, snarling and growling and with steam gushing from its ears.

At the same time, his own very real dog made a sudden lunge forward. Milly had been straining at her lead from the moment they'd arrived at the flat, clearly intent on a more detailed exploration of her new environment, and Trevor had struggled to keep her in check. On this occasion, however, he was distracted by Logan's humiliation and was unprepared for the abruptness and power of Milly's surge. The end of the lead was wrenched from his grasp, and she hurtled across the room and disappeared behind the breakfast bar.

'Get that damn dog under control,' Patterson said in

an exaggerated stage whisper.

Trevor skirted the breakfast bar to find Milly snuffling manically at the base of one of the kitchen units. He bent down to grab her lead, and as he began to straighten again, he glanced indifferently at the notebook display. But his indifference was short-lived. Thrusting his head forward, he stared in disbelief at the face on the screen.

'Blood-ee Nor-a,' he said, each syllable pronounced with slow deliberation.

The woman's dark brown eyes angled towards him, and her forehead creased into a frown, her head tipped slightly to the side as if straining to get a better view. Her lips moved soundlessly, but Trevor thought he could make out the words "Who's that behind you?". He reached for the worktop to steady himself.

'Imelda? Is that… you?'

* * *

Patterson watched from the window until he was sure that Logan and the others had left the building. While he waited, he pondered his future and tried to convince himself it wasn't as bleak as it seemed, even though it was abundantly clear from Statham's conversation with his boss that a letter of resignation would not be unwelcome. So what? He was sick of the job anyway and had only hung on till now to boost his pension by a few more quid. Okay, he wouldn't exactly be able to live a life of luxury, but at least he only had himself to worry about. Maybe he could get some kind of part-time job. It would be something to *do* after all. He detested golf and gardening in equal measure, and other than these two activities, he had no idea what retired people did with their time.

'You bastards just gonna let me bleed to death, are yer?'

Patterson turned slowly and stared down at Harry Vincent's sweat drenched face with undisguised distaste. 'Possibly.'

'Fucking wanker.'

'What *are* we going to do with him?' said Statham. 'The boss wants us to tidy up here and get the hell out of it.'

Tidy up? Patterson found it amusing that she'd used such a seemingly innocuous phrase when what she really meant was: "Get the stiff to some place where he's more likely to have been when he croaked, and as for Vincent—"

'Guv?'

'Sorry, Colin. Miles away.'

'Vincent.'

'Ah yes,' said Patterson. 'Leave him to me. You go next door and tell the others to start packing up. And get rid of the plods, but make sure you scare the crap out of them with the Official Secrets Act and all that stuff.'

'Righto.'

Patterson followed Statham to the door and closed it behind him before taking his gun from his shoulder holster. He walked back over to Vincent, screwing the silencer into place as he went. He knew that he ought to make an effort to find out what had happened to the ransom money, but he doubted Vincent would tell him anything. Besides, it wasn't *his* money. Why should he give a toss any more? He planted his feet either side of Vincent's bulging waistline and aimed at the centre of his forehead, trying to avoid the inevitable look of terror when realisation dawned.

'What the fuck d'you—'

That's something, I suppose, Patterson thought as he began to remove the silencer. This is the last time I'll have to do this sort of shit. Ever. Not that he felt particularly bad about Vincent. The world would be better off without him, and in any case, how could you kill somebody who'd already been dead for two years?

51

Trevor didn't even notice Sandra's hand reaching towards the toast rack in the centre of the table. His eyes just happened to be pointing in that direction.

'What?'

The indignation in Sandra's tone snapped him out of his brooding contemplation. 'Sorry?'

'You're keeping count, aren't you?' she said, her fingertips hovering within half an inch of the last remaining slice of toast.

'Er… sorry?' Trevor said again.

'You're thinking: That's her third piece. No wonder she's fat.'

'No I'm not.' He hadn't a clue what she was on about. His mind was awash with rather more important matters than keeping a tally of how many slices of toast she'd eaten. Besides, he'd told her before that he didn't think she was fat.

'Was Imelda fat?'

Twelve hours or so earlier, Sandra's use of the past tense would scarcely have registered, but in the present circumstances, it was especially poignant. He'd been in denial for over a year that Imelda might actually be dead, and it had taken several more months to get used to the fact that he'd never see her again. Then all of a sudden she pops up large as life on a bloody computer screen. It was bad enough that she'd deliberately subjected him to all that grieving and misery for no reason, but to discover that she'd only married him in the first place for the sake of "convenience"... What a bitch.

'Well?'

Once again, Trevor had no idea what Sandra was asking. 'Well what?'

'Oh never mind,' she said, spreading a liberal amount of butter onto her toast. 'You're not really with me at the moment, are you?'

'And that's surprising, is it? I mean, I've just been told by my missing-presumed-dead wife that all the time I knew her, she was an MI5 field agent, and to cap it all, she tells me she was ordered to get herself wed to any old sucker so her cover would be more convincing.'

'Yes, I think she could have left out the bit about "the more ordinary the better".'

Trevor didn't respond. Imelda's remark had certainly wounded him deeply, but when he'd thought about it later, he'd realised that the depth of the wound was directly proportional to the truth of her statement. He couldn't deny it. He was as ordinary as they came.

'Still,' said Sandra through a mouthful of toast, 'I suppose you've got to be grateful to her in one way.'

'Oh?'

'She got you off a murder charge, didn't she?'

'Yes, but if she hadn't decided to disappear off the face of the planet because – what was it? – some enemy agent was on to her, none of that stuff would ever have happened.' Enemy agent? Good grief, the whole situation was totally bizarre. 'And anyway, it was only by pure fluke that I spotted her on the computer.'

'Gotta thank Milly for that one, I guess.'

'And what if I hadn't? You think if it had gone all the way and I'd been convicted she'd have stepped in and saved the day?'

'Yes, I do actually.'

'Huh.' Trevor slumped back in his chair and folded his arms.

'Your sister thought so too.'

'Oh she did, did she? What is this? Some kind of female conspiracy?'

Trevor was aware of Sandra's mouth moving, but he heard nothing of what she was saying. His mind had already drifted back to the events at Janice's house the night before. It had been close to midnight when they'd got there because Logan had insisted on getting confirmation that Imelda really was who she said she was, and he'd dragged them to the nearest police station and kept them hanging around for almost three hours until he was satisfied. "Satisfied" was perhaps not the most accurate description though. The guy was fuming and had issued all kinds of threats, including charging Trevor's mother with wasting police time if she hadn't been 'completely off her bloody trolley'.

Not surprisingly, Janice had demanded a detailed explanation of exactly what her brother had been up to that had brought the police to her door in full view of all the neighbours. She had fed them soup and sandwiches, and when Trevor had finished explaining and wolfing down the food, she'd rung their mother, who had flatly denied all knowledge of any murder accusation and added that Trevor needed his head seeing to.

As it was so late, Trevor had hoped his sister would put them up for the night, but there was no way his 'hooligan bloody mongrel' would ever cross her threshold again. He had no intention of making Milly sleep in the car, so he and Sandra had found a couple of rooms in a nearby guesthouse which allowed pets.

'So long as it's well behaved,' the guesthouse owner had said, casting a doubtful eye in Milly's direction.

Trevor had lied – convincingly for once – and they'd been shown to their adjacent rooms.

''Night then, Trev,' Sandra had said when the proprietor had headed off back down the hallway. 'Sleep well.'

'Yeah, it's been a long couple of days,' he'd muttered, suddenly aware that Sandra had taken hold of the doorknob to her room several seconds earlier but had so far shown no sign of actually turning it. Afraid that the slight reddening of his cheeks was about to develop into an incandescent beacon of embarrassment, he had mumbled a final goodnight and almost hurled himself and Milly into his own room before she could notice.

Utterly exhausted though he was, it had been almost four in the morning before sleep finally overcame him. Even then, he had slept only fitfully, his subconscious bombarding him with all manner of dreams, none of which were in the least bit pleasant. There was Harry Vincent, brandishing a chainsaw which dripped with blood and tottering towards him on stumps of legs that ended at the knees. Then there was Patterson and his crew carrying him at shoulder height towards an enormous cauldron of boiling water and chanting 'Guts for garters, yum yum yum' over and over again in a quasi religious monotone. Next, he'd lifted the lid of a toilet cistern and inside was Logan's severed head singing *We'll Meet Again* in a heavily Glaswegian accent. But weirdest of all was the sight of Sandra, completely naked and strapped into an armchair with the butt of a gun in her mouth and aiming it directly at his genitals. Blimey, if Sigmund Freud had got hold of any of that lot, he'd be—

'Sssh!'

Trevor shook his head free of unbidden images of trains and cigars and focused on the reality of a fully clothed Sandra with nothing more in her mouth than a generously buttered piece of toast. 'What? I didn't say anything.'

'Look,' she said, pointing in an upward angle above his right shoulder.

He skewed himself round in his chair to see the flat-screen television mounted high up on the wall in a corner of the dining room.

'That's him, isn't it?'

Trevor looked at the picture of a grey-haired man in collar and tie with a Remembrance Day poppy fixed to the lapel of his jacket and recognised him immediately.

'…for Baileyhill and Redbridge,' the newsreader was saying, 'was found dead in the early hours of this morning at the Royal Lansdown Hotel in Bath. Initial reports suggest that the sixty-two year old MP died instantly from a massive heart attack, and police have already ruled out any question of foul play. Other sources have also revealed that Mr Quicke had been suffering from a serious heart disease for several months and that doctors had informed him that it was only a matter of time before—'

'Well there's a surprise,' said Sandra.

The image on the TV then switched to a shot of the Prime Minister being mobbed by reporters and having apparently just emerged from a tour of some factory or other. He wore a suitably solemn expression as he trotted out the usual "deeply saddened", "greatly missed", "thoughts are with Gerald's family at this difficult time" kind of platitudes that drip with insincerity.

'I still don't quite get it,' said Trevor. 'I mean, why all the hush hush?'

Sandra laughed. 'Oh come on, Trev. Even you can't be that naive.'

Still reeling from Imelda's affirmation of his mind-numbing ordinariness, Trevor winced inwardly at this latest assault on his self esteem. He attempted to conceal his hurt by pretending to concentrate on pouring himself a third cup of coffee but realised he had failed when he felt Sandra's palm rest lightly on the back of his hand.

'I'm sorry,' she said. 'I really didn't mean that.'

'No, you're quite right,' said Trevor. 'Ordinary and naïve. Trevor Nice-but-dim.'

'Nobody said you were dim.'

He felt Sandra's hand slide from the top of his and instantly regretted the petulant self pity in his tone. 'Okay,' he said, trying to recover the situation with a show of positivity. 'Let's see if I can work it out for myself. MP gets kidnapped and government pays the ransom – or tries to – but in the meantime, the MP snuffs it. Prime Minister's been banging on for yonks about not giving in to terrorist demands and all that, so it'd be a bit embarrassing if the whole ransom thing ever got out. Um…'

'General election coming up. Plenty of other recent scandals without another one to deal with.'

Trevor felt slightly peeved at Sandra's prompting, but he decided to stifle his irritation in the interests of restoring the amicable equilibrium. 'The Honourable Member's already dead, so where's the harm in playing let's pretend? No kidnap, no ransom. Situation normal.'

'Bravo,' said Sandra, clapping her hands together in mock applause. 'I knew you could do it if you put your mind to it.'

Her accompanying wink reassured him he wasn't meant to take her patronising manner seriously, and he smiled back at her to show that the irony hadn't passed him by.

'All the same,' he said. 'I don't have to be happy about it. I mean, why should we let the bastards get away with it? What's to stop us going straight to the press and—'

'Whoa there, Batman,' said Sandra, her wrists resting on the edge of the table, both palms towards him. 'Before you get too carried away with your new-found role as saviour of the universe, I'll remind you exactly what's stopping us, and that's a little thing called the

Official Secrets Act. Mess with that and you could be talking serious prison time – or worse.'

'Worse?' Trevor genuinely didn't know what she meant.

'You think people like Pitter Patterson give a monkey's who they...' She seemed to be searching for the right word. '... *Liquidate* if they get in the way? It's what they *do*, for Christ's sake.'

Trevor resisted giving voice to any of the thoughts which sprang into his mind. Any one of them would have reinforced Sandra's opinion of his naivety, and besides, he had the distinct impression she was losing patience with him. He stirred his coffee even though he'd added neither milk nor sugar.

'Look, I don't like it any more than you do,' said Sandra, 'but shit like this happens all the time, and there's not a damn thing people like us can do about it.'

Yep, she was definitely getting pissy, but he was grateful she hadn't added "Deal with it" or "Get over it" at the end. He continued pointlessly stirring his coffee, once again in the belief that silence was his best form of defence. After several seconds, however, he was beginning to doubt the effectiveness of his strategy when he heard a sharp tapping sound in front of him. He looked up to see the silver toast rack poised a couple of inches above the table, and his eyes traced a route from Sandra's hand and up her arm to her face. It was wearing a broad grin.

'You want me to order more toast?' she said.

Trevor shook his head. Sandra had arrived in the guesthouse dining room a few minutes before him and ordered the full English for both of them, but he had hardly touched it. By rights, he should have been ravenous since he'd hardly eaten a thing all weekend apart from a handful of biscuits, a Mars bar and the late night snack at his sister's the night before. But his appetite had deserted him. In fact, he felt decidedly nauseous whenever he pondered the events of the past couple of days, which was most of the time. The queasiness was particularly intense when he recalled the shock of seeing Imelda on the— Oh hell, I'm going to throw up.

He jumped to his feet, almost knocking his chair over in the process.

'You okay? You've gone a bit… pale.'

'Need a pee,' said Trevor through ventriloquist lips but was able to appreciate Sandra's look of genuine concern despite his current preoccupation with finding the nearest toilet as quickly as possible.

'Tell you what,' she said as he frantically scanned the room for the appropriate sign. 'I'll sort out the bill while you're gone. It's quite a schlep back to your van, so the sooner we get started, the better.'

He nodded, suddenly remembering there was a Gents in the hallway just outside the dining room, and he was about to set off when Sandra interrupted his mission once again.

'Still, it'll give us plenty of time to talk about how we're going to spend the twenty-five grand. I don't know about you, but I haven't had a decent holiday in years.'

It was as if she had recited some kind of magical healing charm, so rapidly did Trevor's nausea vanish. His mind had no room for anything other than what she had just said. 'We?'

'You got a problem with that?'

'Well no, but—'

'The thing is,' said Sandra, 'you came so close to screwing up this job that I could quite cheerfully have throttled you the moment I caught up with you at the festival.'

Trevor scratched the back of his head and stared down at his feet. 'Yes, I'm sorry about that. All I—'

'But then I was lying in bed last night, thinking it all through, and it struck me that without your untimely and totally unwelcome interference, I'd have ended up with two grand instead of twenty-five. Fair's fair. We split the difference.'

'Are you serious?'

Sandra sat back in her chair. 'I thought you said you needed the loo.'

He didn't any more, but he decided to make the trip anyway if only to give himself the space to try and get his head round what she was suggesting. He weaved his way past the three tables that stood between him and the dining room doorway, each occupied by a solitary man in a suit and tie, all intent on reading their newspapers. As he passed the last of them, he heard Sandra's voice calling out: 'And don't forget to wash your hands.'

There were no urinals in the Gents, just a single toilet and a small washbasin. He locked the door, lowered the lid and sat down. High up on the wall behind him was a small open window through which he could hear Milly's familiar banshee howling. Dogs weren't allowed in the dining room, so he'd taken her for a short walk when he'd come down for breakfast and then left her in Sandra's car.

'Quite an adventure eh, Milly?' he said aloud. 'Bet you never thought it'd turn out like this.'

As if in response, Milly gave a particularly ear-piercing shriek, and Trevor laughed for the first time in days. It gave him a much needed boost, and the conversation he'd just had with Sandra meant that – for now at least – his mind no longer had room for the nausea-inducing thoughts of Imelda, Harry Vincent, Logan, Patterson and all the rest of them.

What was it she'd said about a holiday? Did she mean they should go somewhere *together*? He closed his eyes and concentrated hard to conjure up the vision of a tropical beach, complete with white sand, palm trees and gently lapping turquoise waves with Sandra lying beside him in an exceptionally skimpy bikini. But try as he might, all he could come up with was a depressingly vivid evocation of the last beach he'd visited about three years ago – a windswept Cleethorpes, complete with a relentless grey drizzle and the fetid stink of seaweed and fried onions. Fortunately, however, he was still able to picture the scantily clad Sandra with impressive clarity even though he wasn't quite sure why she was leaping up and down on the floor of a bouncy castle with an enormous piece of toast in her mouth.

The image began to fade and then evaporated entirely with the sudden awareness that Milly had stopped howling. Whereas most dog owners would have heaved a sigh of relief at the lull in the mayhem, Milly's silence instantly pushed all of Trevor's alarm buttons at once. It could only mean one thing. Frustrated that her baying wolf impersonation had failed to produce any tangibly positive results – particularly the reappearance of her so-called master – she had turned her attention instead to the upholstery of Sandra's car.

'Oh bloody Nora,' he said and sprang to his feet.

Although there was no reason to do so, he automatically grabbed the flush handle of the toilet and pushed it downwards. He had already unlocked the door when he realised that all he had heard was a dull clunking sound from somewhere inside the cistern. Turning back, his hand reached out towards the porcelain lid, but it had travelled no more than two or three inches before he abruptly withdrew it.

'Uh-uh,' he said, shaking his head. 'You might have caught me out once, but that's your lot, pal. You can get yourself a proper plumber this time.'

THE END

ABOUT THE AUTHOR

Some readers have asked me if *Lifting the Lid* is partly autobiographical. Am I anything like the main character, Trevor Hawkins? The answer, quite simply, is: 'No, I'm not.' Okay, so I do own an elderly VW camper van (currently off the road), I do have a dog (five rescue dogs actually), I do have a low pain threshold, and I can occasionally be accused of 'anally retentive faffing'. But there the similarity ends.

Unlike Trevor, I live in Greece with my partner, Penny, two cats and the aforementioned rescue dogs. As far as I'm aware, Trevor has never written anything longer than a shopping list in his life, whereas I'm working on the sequel to *Lifting the Lid* and two screenplays.

I hope you enjoy *Lifting the Lid*, and if you'd like any more information, please...

- visit my website at
  http://www.rob-johnson.org.uk (where you can also listen to my series of short, hopefully humorous podcasts)

- follow **@RobJohnson999** on Twitter

- check out (and please like!) my Facebook author page at
  https://www.facebook.com/RobJohnsonAuthor

REVIEWS

Authors always appreciate reviews – especially if they're good ones of course – so I'd be eternally grateful if you could spare the time to write a few words about *Lifting the Lid* on Amazon or anywhere else you can think of. It really can make a difference. Reviews also help other readers decide whether to buy a book or not, so you'll be doing them a service as well.

AND FINALLY...

I'm always interested to hear from my readers, so please do take a couple of minutes to contact me via my website at **http://rob-johnson.org.uk/contact/**

Made in the USA
Monee, IL
25 September 2020